"Henry is able to keep all the strands of her spiderweb woven together in a neat and concise way.... The end result is a complex, interesting story that maintains suspense and intrigue page after page after page."   —Sadie Hartman, author of *Cemetery Dance*

PRAISE FOR
LOOKING GLASS

"Mesmerizing.... These somber, occasionally disturbing novellas offer a mature take on the children's story but balance the horrors of the City with hope."   —*Publishers Weekly*

"Fans will delight in discovering the unknown family backgrounds and future fate of Alice and her wild and bloody Hatcher."   —*Booklist* (starred review)

PRAISE FOR
THE GIRL IN RED

"An engrossing page-turner that will delight anyone who loves running through thought experiments about the apocalypse."   —Paste

"With *The Girl in Red*, Christina Henry once again proves that retellings don't necessarily lack originality."   —*Kirkus Reviews*

"Multiple twists keep the reader guessing, and the fluid writing is enthralling. . . . Henry immerses the reader in Neverland and genuinely shocks. . . . This is a fine addition to the shelves of any fan of children's classics and their modern subversions."

—*Publishers Weekly* (starred review)

"This wild, unrelenting tale, full to the brim with the freedom and violence of young boys who never want to grow up, will appeal to fans of dark fantasy."

—*Booklist*

"Turns Neverland into a claustrophobic world where time is disturbingly nebulous and identity is chillingly manipulated. . . . A deeply impactful, imaginative, and haunting story of loyalty, disillusionment, and self-discovery." —RT Book Reviews (top pick)

PRAISE FOR
ALICE

"I loved falling down the rabbit hole with this dark, gritty tale. A unique spin on a classic and one wild ride!".

—Gena Showalter, *New York Times* bestselling author
of *The Phantom*

"*Alice* takes the darker elements of Lewis Carroll's original, amplifies Tim Burton's cinematic reimagining of the story, and adds a layer of grotesquery from [Henry's] own alarmingly fecund imagination to produce a novel that reads like a Jacobean revenge drama crossed with a slasher movie." —*The Guardian* (UK)

"A psychotic journey through the bowels of magic and madness. I, for one, thoroughly enjoyed the ride."

—Brom, author of *The Child Thief*

"A horrifying fantasy that will have you reexamining your love for this childhood favorite." —RT Book Reviews (top pick)

PRAISE FOR
RED QUEEN

"Henry takes the best elements from Carroll's iconic world and mixes them with dark fantasy elements. . . . [Her] writing is so seamless you won't be able to stop reading."

—Pop Culture Uncovered

"Alice's ongoing struggle is to distinguish reality from illusion, and Henry excels in mingling the two for the reader as well as her characters. The darkness in this book is that of fairy tales, owing more to Grimm's matter-of-fact violence than to the underworld of the first book." —*Publishers Weekly* (starred review)

TITLES BY CHRISTINA HENRY

The House That Horror Built

Good Girls Don't Die

Horseman

Near the Bone

The Ghost Tree

The Girl in Red

The Mermaid

Lost Boy

THE CHRONICLES OF ALICE

Alice

Red Queen

Looking Glass
(novellas)

THE BLACK WINGS NOVELS

Black Wings

Black Night

Black Howl

Black Lament

Black City

Black Heart

Black Spring

THE HOUSE THAT HORROR BUILT

CHRISTINA HENRY

BERKLEY

New York

BERKLEY
An imprint of Penguin Random House LLC
penguinrandomhouse.com

Copyright © 2024 by Tina Raffaele
Penguin Random House supports copyright. Copyright fuels creativity, encourages
diverse voices, promotes free speech, and creates a vibrant culture. Thank you for buying
an authorized edition of this book and for complying with copyright laws by not
reproducing, scanning, or distributing any part of it in any form without permission.
You are supporting writers and allowing Penguin Random House to continue to
publish books for every reader.

BERKLEY and the BERKLEY & B colophon are registered trademarks of
Penguin Random House LLC.

Library of Congress Cataloging-in-Publication Data

Names: Henry, Christina, 1974- author.
Title: The house that horror built / Christina Henry.
Description: First Edition. | New York : Berkley, 2024.
Identifiers: LCCN 2023042004 (print) | LCCN 2023042005 (ebook) |
ISBN 9780593638217 (trade paperback) | ISBN 9780593638224 (ebook)
Subjects: LCGFT: Gothic fiction. | Horror fiction. | Novels.
Classification: LCC PS3608.E568 H68 2024 (print) |
LCC PS3608.E568 (ebook) | DDC 813/.6—dc23/eng/20231011
LC record available at https://lccn.loc.gov/2023042004
LC ebook record available at https://lccn.loc.gov/2023042005

First Edition: May 2024

Printed in the United States of America
1st Printing

Book design by George Towne
Interior art: Grunge Interior © Valentin Agapov/Shutterstock.com

For Henry, who is only just beginning

Imagination, of course, can open any door—
turn the key and let terror walk right in.

—Truman Capote, *In Cold Blood*

THE
HOUSE THAT
HORROR
BUILT

HARRY

before

SHE REMEMBERED FALLING IN love with movies when she was very young, remembered disappearing into the dark with only the flickering screen to guide her. She remembered the feeling of drifting away from the seat and the small bag of too-salty popcorn and into the movie as the restless sounds of her mother and father and sister shifting and coughing and whispering faded to another time and place, another time and place that Harry had left behind.

Her parents took her to very few films, and even then only films that were considered "clean"—while the rest of her fourth-grade class chattered excitedly about *Titanic* she had to content herself with occasional glimpses of clips seen during television commercial breaks. Her parents were half-convinced that film and television were actual tools of the devil, and Harry and her sister Margaret (always Margaret, never Maggie) weren't allowed to see anything that had higher than a G rating. But Harry didn't care. She loved the movies—loved the drive to the theater and the way everything smelled like hot butter and Raisinets, loved watching the coming attractions before the film started and the hush of anticipation that fell when the title sequence began. Even if she was only allowed to see G movies at least she was seeing movies. At least she was someplace besides her sober, judgmental household, a place where the only acceptable conversation was prayer and the only acceptable attitude was piety.

Harry knew her family was different than other families, even different from most of the families who attended the same church. Her school friends attended Sunday school with her and went to Christian summer camp, but they also were allowed to walk the mall in small groups. They had cable television and saw rated R movies late at night after their parents had gone to bed. They had new clothes from places like the Gap and American Eagle and Aeropostale, while Harry and Margaret were only allowed Salvation Army secondhands.

Harry was eleven when she was permitted to attend her first sleepover birthday party. She'd begged her mother to allow her to go, having always been the only girl left out when she had to turn down previous invitations. For some reason, on that particular occasion, her normally stern mother relented—a decision she would likely regret for the rest of her life, because it was on that night that Harry was irredeemably corrupted.

The friend, Jessica Piniansky, had an older sister named Erin who had been left in charge of the menagerie of girls for the evening while Jessica's parents wisely went out to dinner after the birthday cake was served. Erin had been dispatched to the local video store to rent Kiefer Sutherland movies, as Kiefer was Jessica's current obsession and her bedroom was plastered with photographs of him torn from *Us* and *Entertainment Weekly* and *People* that she'd taken from the library. Jessica always had slightly out-of-date obsessions, like she ought to have been born ten years earlier.

Erin had returned with copies of *The Lost Boys* and *Flatliners,* two films that Harry would never have been permitted to watch under normal circumstances. Her hands were sweaty as *The Lost Boys* slid into the DVD player, as she stared down the barrel of doing something her parents would not approve of.

All around her the other girls argued over the relative merits of Jason Patric vs. Corey Haim vs. Kiefer Sutherland, but Harry didn't join in. She was in love with the dark, with the lost boys swinging and flying under the railroad track, with the arterial spray of the first vampire attack, with the blood gushing from the sinks and spattering all over the house. She relished the thrumming of her heart, the pulse of her own blood, the terror and the splendor and the excitement she'd never felt before.

When the movie was over she felt reborn, reborn as an addict seeking another thrill. She didn't know how she would find it again, how such a visceral pleasure would ever be allowed in a home where pleasure of any kind was a sin.

She began to sneakily read copies of *Fangoria* magazine whenever she saw them—at the corner store when she was sent out to buy milk, or at the bookstore when her mother wasn't paying attention. As she entered high school and she got a job of her own—making ice cream cones and sundaes at Dairy Queen after school—she had more time and money to do what she liked, to stop and buy those copies of *Fangoria* on the way home and ferret them away between her mattress and box spring, taking them out only when everyone else in the house was asleep and scanning the pages, flashlight in hand, seeing hints of worlds where she still wasn't permitted to travel—places where regular people were

ONE

IT WAS THE SIZE of the house that got Harry every time she saw it. Of course she'd seen houses that size before, in Certain Neighborhoods around Chicago, giant houses whose sheer enormity should have relegated them to the suburbs. This city house wasn't a McMansion, though—one of those classless boxes, bulging oversized dwellings for those who wanted to display their money, or at least their debt.

It was decidedly not new, not the province of some futures broker or investment banker. It had the same greystone face as her own two-flat apartment building—a fifteen-minute bus ride and half a world away, economically speaking—but it was twice the size. The house covered two lots, with a third lot for a side yard. As an apartment dweller she didn't often contemplate property taxes, but just the fact of those three lots made queasy multi-digit numbers dance before her eyes.

The building was three stories plus a basement level. The windows were tall on the lowest story, less so on the second one, and downright tiny on the topmost, giving the overall effect of slowly closing eyes if you glanced from the bottom to the top.

Other than the oddly sized windows there were no particular architectural flourishes save two. At the northeast corner of the roof a sculpture protruded like a Notre Dame gargoyle—a horse's head and neck carved in stone, the horse's lips pulled back, its eyes wild. All around the horse, stone flames rose, waiting to burn. Harry thought she'd grimace, too, if she was trapped in fire for all eternity.

In addition to the frantic stallion, there was a name carved in an arc above the door—***BRIGHT HORSES***.

The entire property was surrounded by a ten-foot-high black iron fence. The only two entry points were the gate in front of her and the sliding gate in front of the garage in the back.

Harry reached toward the call box so she could be buzzed in, but paused as she heard her phone chirp in her pocket. She pulled it out and saw a text from her son, Gabe.

FORGOT MY CHEM REPORT! IT'S ON MY DESK? followed by a praying hands emoji.

Already at work, she texted back, and tacked on the woman shrugging and holding her hands up.

She only worked three days a week, so if Gabe had tried on a different day she might have hopped the bus and brought his report to him. Maybe. Part of her thought he needed to learn the consequences of not thinking ahead and putting the report in his bag the night before. The other part of her wanted to cut him some slack, given that it was his freshman year and the first time the kids were back at school post-pandemic, even if it was only three days a week.

She was grateful that it was only two days off in-person schooling, as her unemployed spring (furloughed from her server job, never to return) coupled with overseeing remote learning for a thirteen-year-old with ADHD had resulted in screaming, emotional breakdowns for both of them. Having Gabe's learning monitored by qualified teachers was a profound relief.

Harry watched the reply bubbles churn on her screen until Gabe's answer popped up. A sad face emoji, followed by a shrugging boy.

Noise crackled from the call box and a deep baritone voice emitted from it. "Are you going to stand there all day, or perhaps you'd like to work?"

Harry glanced up at the camera perched on the top corner of the fence. The preponderance of cameras in and around the house always left her feeling uneasy, even though she understood the necessity of them. There were a few too many, in Harry's opinion, though she was careful to keep that opinion to herself.

"Sorry, Mr. Castillo," she said, and the gate buzzed.

Harry pushed the gate open and hurried up the walk as Javier Castillo opened the front door, watching her approach.

"We'll start in the blue room today," he said as she jogged up the steps.

"No problem," she said, pausing in the doorway. She pulled her slippers—plain gray terry cloth scuffs, bought expressly for and used only at the Castillo residence—out of her backpack, placed them on the floor in the entryway and toed out of her sneakers one by one, sliding each foot into a slipper without ever touching the ground.

Harry picked up her sneakers and carried them inside, placing them on the special shelf to the left of the doorway. No outside dirt, damp or germs touched the floors in Bright Horses.

The shelf that housed her sneakers was something like a preschooler's cubby, with a space for shoes at the bottom, hooks for bags and coats in the center, and a top shelf for hats and other items. Harry pulled off her black windbreaker and hung it on a hook. She slid her cell phone into her backpack as Mr. Castillo watched. There was a strict no-phone policy inside the house. Violation of this rule was grounds for immediate dismissal, though she was allowed to go outside during her lunch break to check messages.

Mr. Castillo held out the box of latex gloves stored on a side table behind the door. Harry pulled on the gloves, wincing a little as she did. She hated the feeling of pulling on the gloves, the way the material seemed to grab and yank at her skin. Once the gloves were actually on she didn't mind them as much, although she still liked the moment at the end of the day when she was allowed to peel them off and let her skin breathe again.

Harry adjusted her medical mask—Mr. Castillo never allowed her to remove it inside the house except in the kitchen when eating or drinking—so that all that was visible were her faded blue eyes and the bit of her forehead that showed when she pulled her pin-straight blond hair into a ponytail. She followed him down the hallway and up the stairs to the second floor.

The entry to the house was deliberately neutral—the plain gray carpet and faded wallpaper practically screamed, *There's nothing to see here!* But upon leaving the downstairs hall and passing into any other room the true nature of Bright Horses was revealed.

It started on the stairway, after the first few steps, when the stairs curved to the left, out of sight from anyone standing in the entryway. A large framed poster of a voluptuous blonde in a red dress hung on the wall there. A snarling cat, blood dripping from its mouth, curled over her right shoulder, and over her left were the words **SHE WAS MARKED WITH THE CURSE OF THOSE WHO SLINK**

AND COURT AND KILL BY NIGHT! Above her head the words **CAT PEOPLE** floated over a clock whose hands showed midnight.

Harry always smiled at this poster, as *Cat People* was one of her favorite films, though Mr. Castillo had hastened to point out that the poster wasn't an original print. Most of the posters that lined the wall along the stairs were contemporary copies, though there were a few genuine articles—the original U.K. quad poster for Hammer's *The Curse of Frankenstein*, the lurid red French theatrical poster for *Eyes Without a Face*, a U.S. lobby poster for *An American Werewolf in London*.

It was slow going to the top of the stairs, as Mr. Castillo always got out of breath halfway up and had to stop. Harry didn't remark on this, or offer any help. She'd made the mistake of offering assistance once, saying she would fetch a glass of water.

"I'm fine," Mr. Castillo snapped. "I'm just fat."

Harry attributed his breathlessness to lack of regular exercise rather than size—she knew plenty of heavier people who had no trouble with stairs because they ran or lifted weights on the regular, and plenty of thin people who tired after walking half a block. But she hadn't said this.

She hadn't said anything unnecessary or even vaguely personal, because it had been her first day. She was grateful to have work again, and desperately averse to jeopardizing her new source of income.

Even now, more than a month later, she never said anything that might be construed as personal. She was too much in awe of him, in awe of this person who'd let her into his home.

Javier Castillo had brown hair going gray, brown eyes behind steel-rimmed spectacles, was on the shorter side (though not as short as Harry, who had reached five feet at age thirteen and never grown again) and overall had the completely nondescript appearance of any random person on the block. He was the sort who would never attract attention unless you knew who he was, would never be whispered about if he went to the grocery store—which he never did. He never went anywhere if he could help it.

Because of this, very few people in his neighborhood realized one of the world's greatest living horror directors lived among them: Javier Castillo, director and writer of fifteen films, most of them visually groundbreaking, genre-defying masterpieces. His film *The Monster* had won the Oscar for Best Picture five years earlier and swept most of the other major categories along the way, including Best Director and Best Original Screenplay. The world had waited breathlessly for the announcement of his next project.

Then a shocking, unthinkable incident happened, and Castillo withdrew into his California home, and there was no mention of potential new movies while the paparazzi stood outside his house with their cameras ready for any sign of life within.

After one too many wildfires came too close to his residence he decided to move, somewhat incongruously, to Chicago. He packed up his legendary and possibly priceless collection of movie props and memorabilia and brought them to a cold Midwestern city where the last major urban burning was decidedly in the distant past.

If it wasn't for those California wildfires Harry would still be collecting unemployment, frantically responding to job ads with a horde of other desperate people, never hearing back, wondering how long Gabe would believe her tight smile followed by, "Everything's going to be fine."

But instead there was this miracle, this miracle of a strange and reclusive director who needed someone to help him clean his collection of weird stuff three days a week, and so Harry climbed up the stairs and listened to Javier Castillo huff and puff.

The second floor was essentially one big room divided by a load-bearing archway. The stairs curved up to the southwest corner of this room and stopped there. The stair to the third floor was on the northeast corner, which always made Harry think of a Clue board, with its seemingly random staircases scattered all around. There was a black railing running along from the southeast corner of the room to the top of the stairs to keep people from falling straight down the first-floor stairwell.

The bucket of cleaning supplies was ready at the top of the stairs. Harry and Mr. Castillo each took a long-handled duster. Mr. Castillo went to the far end of the room while Harry started on the closest figure.

The blue room wasn't entirely blue. The carpet was blue—and Harry really thought he ought to get rid of the carpet; it collected dust and it was such a difficult room to vacuum. The wallpaper had blue flowers patterned on it, blue flowers that made Harry think of Agatha Christie's story "The Blue Geranium."

Except that's not quite right, Harry thought. *In "The Blue Geranium" the color of the flower on the wall changed to blue because of a chemical in the air—proof of poison.*

Nobody was in danger of poisoning in Bright Horses. Nobody lived there except Mr. Castillo—and his props, of course, and some of those were so lifelike that Harry sometimes thought they really were watching her, just out of the corner of her eye. When she'd turn, the figures would be still and glassy-eyed, the artificial pupils staring off into the middle distance, never having focused on her or anything else at all.

Harry loved most of the films that the props came from, but despite this the blue room, in particular, gave her a creepy-crawly itch on the back of her neck. She didn't know why. She knew the props were make-believe, knew they were just elements of the movie magic that she loved so much. But the feeling still persisted—a feeling of something not quite right.

All the various members of the collection were posed on skeleton-like frames, so that the overall result was a museum diorama grouped according to some internal catalog system of Mr. Castillo's devising.

Harry dusted a Xenomorph puppet from *Alien³*. The creature's jaw extended from the head as if it was about to bite. Harry liked the *Alien* movies. She was a fan of most of the source material for the props littered around Bright Horses. But she'd discovered, to her surprise, that she didn't like the pieces separated from their performers, didn't see the appeal of latex and foam rubber without animation. Devoid of both life and context, the costumes were nothing but shed snakeskin, a pantomime of their original intent.

Harry moved from the Xenomorph to a figure that had been featured in one of Mr. Castillo's films, a kind of half-goat/half-demon hybrid. In the film, *A Messenger from Hell*, the creature, Sten, had acted as a sort of sinister guardian to the main character, Flora. It was one of Harry's favorite movies, a transcendently beautiful piece of art that was also deeply grotesque—in other words, a Castillo film.

But the first time she was confronted with the mask and costume she found herself deeply, viscerally repulsed, barely able to look at it and unable to explain why.

As Harry fluttered the duster over the face she caught, as she always did, the faint odor of sweat and talcum powder. She'd thought, on the first occasion, that this was simply the scent of the actor who'd worn the mask, lingering inside the rubber. But then she realized that was absurd, that all these pieces were specially cleaned and treated before Mr. Castillo displayed them. Of course it didn't still smell like the actor.

Still, every time Harry dusted the sharp distended chin, the high cheekbones, the pointed ears, the curling horns, she was certain that the fanged mouth would curl up in a terrible smile, that the icy blue eyes would shift in her direction a moment before long-fingered hands grasped her shoulders. And every time she felt this way she shook off her unease, recognizing it as irrational. She loved the character in the movie, and a costume and mask were just that—empty props. They were nothing to be frightened of.

On a deep level, though, she recognized that this half belief—or maybe willingness to believe—that the mask would come to life was one of the reasons why she loved horror movies so much. She never saw the props and the fake blood and the clear unreality of it all. She was perfectly credulous, always, perfectly willing to believe in what the filmmakers put on-screen. Harry never held herself away from what she viewed. She was a part of it.

Harry moved on to brush the elaborate folds of the silken costume, absolutely positive that the head was tilted down, watching her as she worked, and just as equally certain that the idea was absurd.

She was thirty-four years old, well past the point in life when she was allowed to be scared of inanimate objects. Still, it was a relief, as always, to move away from the figure to the other costumes behind it, to feel the pressure of that terrible gaze lift.

A number of the figures on this side of the room were also from Mr. Castillo's own films—a massive demon, red-skinned and black-clawed; an eyeless troll, the folds of its body the same texture as elephant skin; a tiny, gauzy-winged fairy with terribly sharp teeth.

Harry knew all the movies the props came from, loved some of them enough to have watched and rewatched over and over. She never mentioned this. She had sensed during the interview that gushing fandom would be a detriment to her job prospects, and Harry really needed the job. Her unemployment check had barely covered the rent, even though she had one of the few affordable apartments in a neighborhood that had progressed rapidly from "gentrifying" to "upwardly mobile."

Harry had been one of the few parents in Gabe's elementary school whose income didn't remotely approach six figures, which led to increasing embarrassment as the years passed and the financial expectations grew.

First it had been "fundraising" for full-day kindergarten (the state only paid for a half day) with an "expected donation" of "$2,000 per family." It was a public school, and Harry had never had two thousand dollars in one place in her entire life, so she'd shrugged and said she couldn't pay, and that was that.

She hadn't minded the idea of Gabe in half-day kindergarten anyway, as she possessed the apparently radical notion that five-year-olds should spend more time running around than drilling reading skills.

Harry had mentioned this to another mom once (full-day kindergarten having been fully funded despite Harry's lack of contribution) and the other parent had given Harry the kind of look normally reserved for serial killers or politicians she disagreed with.

"It's absolutely *vital* that young kids get a head start on learning. Statistics show that full-day kindergarten is a predictor of future success," the mom had said.

Or a predictor of future burnout, Harry had thought as the woman continued to lecture. Harry had nodded and privately vowed never to mention her personal opinion on anything school-related ever again.

As the years passed there had been one expectation after another—the yearly gala, for which the wealthy and well-connected donated things like Cubs tickets and spa days and wine country vacations for auction. Harry never had anything to donate or any money to bid, so she always gave vague answers when asked about the gala and made sure she had something else to do that night—and usually she did, because unlike almost every other mom at pickup she sometimes had to work evenings.

Then there was an "expected donation" of "$200 per family" per year, used toward arts and theater programs. Harry tried to scrape this up every year, carefully saving a portion of her summer tips, since she believed school should be about more than just math. Still, there always seemed to be some new thing to contribute to—the walk-a-thon, the science lab, the ticket money for the yearly musical.

Harry had moved to the neighborhood because it had one of the best K–8 schools in the city, and entry was only guaranteed for residents. But the constant flood of financial requests had drained her, and the additional expectation that she had the time or the energy to volunteer in various capacities had been equally frustrating.

She worked during school hours, unlike most of the Lululemon moms of Gabe's classmates—women who wore Canada Goose jackets in winter and expensive blonde highlights year-round, women who drove Lexus SUVs and spent their children's school hours taking barre classes and chatting with other moms at Starbucks. It had been hard for Harry not to resent these women and their clueless privilege. But Harry had gritted her teeth and stuck it out so that Gabe could have a better chance at one of the top high schools in the city.

She'd worked—before the pandemic, before everything came crashing down—at an upscale-ish restaurant only a couple of blocks from her apartment, a place where many of those school moms with unlimited leisure time lunched during the school week. They always gave her fake smiles while ordering their grilled chicken salads, but they left nice tips (probably worried that Harry would tell the other moms that they were cheap otherwise), so Harry fake-smiled them right back and thought about Gabe.

Gabe. The best kid in the world. She knew every mother thought that about her kids but in Gabe's case she was firmly convinced it was true. Whenever Harry looked at Gabe she felt a fierce, almost incomprehensible love inside her, a love that was sometimes painful in its intensity. She was a bottle filled with hopes and dreams for him, tempered only by free-form anxiety that Something Might Happen to her only, most beloved child—COVID, cancer, a bus accident, a school shooting.

She never expressed these fears except to sometimes give Gabe an extra-long hug before he left for school, which he patiently tolerated for a few moments before saying, "Okay, Mom." That was her cue to release him, and she would, hiding the sudden emptiness she felt with an offhand "Be safe and learn stuff, okay, kiddo?" He would duck his head and grin and leave, and she'd fight the urge to call him back, to keep him home where the world couldn't harm him.

Mr. Castillo's voice broke into her reverie. "I have several calls to make, so as soon as we're finished here you can go upstairs. After lunch we will tackle the first-floor and basement rooms."

Mr. Castillo was always present whenever Harry cleaned one

of the prop rooms, and in fact he did half the work, lovingly caring for his masks and costumes and maquettes. Harry's sole purpose was to assist, for he couldn't keep everything clean on his own. But the "regular" rooms—rooms without film collectibles, of which there were very few—were Harry's responsibility.

These included three bedrooms upstairs—Mr. Castillo's room and two guest rooms—the bathrooms on the first and third floors, the kitchen, and what Mr. Castillo referred to as "the small library."

The small library was essentially a reading room on the third floor, a place for him to store paperbacks that had no special monetary value. It was Harry's favorite room in the house, much nicer than the formal library downstairs. There were shelves stuffed with books stacked every which way, following no particular organizational system, and two big soft armchairs, each with its own side table and reading lamp.

Her second-favorite room was downstairs off the dining room. Mr. Castillo called it "the screening room." There was a large movie screen at one end, maybe eight feet across, and about twenty extremely comfortable chairs in rows to watch movies. He had even added a little mobile popcorn cart in the corner.

It was the sort of room Harry had always wanted in her own place, except they lived in a two-bedroom apartment and there was no extra space for a broom closet, never mind anything as extravagant as a reading room or a special room to watch films.

Someday, she told herself, but deep down she knew she'd been saying "someday" for ten years or more and that someday might never come.

Especially not if you keep working as a house cleaner, she thought as she ran the vacuum carefully around the blue room under Mr. Castillo's watchful eye. She was grateful for the job, for the money, but it was not exactly a path to wealth or even the stability of the middle class. It just meant she worried about money every five minutes instead of every single second.

As soon as she was finished vacuuming she rewrapped the cord around the machine and carried it to the upstairs hallway before returning to the blue room for the rest of the cleaning supplies. Mr. Castillo had already left to make his calls from his downstairs office.

He often did this, disappearing without a word and reappearing suddenly, always silent, like he was expecting to catch her goofing off or thought that he might discover the existence of a second, secret cell phone being used to take photographs. Harry tried not to be offended by the unspoken implications. Mr. Castillo wasn't unkind—a little on the stern side, perhaps, but he was fiercely protective of his privacy. She was there to do a job and he wanted her to do it and leave, not poke around in his things or stare out a window.

Harry understood that. Really, she did. So she tried not to feel offended by his monitoring, and mostly she succeeded, and if resentment stuck in her craw she just swallowed it down. Resentment is a familiar meal when you can't afford contentment.

Harry went into the first guest room on the right on the third floor. There wasn't much to do in there, just run a duster over the furniture and vacuum the carpet. Once a week she changed the sheets and shook out the duvet. It seemed a ridiculous waste of effort and washing water to keep the guest room beds fresh and ready for anyone arriving at a moment's notice, particularly when Mr. Castillo never even appeared to invite anyone over for dinner. Harry considered it would be much more practical to wrap the mattress in plastic until it was needed, but it was not her house, nor was it her place to make suggestions.

She finished the first room and moved down the hall to the next guest room on the right. As she ran the duster over the dresser a soft thump sounded from the far wall, seemingly coming from the room next door.

Harry had expected this noise, so she didn't jump the way she had the first several times it happened, nor did she attempt to investigate its source. She hummed a little tune, the way a child might whistle in the dark to keep the monsters away.

She first heard the noise maybe two weeks after she'd started working for Mr. Castillo, and it had recurred intermittently since then.

The thump came again, louder than before, but her breath and her tone remained even as she kept humming.

The noise sounded once again, and she thought, not for the first time, *It sounds like someone kicking the wall.*

But no one lived at Bright Horses except Mr. Castillo, so it couldn't be someone kicking the wall. Likely it was just an oddity in the pipes—the old heating systems in a lot of houses made noises like that.

As she exited the second guest room and crossed the hall to the small library she kept her eyes averted from the closed door to her right, the last room on the guest room side.

That door was always locked, and it wasn't her job to be curious about it.

JAVIER CASTILLO

before

IN 1970, WHEN HE was eight years old, his mother dropped Javier and his brother Luis off at the cinema so she could shop for a couple of hours without dealing with their constant bickering. They loved each other, the way that brothers do, but they also loved needling each other, the way that brothers do.

There was visible relief in her eyes as she called to them, "Have fun, be careful," but Javier barely noticed. He was already thinking of hot buttered popcorn slipping between his fingers, the click of the projector, the curtains parting to reveal the white screen in the moments before it filled with giant monsters.

Luis was four years older than Javier and loved Godzilla movies, or anything close to a Godzilla movie (he'd take a Gamera film in a pinch, though he didn't prefer the giant turtle, who was a little too cute for Luis's taste). Fortunately for Luis, the owner of the Majestic Theater also loved Godzilla movies, and that meant they were going to see *Destroy All Monsters*.

Javier didn't remember the exact plot of the movie later, when their mother (bearing a fresh manicure and fewer lines in her forehead) picked them up and bore them home. He only remembered the monsters—Rodan, the flying dinosaur who moved at great speeds; Mothra, the giant caterpillar who could become a magical butterfly; Manda, an enormous sea dragon with an incredibly long neck; Anguirus, who looked like a cross between a dinosaur and a turtle and a roly-poly bug, and who always made Javier laugh.

Of course, his number-one monster was Godzilla, the king of them all—Godzilla with his deliberate, destructive walk and the terrible flash of his nuclear breath. Godzilla, who was feared by everyone but also loved—what a strange thought this was for young Javier. If he ever saw Godzilla in real life, he didn't know if he would cheer or run screaming.

In the movies, people always did a little bit of both. Maybe that was how monsters were supposed to make you feel. Maybe they were supposed to make your heart thrill and your blood run cold at the same time. Maybe they made you want to run and to stay, to escape but always to look back because you had to see.

And the exhilaration of Monster Island—a place just for giant monsters to live! Javier dreamt of this island at night, dreamt of being allowed to live there, to wake each morning in a tent on the beach and see Minilla laughing and blowing smoke bubbles instead of fiery breath like his great father.

As he grew older, all he wanted was to live among monsters, to make their monstrosity a part of him, to feel that he too was terrible and beautiful, that perhaps even when others wanted to run from him they would stand and stare, and be unable to look away.

TWO

GABE WAS AT THE dining room table with his homework spread out before him when Harry got home. He was tall and gangly like his father, all long limbs and sharp joints, and his legs stuck out in front of him. He had dark curly hair the exact opposite of her own and he wore it shaggy, which was apparently the fashion now. He was just starting to get a little hair above his upper lip, that wispy-nothing of a mustache that most boys in their early teens have.

His head and shoulders hunched over an open workbook, and as Harry dropped a kiss on the back of his head she saw his left hand carefully writing out solutions to algebra problems that appeared frighteningly incomprehensible to her. Harry was relieved Gabe had an aptitude for math, since it had been her worst subject and she wouldn't be able to help him with it if she tried.

"There's a letter from Mr. Howell for you," Gabe said, not looking up. "He was leaving when I was coming in and he gave it to me."

Harry frowned. Ted Howell Jr. was the son of the original owner of the building. Howell Sr. had always kept the rent in the building artificially low, which had allowed Harry and Gabe to stay in one place for more than ten years.

The apartment above theirs had been host to a rotating wheel of tenants who stayed, on average, two years before moving on. Their current neighbors were two twentysomething girls who both worked office-jobs-gone-remote since the pandemic. They were nice enough, if a little bland. They didn't make a lot of noise, though—that was the important thing.

Harry and Gabe had once spent a nightmarish year with a couple of party-all-the-time college boys living upstairs. Harry remembered feeling constantly snappish and irritable, never able to get a decent night's sleep because the neighbors always decided the exact right time to turn on their music to soul-crushing volume was eleven p.m. or later.

Howell Sr. had informed Harry about six months previous that he was handing over administration of his business—he owned three apartment buildings in the neighborhood—to his son. Ever since, Harry had felt a continuous, low-frequency dread that Howell Jr. would raise the rent to something more in line with the rest of the neighborhood and they would be forced out.

It wasn't so essential that Harry and Gabe stay in this neighborhood now that Gabe was out of elementary school; it was simply that Harry was completely unable to manage the cost of a move at the moment. Her "savings account" (she always thought of it in air quotes, since no matter how hard she tried she never managed to get ahead of her expenses long enough to do any significant saving) was completely depleted by the long months without work. She couldn't afford to pay a security deposit and first month's rent plus the current rent on her new place, never mind the cost of a moving truck.

Gabe had left the envelope from Ted Howell on the counter next to the mail. Harry's hand hovered over the envelope, trying to decide if it was better to rip the bandage off right away or to wait until later, when she was alone.

As a single mother she was always deeply conscious of how easy it would be to burden Gabe with adult concerns that weren't his to bear. It would be easy to complain to her son about her worries, to make him the second adult in the house when that role should be filled by a partner, not a child.

It had been just Harry and Gabe since he was born, the two of them against the world. But it wasn't his responsibility to worry about the rent or food or doctor's appointments. His job was to go to school and play video games and mess around with his friends, to make mistakes, to get in trouble, to learn, to grow up to be a better adult than she was herself.

She'd wait until later to read Howell's note. *In fact,* she thought as she separated the junk mail from the first class and saw that all that remained was bills, *I'll just save all the bad news for after Gabe has gone to bed.*

A thump came from above her head, the sound of one of her neighbors dropping an object on the hardwood floor. Harry started, and Gabe laughed.

"Jumpy much, Mom?"

Normally she'd laugh and make some sarcastic comment back, but she found it was caught in her throat. The noise sounded exactly like the one that had come from the other side of the wall in Mr. Castillo's second bedroom. The sounds happened every time she went in there, usually intermittently. That day the noise had been consistent and determined, so much so that for a moment she thought someone was trapped in the room.

That's ridiculous, she thought. *One of the most prominent filmmakers in the world has not imprisoned someone in his spare room. Probably.*

(What if someone is trapped in there and you're ignoring it and you could save them? What if it's like that movie with Catherine Keener that was based on a true story—the one where she kept the girl in her basement and tortured her and nobody did anything about it?)

"What's that movie, that true-crime movie about the mom who kept the girl in the basement?" Harry asked as she rummaged in the cupboards, trying to decide what to cook for dinner.

"Are you trying to tell me something? Should I be worried if I come home with an F?" Gabe said.

"I can't imagine you failing anything."

"You never know. It could happen."

Something in his tone made Harry stop rummaging and look at Gabe. "Are *you* trying to tell me something?"

His shoulders hunched in more and he continued scrawling answers to his algebra work as he said, "No. I'm just saying it could happen. High school is a lot harder than eighth grade."

Harry stared. Was Gabe struggling? Was a teacher giving him a hard time? Maybe she should have asked Mr. Castillo if she could run Gabe's missing report up to school that morning after all. Did he need extra help? Should she arrange for a tutor?

"If you're struggling—"

"I'm not. I'm *not.* Don't start that panic spiral thing you do."

Harry frowned. "What panic spiral thing?"

"That thing where you start imagining every possible permutation of doom, and you just sit there getting more and more worked up behind your eyes and you think I don't notice."

"I don't do that," Harry said. She did do that, but she'd thought—or rather, hoped—he hadn't noticed.

"Yeah, you do," Gabe said.

"No, I don't."

"You do."

They glared at each other for a moment, and Harry really noticed for the first time how much older he looked. There was an adult lurking behind Gabe's eyes, and she felt a pang of preemptive loss, like a memory she didn't have yet.

Gabe dropped his eyes first. Harry opened her mouth, not sure what she intended to say, but then Gabe spoke.

"*An American Crime.*"

"What?" Harry said. She was wrong-footed, lost in a different thread of conversation.

"*An American Crime.* That's the Catherine Keener movie you were talking about before."

"Oh. Right."

She felt disoriented, which always made her grumpy, but she didn't want to take it out on Gabe, so she pulled a box of spaghetti out of the cabinet and began filling a pot with water.

"Did you like my use of the word 'permutation'?"

"Huh?"

"When I said 'permutation of doom.' I thought that was pretty good."

She shut off the water and found him grinning at her, and she grinned back. Something clenched tight inside her eased then, and the slightly out-of-sync feeling she'd had all day cleared up.

"New vocabulary word?" she asked.

"Yup," he said. "Probably the only one I'll remember."

"Guess you'd better study your vocabulary words then," she said.

Her eyes found the envelope from Howell Jr., but she turned away from it, wanting to keep the anxiety away for a little longer.

Later. Later, when Gabe won't see.

"ARE YOU FEELING WELL?" Mr. Castillo asked.

"Hm?" Harry asked, her brain one million miles from her current location.

"Are you feeling well?" he repeated. "You seem very distracted today. I thought you might be unwell."

Harry was sure she did a terrible job keeping the shock off her face. Mr. Castillo had never before appeared to notice her mood, or even notice her beyond her value as a human dust remover.

He frowned at her now, his own duster in hand, his slightly-too-small maroon sweater bunching up around the roll just above his trouser belt. Harry never saw him in casual clothes, and since she vacuumed inside his closet she knew he didn't own any. Not a sweatshirt or jeans or a ratty pair of sneakers in sight.

The crinkled line between his eyes became more pronounced and she realized she hadn't actually answered his question.

"I'm sorry," she said. "I didn't get a good night's sleep and I'm a little out of it."

That much, at least, was true. She hadn't slept except in fitful snatches the night before, or the night before that. When she closed her eyes she saw the lines of the letter Ted Howell Jr. had sent, the stark, unrelenting cruelty of them. Worse, she'd replay the humiliating conversation they'd had after she'd worked up the nerve to call him.

Mr. Castillo's lips moved and she realized he was talking again. She forced herself to concentrate on him, to make sense of the noise emitting from his mouth.

". . . cup of coffee in the kitchen. There are some blueberry muffins as well. Did you eat breakfast?"

Harry shook her head. She'd barely eaten a thing the last two days. It was hard to think about food when there was a cold knot in her stomach that never loosened, taking up all the space where a meal should go.

"Have something to eat and a cup of coffee and come back in twenty minutes. I will have finished the shelves on this side by then."

They were in the big library, which housed not only Mr. Castillo's special editions—rare and collectible volumes, many of them perfectly preserved or restored—but many smaller props from film sets—the gold box from *Cronos,* the Necronomicon from *Army of Darkness,* Sweeney Todd's silver-chased blades.

These were the props that Harry liked, things from the films she loved that didn't seem to have agency or personality like the costumes and puppets on the upper floor. They were just incredibly cool objects, and she would marvel that she got to touch them even with gloves.

Today she'd barely noticed what she touched, though her hands had moved automatically through her tasks. She didn't know what she was going to do, and worrying about it took up every cell of her body.

"Go on, go on," Mr. Castillo said as she stood in a stupor. He made a *hurry along* gesture with his arms. "Eat something, drink coffee. You'll feel better."

Harry nodded and moved toward the kitchen like a sleepwalker, unsure what to say or do in the face of Mr. Castillo's sudden gesture of humanity. He usually treated her like an automaton, a cleaning robot that arrived at his home at ten a.m. and left at five p.m. three days a week. He wasn't unkind; he just wasn't familiar. He didn't make idle chitchat. He didn't invite confidences.

Harry understood why. The press, she knew, had been very intrusive after the tragedy. And Mr. Castillo had made it clear that their relationship was a professional one, even though—or perhaps especially because—she was in his house and among his things.

Now he was telling her to take a break—a break, a thing she'd never been offered before. Mr. Castillo didn't seem to think breaks were necessary things. He never appeared to take one himself. Normally the only time Harry was able to sit down was at lunch.

I must have been really out of it, Harry thought as she pushed open the door into the kitchen. It was one of those doors that had hinges that swung both ways, which always made Harry think of a housekeeper carrying a tray of dishes, nudging the door open with her hip.

The kitchen itself looked like it belonged to another house, like it had been dropped in Bright Horses by aliens who'd missed their correct stop. The furniture throughout the rest of the house was heavy and dark, with brocaded fabrics and thick curtains and old-fashioned wallpaper all around. The rooms gave off the impression of cobwebs and dust even though everything was spotlessly clean.

But the kitchen was like a display model for a new condo showing. White cabinets, subzero refrigerator, Wolf oven and range, chrome appliances, marble countertops. It was an entertainer's kitchen, the kind of room made for someone who loved to cook, who loved to arrange plates of food just so and carry them out to guests who oohed and aahed. It was incongruous with Mr. Castillo's hermit-like nature, just like the guest rooms that were always prepared for anyone who might drop in.

She wondered if these habits were a remnant from his life before, when he did throw parties and have guests stay at his home.
Now the beautiful kitchen and the fresh sheets on the beds were
phantom limbs, memories of a life he couldn't feel properly any
longer.

Harry made a cup of dark roast coffee. Mr. Castillo had one of
those pod machines that she considered too expensive and waste-
ful. She didn't think the coffee tasted that great, but it was better
than the instant she kept at home.

She found a basket of muffins on the counter and took one,
eating it while standing over the sink. Harry wondered who baked
the muffins. It was hard to picture Mr. Castillo with an apron over
his nice trousers, surrounded by flour and butter and sugar, splat-
ters of blueberry juice on his hands.

Perhaps he had a cook who only came in when Harry wasn't
around, a cook who kept all the surfaces gleaming, because Harry
found there was never much for her to clean.

She heard a muffled thud from the other room, a thud that
reminded her of the room upstairs.

(*And I never clean that room at the end of the hall on the third floor but
there's nothing sinister about it and there's no one being kept in that room
against their will, definitely not.*)

Thinking about the locked door upstairs made Harry feel sick,
made the muffin she'd just swallowed catch in her throat. If there
was someone in that room and she didn't do anything about it . . .
but if there wasn't some secret attic wife and she broke into a room
Mr. Castillo had expressly told her to stay out of, she'd lose her
job. She needed this job more than ever after Howell's news.

*Mr. Castillo isn't the kind of person who'd do something like that, keep
someone locked away. He isn't. He isn't.*

(*maybe he's grooming you to be his next victim*)

Harry shook that thought away and told herself firmly, "Stop it." She was doing the very thing Gabe had accused her of doing—letting panic bubble up and then following it into an impossible spiral, letting it morph into every absurd permutation (*vocabulary word*, she thought in Gabe's voice).

Mr. Castillo wasn't a serial killer. He did not have Harry clean his house just so he could murder her at his leisure.

(but his wife disappeared)

She shook her head again, took a deep breath, made a conscious effort to dismiss all thoughts of the room upstairs from her mind. This was the kind of behavior that made people start spouting conspiracy theories, talking about lizard people and who-knew-what-else absurdities.

She was just stressed out and scared about her future, and her brain was trying to latch onto something else, anything else, so she wouldn't think about the Letter.

That was what it had become in her mind—no longer a benign piece of paper fulfilling its purpose of delivering a message. It was an event, a crisis of epic proportions. The Letter stated not, as she'd feared, that her rent would be raised. Such fear seemed profoundly quaint now, in light of actual events. No, the Letter said that Howell Jr. had sold the building to a developer who planned on converting it into a single-family home.

This was happening all over the North Side, had been for some time. Beautiful old greystones that housed two or three families transformed into monstrosities with six bedrooms and seven and a half baths, the rear half of each building extended until there was no green space to be found. These houses always sold for seven figures to the futures brokers and investment bankers married to the Lululemon moms.

These houses (and their occupants) propagated like a virus,

single-family conversions begat more single-family conversions which begat more investment bankers and Lululemon moms. And now her building, her and Gabe's home for the last decade, was going to be one of those places, housing the kind of person she couldn't stand, the kind of person who thought it was a personal failing to be poor.

Harry had waited until Gabe was out of the house the next morning before calling Howell Jr., who'd informed her in the Letter that they had two months to vacate.

"That's not enough time," Harry had protested.

"It's more than generous," Howell Jr. said. Harry could practically hear his shrug over the phone.

"I've lived here for ten years. Aren't you required to give us more notice?"

"In point of fact, I'm only *required* to give thirty days' notice. You can go look it up, if you want," Howell Jr. said.

"Look," Harry said. "I've been a good tenant to your father."

"I'm sorry," he said, not sounding sorry at all. "The sale is already done and the developer wants to get moving. The housing market is hot right now. Everyone wants more space because they're sick of being cramped in tiny apartments."

"Mr. Howell, please." Harry hated how craven she sounded, how desperate. "I lost my job because of the pandemic and was only able to restart work a month ago. I'm not in a position to pay a deposit and moving costs for a new place. Can't you find space for us at one of your other properties?"

"Nope. I sold them all. My father liked being a landlord, but personally, I'm not interested. Once all the sales are complete and the property transferred over I'll be moving to Arizona." He sounded so cheerful, so pleased he was about to come into money that he hadn't earned.

Harry gritted her teeth and asked, "Well, maybe you know some other landlords in the area looking for tenants?"

Howell Jr. chuckled. "Nobody around here is going to charge what Dad's been charging you. He's been losing money on you for years. He kept the rent that low as a favor."

"But do you know anybody?" Harry asked. She clung to the vague hope that if Howell Jr. recommended her personally to someone she might get away without paying a deposit.

"Sorry, no," he said. Harry hoped that when he moved to Arizona a bark scorpion would crawl into his shoe and bite him.

The kitchen door swung open and Mr. Castillo came in, found Harry standing at the sink holding a cold cup of coffee in one hand and muffin with one bite taken out of it in the other. Harry hastily dumped the coffee in the sink and shoved the rest of the muffin in her mouth. It tasted like ash and bile, and she only just forced herself to swallow it down.

"I'm sorry, Mr. Castillo. I lost track of time."

He gave her a long look as Harry pulled her mask back up. With the coverage of the mask all he could see of her expression was her eyes. He seemed to be studying the dark circles underneath them.

"You appear to be getting less sleep," Mr. Castillo said. "Anything worrying you?"

So many things, I don't even know where to start, Harry thought. But she absolutely, positively wasn't going to talk about those things with Mr. Castillo.

He watched her expectantly, and she realized she ought to say something, justify her behavior in some way.

"I'm just worried about my son," she said. "The transition to high school, you know . . ."

She trailed off, her words trickling to a halt. Mr. Castillo's face had frozen in place the moment Harry said, "My son."

Stupid, stupid. Why did I bring up Gabe?

"Your son," he said. He seemed to drift off for a moment, somewhere far away.

His son is out there somewhere, someplace. But he doesn't know where that place is, Harry thought, feeling desperately sorry for him.

Then he said, "Sons need guidance from their fathers. They shouldn't make their mothers worry like this."

"Oh," Harry said, regretting more every second that she'd mentioned Gabe. "His father is, um, not in the picture."

That was a nice way of saying Gabe's father walked out before Gabe was even born, making it clear that being a father just wasn't his preferred vocation. He'd never been in contact again after that. Harry could have pursued him for child support at least, but she'd have had to find him first. And it had hurt that he hadn't wanted her—or their child—enough to stay.

"I see," Mr. Castillo said.

Harry had the uncomfortable feeling that he did see, that he'd gleaned a lot more from her one sentence than she wanted him to know.

"Let's finish in the library, shall we?" he said.

Harry nodded, and followed him out.

HARRY

before

IT WAS INEVITABLE THAT her mother would discover her secret life. Like most teenagers, Harry had done a poor job of hiding that she was hiding something. One night, while Harry was at work blending Blizzards and piling fries into baskets, her mother went through Harry's room with a fine-toothed comb. She opened all of Harry's dresser drawers and looked under the bed and searched through the closet, worming out every passed note from a friend that Harry had saved, every Stephen King book stacked inside a shoebox for safekeeping, and most importantly, the stash of *Fangoria* and *Famous Monsters* issues in between Harry's mattress and box spring.

In other households this might be a cause for relief, for when most parents worry about their teens they're worrying that they'll find dime bags of weed or pornography or boxes of condoms. They don't worry about horror movie magazines.

But to Harry's mother this was proof that her daughter had been possessed by the devil—that and the Stephen King books, because there wasn't an author on earth more ungodly in Mrs. Schorr's opinion. The sort of things that man wrote about were most decidedly not in line with Christian values.

Harry returned home from work that night to find her mother and her father and her sister at the kitchen table—her parents stone-faced, her sister barely able to suppress her glee that Harry was about to get her comeuppance.

On the table Harry's mother had piled the magazines and the books and the few saved notes, notes in which Harry and her friends talked about cute boys and their cute asses, or drew stupid pictures for one another. Just teenage girl foolishness, but Harry's mother didn't see it that way.

Harry's heart sank when she saw all her belongings, her most precious things, piled there like so much trash. And as her mother launched into a lecture about letting Satan into her heart, Harry felt her anger swell and swell. Why was it so wrong? Why was what she wanted, what she *needed*, something so bad?

She sat there, feeling her rage stoke more with every word of the lecture, her teeth clenched while a scream rose in her throat.

Then her mother picked up the pile of precious things and ordered Harry to follow her outside. Harry thought that her books and magazines would be thrown in the trash, and planned to retrieve them later, hide them in some better place outside of the house.

Instead she saw that wood had been stacked in the outdoor firepit, and her nostrils filled with the scent of lighter fluid.

Her beautiful things were thrown there, and Harry's father poured more lighter fluid on top of them, and her sister dropped in the match. Harry did scream then, screamed because a part of her heart was burning, and her family looked like gleeful demons, their faces lit and shadowed by flame.

THREE

ON THE WAY HOME Harry did a quick search on her phone for the details of the Castillo family tragedy. When Mr. Castillo had first hired her she hadn't wanted to look up the information, felt like it was a violation of his privacy even though it was public knowledge. She'd reasoned that she remembered the basics, and that since she planned to never, ever mention the events it would be fine.

After the encounter in the kitchen Harry felt more than ever the importance of avoiding conversational land mines. She couldn't jeopardize her job. She didn't have a ton of skills, and most of those skills involved carrying a tray of food. Restaurants weren't back at their pre-pandemic capacity yet and most places, including her former employer, operated at half-staff. More restaurants closed every day.

Harry felt, deep in her soul, the looming terror of being both jobless and homeless. She'd been both in the past, and it was one thing to have no roof over your head when you were alone. It was quite another to do so when you had a teenager who relied on you to be a responsible adult.

The fear was a near-constant prickling of anxiety, like a rash underneath the skin. She'd worked hard all her life, had scrimped and struggled to create some degree of respectability for Gabe, but it was nothing but a card house vulnerable to a hard gust of wind.

She scrolled through the search results on her phone—she'd entered **Javier Castillo** in the search bar and found a jumble of topics ranging from his award wins to interviews with *Entertainment Weekly* and the *Hollywood Reporter*. She found what she was looking for on the second page of results, and wondered who Mr. Castillo had to pay to make sure it wasn't the first story that popped up.

Harry tapped on one with the headline **SON OF OSCAR-WINNING DIRECTOR ARRESTED**. It was dated five years earlier, pretty soon after Mr. Castillo won the Academy Award. Harry read, "Michael Castillo, just thirteen years old, was today charged with driving a stolen vehicle and driving without a license. His blood alcohol level at the time of the arrest was well above the legal limit, according to sources familiar with the matter. Castillo's father, Javier Castillo, could not be reached for comment. Michael Castillo will be charged as a juvenile."

Harry followed a link at the bottom of the page that led to a story about a plea deal in which Michael Castillo was given two hundred hours of community service, "according to an anonymous source." There was a picture of Mr. Castillo and his wife, Lena, both looking grim as they exited the courthouse behind their son.

At thirteen Michael was very tall, taller than both his parents, and resembled them only in coloring—both had passed their own dark hair and eyes on to their son. Michael's features were already sculpting into the kind of good looks that might result in a modeling career, or at least would pave the way for a lifetime of what Harry thought of as "beauty privilege." There was none of the gangly awkwardness of the adolescent about him. Harry imagined he got his way often and easily—if he possessed even a tenth of his looks in charm then most people would find him irresistible.

The article, again, led to another. This one had paparazzi photographs of young Michael, roughly the same age as the picture of him leaving the courthouse, partying at a club with a bevy of Victoria's Secret models. Harry traced the photo of Michael with her finger, enlarged it on her phone. His perfect white teeth were displayed in a wide smile, his arms in the air as he danced with a woman at least ten years his senior. Harry imagined he felt on top of the world, like he could do anything he wanted and get away with it. There was a reckless light in his eyes, a giddy arrogance that Harry had seen before.

Money and privilege are truly magic powers, Harry thought.

Even after Michael Castillo was caught drinking again, caught fighting with an A-list actor at a party, caught doing cocaine in a restaurant bathroom, caught using his (much older) girlfriend's credit card without her permission—even after all that he never went to a juvenile detention center, which in Harry's opinion was clearly where he belonged. He didn't even wind up in rehab, which seemed the bare minimum that should have been done to address the boy's issues.

Throughout it all there were pictures of Javier Castillo and his wife, always grim, their lips set, their eyes blank, ignoring the microphones waved in their faces. Over time, only one significant thing changed in the photos.

In the first one, taken after Michael was caught driving the stolen car, Javier Castillo had his arm around Lena. Her head was tucked into his shoulder, and the two of them appeared as a team uniting against an onslaught.

In the second photo his arm was still around her but she looked away from him, as if they'd had an argument a moment before.

The third photo showed them holding hands, but by the fourth even that pretense was gone. The two of them stood a few inches apart, Javier Castillo's hands curled into fists, Lena's arms folded tightly in front of her body like a shield.

Michael was a wedge driven into their marriage, prising them apart by degrees.

Harry clicked on the next link, the one she'd really been looking for all along but was half hoping to avoid.

MICHAEL CASTILLO—MURDERER? the headline blared. The copy underneath was nearly as salacious as the title.

The troubled son of Academy Award–winning director Javier Castillo has been questioned by police in regard to the homicide of Adelaide Walker, 19, a model and actress known to be linked to Michael Castillo, 17.

Police responded to a 911 call from a neighbor of Walker's, claiming she heard "sounds like fighting, like someone was hitting her and she was screaming." The neighbor reports that she looked out the window and saw a figure leaving Walker's house and getting into a sedan that appeared to be waiting for a passenger. The neighbor was unable to say conclusively if the person seen leaving Walker's house was, in fact, Michael Castillo, although the neighbor claimed "he's in and out of there all the time."

Walker was found dead a short time later by emergency responders.

Michael Castillo was at his parents' home when police arrived to question him. A lawyer for the family has stated that Michael Castillo has not been arrested and is fully cooperating with the investigation.

This time there were no photos of Michael with his parents, just a shot of the gate outside their home, followed by a glamorous headshot of Adelaide Walker and some paparazzi photos of Castillo and Walker on a beach.

The article, and related articles that Harry found, strongly hinted that Michael Castillo's arrest was inevitable.

Then, inexplicably, the police did nothing.

Three days, four days, five days, two weeks. They claimed to be waiting for lab results. No arrests were made, no progress visible to the public. They said they were pursuing multiple lines of inquiry.

In the interim Adelaide Walker's parents began appearing before the press. Peter and Johnna Walker were an ordinary-looking, corn-fed Midwestern couple made luminous by their despair. In photos the couple, especially Peter, appeared lit from within by a righteous fury. The lines of grief drew his skin tight around his cheekbones, the same bone structure he'd passed on to his beautiful daughter. Johnna stood at his side in every photo, a sentinel of justice—her face pale, her blue eyes welling with tears that never fell.

And in every interview they said the same thing—"Michael Castillo killed our daughter and the police should arrest him."

They said this to anyone who would listen, anyone with a

video camera and a recording device. They hinted that police corruption was at the heart of this injustice, that Javier Castillo's money kept his son out of jail. Speculative stories began to appear on blogs, followed by the inevitable weigh-in of social media users desperate to express an opinion. The hashtag #JusticeForAdelaide began trending.

Many people, wondering exactly how a boy from such a privileged background could go so wrong, started blaming his parents. His father was never home, cared more about making movies and collecting props than about his own son. The hashtag #CancelCastillo began trending.

People posted videos of themselves breaking Castillo-directed DVDs or burning T-shirts of his film characters. The police still didn't arrest Michael Castillo, or anyone else.

Then the mob turned on Lena Castillo, and, like all women, she took the brunt of the wrath. At least Javier Castillo had an excuse, the court of public opinion reasoned. He was a filmmaker. He was *working*. What was his wife doing while Michael ran wild? The boy was seventeen. She should have watched him more closely, done more to discipline him. What was she doing while Michael, a minor, went partying? Was she shopping, getting her nails done, having facials?

She should have removed him from that dangerous environment, put him in rehab, sent him to military school. If only Lena Castillo had done more, been a better, more attentive mother, then Adelaide Walker would still be alive.

Michael Castillo might be a murderer but everyone knew he didn't get that way on his own. He was obviously acting out because his mother didn't love him enough.

Harry felt sick as she read things like this, got caught in a rabbit hole of old comments and hashtags. She looked up from her phone and realized she'd missed her bus stop. She pulled the wire and got off at the next stop, trudging back the four blocks to Jewel, where she'd meant to stop and collect some groceries before going home. There was no time to think about Lena Castillo then, about the stark unfairness of blaming the mother of an alleged (*Michael Castillo was never actually arrested; there must have been a reason for that*) murderer.

Why was it always the mother's fault? Why didn't the father receive the same degree of criticism? Or really, Harry thought as she wiped the handle of a grocery basket with a sanitizing wipe, *why can't people accept that sometimes children's actions have nothing to do with their parents at all?*

Harry took a bunch of bananas, weighed them, added the bananas to the basket and the cost to the calculator on her phone. She had a very strict budget and always kept a running tally of what went into her grocery basket. Sometimes Harry dreamed of having the freedom to put whatever she wanted in her cart, without worry about cost.

She always tried to leave a little money to buy treats for Gabe, because she didn't want him to think life was nothing but penurious misery. He deserved to have as normal a life as possible.

Doritos were on sale and Gabe loved them. Harry grabbed a bag even though every time Gabe ate Doritos he used his T-shirt as a napkin and that made her crazy. It didn't matter if he had an actual napkin in front of him. He'd take a handful of chips, chomp them the way a horse chomps on its feed, and then swipe his cheese-dust-covered hand across his chest, leaving a thin line of orange powder on his clothes. No matter how many times Harry pointed out this behavior he kept doing it, like it was a compulsion he couldn't help.

She picked up some corn tortillas—two packages were less

than a dollar—a couple of cans of black beans, three sweet potatoes, salsa and a block of cheddar. Gabe loved black bean and sweet potato tacos, and she could cook a lot for a little money and it would fill him up.

Gabe's appetite, especially in the last few months, had become this ravenous, appalling thing. He was always looking for something to eat. Harry felt like keeping him in a steady supply of snacks was like trying to shovel her way out of a blizzard.

She finished her shopping and got into a long line of people with packed carts. There were only a few items in her basket and normally she'd use the self-check, which would be a lot faster, but she had to pay in cash and cash wasn't accepted in the self-check at the moment because of the national coin shortage.

Harry watched a blond woman with two young kids and a cart piled high with food swipe a platinum credit card. She swallowed the bile that burned in her throat. Resenting people who had more than her wouldn't do her any good. It wouldn't make a comfortable life magically appear, and it wouldn't make her current one any easier to bear.

Gabe was in his bedroom when she got home, but he came into the kitchen when he heard her enter. He liked to see what she'd bought so he'd know what was available for future consumption. He hugged the bag of Doritos to his chest and kissed her cheek.

"Thanks, Mom," he said, then added in a rush, "Is it true we have to move out of the apartment?"

Harry kept unloading her few items onto the counter and then crumpled up the plastic bag in her hand.

"Where did you hear that?" she asked casually, though her heart had started a rapid tattoo in her chest.

"I bumped into Tiffany from upstairs when I came back from

my run." Gabe was on the cross-country team, so even on remote learning days like today he went out to practice on his own. "She said that Mr. Howell's son sold the building and everyone has to leave. She sounded pretty stressed about it, was saying it's hard to find a place this cheap around here."

Damn that Tiffany, Harry thought.

"That's not the way I wanted you to hear about it. I was going to tell you myself later."

"So it's true? We have to leave?"

A line formed between his brows, a line Harry hated to see. This wasn't something he should have to worry about.

"Yes," she said, infusing her tone with a calm she didn't feel. "But not for two months, which means we have plenty of time to look for something new."

"Oh. Okay," he said, but the line in between his brows did not soften. "But what about the rent? Tiffany said this place was really good."

"Well, we don't have to stay right in this neighborhood now that you're out of elementary school," Harry said. "We can look for something closer to your high school. Wouldn't it be nice to have a shorter bus ride?"

"I don't mind it," Gabe said. "I just listen to music and stare out the window."

"If you have a shorter bus ride you can listen to music and stare out the window at home," Harry said.

"I know. But I like it here."

They'd lived in the apartment for so long that Gabe didn't really remember living anywhere else.

"I know. I like it here, too." She ran her hand over his hair. He was so tall now. What had happened to her baby? Anxiety filled her, anxiety that she was failing him when she loved him so much. "Don't worry. It will be a change, but change isn't always a bad thing."

"If you say so," Gabe said.

"I say so," Harry said. "Let's make tacos."

As she peeled the potatoes Harry resolved not to think anymore about Michael Castillo. She had enough on her plate without worrying about what happened to him. She just needed to remember not to say anything stupid that might remind Javier Castillo of his lost child. As Harry fried the potatoes and supervised Gabe while he heated the tortillas, she couldn't help thinking of Lena Castillo again.

Everyone had blamed her for what Michael did, or supposedly had done. But Harry found she couldn't blame Javier Castillo's wife for what Lena had done next. Harry, too, thought she would do anything to protect her son. Even if he had committed a murder.

One night, when Javier Castillo wasn't at home, Lena had taken Michael and disappeared. They'd disappeared so thoroughly that not a hint, not a trace of them had ever been found.

I might have done that. I might have done something exactly like that to keep Gabe safe.

Much later, though, when she was watching Gabe laugh at *Abbott and Costello Meet Frankenstein*—he had old-fashioned taste for a modern kid—Harry thought about the look on Javier Castillo's face that day in the kitchen.

Lena Castillo might have saved Michael, Harry thought, *but she left Javier Castillo alone.*

HARRY SPENT HER DAY off checking Craigslist and Redfin and other websites looking for potential new apartments. This was disheartening work. So many places were out of her price range, and the ones that weren't were very far from both Gabe's school and her current workplace.

You'll have to make do, she told herself. *There's no two ways about it. You can't live in a tent under the Montrose overpass. A longer bus ride is a small price to pay for a roof over your head.*

But it would be a very, very long bus ride if any of these apartments worked out for them. Harry tried to be philosophical about it. She could read more on a long bus ride. Or listen to a podcast. Or learn how to crochet.

Scratch that, she thought. Harry wasn't coordinated enough to learn how to crochet.

Finding an apartment within her price range, if not her preferred geographic range, was less of a problem than working out the issues with the deposit. The fact remained that her checking account did not have enough zeros in it to accommodate the payment of the first month's rent and security deposit plus payment of her current place. That wasn't even taking into account all the associated costs that took up both time and money—paying for a U-Haul, setting up new utilities, collecting and packing boxes, unpacking and disposing of boxes. Plus moving to a new place inevitably meant new furniture, because her old things wouldn't fit in the new space or were so worn out that it didn't make sense to move them.

Harry shifted on the couch, which was older than Gabe and weighed about as much as a compact car. She couldn't imagine trying to get it down the stairs in her current building, much less up the stairs in a new one.

She made some notes about potential places, writing down phone numbers and locations, but after a few hours she was too exhausted and upset to try to call anyone. She genuinely thought she might burst into tears on the phone.

Harry knew she was working herself up into a state, that her anxiety over a potential future could paralyze her in the present. This had happened to her before. And finding a new apartment was important—so, so important. She shouldn't be selfish. She shouldn't be stuck in her own feelings. She had to think about Gabe.

I am thinking about Gabe. I'm thinking about him all the time, every second of the day. I'm thinking about how I need to make things good and right and stable for him so he can grow up and be a success, and not struggle all the time like me. I want that for him. I want that so much.

But she still couldn't trust herself to keep on an even keel, so she decided to put off the phone calls for another day.

The next day was Friday, and the pace of work at Bright Horses was the same as always. She dusted and vacuumed and mopped in silence, and if it seemed that Mr. Castillo glanced at her more frequently she was careful to pretend that she didn't see. Harry didn't want to be drawn into another personal conversation where she might mention her son, her son who was close to the same age as Mr. Castillo's son when he'd (possibly) murdered someone and then disappeared. It might lead to awkward confidences. Awkward confidences might have Mr. Castillo rethinking their arrangement, and then Harry would be fired and a new, more anonymous cleaner brought in.

She couldn't have that. So she kept her eyes on her own work.

Soon enough she was in the upstairs bedrooms, changing sheets that were never slept on, cleaning floors that were never walked on. Harry was dusting the blinds—Mr. Castillo was absolutely maniacal about the condition of window blinds, he hated to see even a speck of dust on them—when the knock sounded from next door.

It had been a few days since Harry had heard the noise, which was unusual. Normally there was some kind of communication—

(it's not communication because there's not a person in there, you have to get that idea right out of your head)

—or rather, knocks, they were knocks like the kind that came from old heating systems, every time she was in the spare bedroom. But all had been quiet for a few days since the last incident, the one that had made her think of the Catherine Keener movie where the girl was held captive and Harry had forgotten the name of it again because she was standing with the duster suspended in air, staring at the place where the knock had sounded and wondering if it would happen again.

The knock came, and, though Harry was waiting for it, she dropped the duster. She saw the dust scattering in the air, little motes dancing in the thin sunlight that made it through the closed blinds.

All I did was put the dust back on the window blinds, she thought in frustration. *And on the floor, though at least I haven't vacuumed it yet.*

As she bent to pick up the duster the knock sounded again. Harry realized, for the first time, that the sound was coming from a low place on the wall. She ignored the duster and walked toward the place where the knocking was loudest. She was hunched over, like she was searching for something on the ground, and when she reached the place where she thought the noise had emanated she stopped and put her hand to the wall.

She felt the pulse of blood in her body, felt it running through her arm and her hand.

It's nothing, it's nothing, it's nothing, she repeated to herself. *In a second I'll feel the water rushing through the pipes, or the bang of forced air and I'll have my answer, it's just an old house stretching and straining, there's nothing strange about it at all.*

Instead of any of those things, though, Harry heard something else.

Whispers.

"Help me."

Harry pushed away from the wall so violently that she fell backward onto her butt. She scrabbled frantically on the floor, her legs kicking out, her hands crawling away, away, away from what she'd heard.

"Help me."

"No," Harry said, but it wasn't a response to the voice, just a reflexive denial. She couldn't have heard what she thought she heard. This house was full of atmosphere, and she'd been imagining things that weren't there, that couldn't possibly be there.

Because if Harry had heard someone say *"Help me"* then that meant there *was* someone in the room next door. There was someone in there who needed help and she was the only one who could give it.

Is there really someone being held captive in that room, someone trying to get out? And if there is, what will Javier Castillo do to me if he knows that I know? If something happens to me, then what will happen to Gabe? Who will take care of him?

All this sped through Harry's brain in an instant, and a moment later she heard a voice.

"Are you well? What are you doing on the floor?"

Mr. Castillo, standing in the doorway. He seemed somehow menacing, like he was preventing her from escaping. His voice, which had always had the slightly stern and clipped notes of the natural introvert, was now a baritone of doom.

He stared at her, and Harry realized he was waiting for an answer. She hurried to think of something plausible, to keep herself from asking, *Are you holding someone captive in the next room?*, which was the only thing running through her mind at the moment.

"I dropped the duster," she said, "and when I bent over to pick it up I got a little dizzy, so I sat down."

"Are you feeling better now? Would you like some water?" His mouth was making all the correct words but Harry found she didn't believe in them, didn't believe that *he* believed what she had said.

"No, I think I'm fine now," Harry said, standing slowly so that she appeared to be a person recovering from dizziness.

"Are you eating properly?" Mr. Castillo asked. "You're very thin, and you have appeared more tired lately."

Harry bristled. Her employer shouldn't be commenting on her weight, no matter what her size. And she thought she'd done a pretty good job of concealing the dark circles under her eyes.

Don't snap at him. He thinks he's being helpful.

(or he's pretending to be)

She forced herself to say something mild. "I'm doing okay. Really, it was just a momentary thing. I'll finish up in this room. I just need to do the blinds and then run the vacuum."

Mr. Castillo stared at her for a few moments longer, like he wanted to say something else. Then he appeared to change his mind.

"Very well," he said. "After you finish this room please join me in the green room."

The green room was in the basement, where Mr. Castillo kept some of the largest props he'd collected—oversized things like vehicles and giant puppets. They cleaned down there only once every few weeks, because the items in question were so large it generally took most of the day.

"Of course," Harry said, but her heart pounded as he turned away.

She couldn't help wondering if the reason why he'd chosen today, of all days, to do the green room cleaning was because in the basement no one would hear her scream. And then she told herself to stop being ridiculous, that this wasn't a horror movie.

There's no one in the next room. It's all in your mind.

Still, Harry was certain she heard the echo all around as she finished up, even over the drone of the vacuum.

Help me. Help me. Help me.

JAVIER CASTILLO

before

HIS FIRST FILM DIDN'T make any money. This was not un-usual, even for a film with a small budget. "Budget" had been stretching the use of the term, in any case. He'd mostly funded the project out of his own pocket, taking out a line of credit on his house and getting some funds from his parents and brother.

It was a little mood piece, a story of a lonely vampire, and all of Javier's heart was in the project, in every angle of the camera, in every line that was spoken, in every piece of set design and cos-tume and makeup. He acted as the camera operator himself, not knowing that this was unusual for a director, but he wanted to see the film through the lens, to see it come to life as the audience would.

Everything about making it was hard. He couldn't afford a lot of location changes, nor was it particularly easy to get permission to shoot in some of the places he chose. Film reels were astonish-ingly expensive, and Javier lived in terror each day that something would happen to the footage, that it would be lost or destroyed, or that there would be a terrible fire. His dreams, his very sense of self, was completely wrapped up in the making of this movie.

It was the only place where he'd ever felt he truly belonged—making monsters come to life, willing something terrible and beautiful into existence.

When he finished he was both thrilled and disappointed. It was a significant achievement to have made a movie, to have gone through the process, to have something whole and wonderful in his hands.

Except that he knew it wasn't quite as wonderful as he wanted it to be, that if only he'd had proper funding he could have made something bigger, better, more spectacular.

Still, it was a start. And he told himself that everyone had to start somewhere, but they didn't have to finish in the same place they started. One day he would be able to name his price, and the world would see his genius. Javier knew that he was brilliant, knew this without any ego. He knew that he'd created something few would be able to create with such a small amount of funding. He knew that his true vision would shine through and that studios would be able to recognize the diamond in the rough.

Javier submitted his moody vampire film to all the noteworthy festivals, hoping to get it picked up by a major distributor. A few studio reps expressed interest, but not enough to actually spend money. He went to festival after festival, big and small, and watched lesser directors get feted while he languished. He didn't tell anybody, but he began to despair. Why would nobody see him for what he was? Why was no one recognizing the beautiful heart inside his monster movie?

He decided to take the movie out on the road himself—a costly and possibly disastrous proposition. No one did this, because getting a film into theaters usually depended on a distributor.

Roadshowing the film himself would mean physically taking the reels of film from town to town, and that would also necessarily limit the run of the film at each theater. Javier had to weigh a limited run in a few places versus no run at all.

No run at all was unacceptable. He was a filmmaker, and people needed to see his film.

He managed to scrape up the money to have five copies of the film made, so that if he died in a fiery car accident there would still be some evidence that he'd existed, that he'd created. His brother agreed to take a copy of the film to half of the theaters, if Javier managed to get any to agree to this crazy idea.

Javier called independent theaters and semi-independent small chains. These were the homes of people who loved movies, passionate cinephiles who ran Charlie Chaplin film festivals with live musical accompaniment or who spent a week screening nothing but samurai films. The kinds of people who went to those theaters would love his vampire story. He was sure of it.

In the end fifteen theaters across the country agreed to show his first movie. He drove to ten of the theaters himself, agreeing to do Q&As with audiences after several showings.

And people loved him, loved his film. People applauded.

Their applause, their adulation, slipped into his bloodstream, slithered around in his brain. It settled there, and would thereafter be a part of making movies for Javier Castillo—not just the thrill of creativity, of making something no one else could make, but the poisonous, delicious burn of love, of worship.

FOUR

"WOULD YOU AND YOUR son like to have dinner with me next Friday?"

Harry was perched on a ladder, sweeping a long-handled duster over the top of a space pod that had been used in an SF movie from the eighties. Mr. Castillo was also on a ladder, a few feet away from her, carefully cleaning the face of a fifteen-foot-tall yeti puppet. He'd paused in his work to look at her, to ask the question. She didn't think she'd heard right at first. Mr. Castillo wanted her to come to dinner? Her and Gabe?

Does that mean he doesn't *want to murder me in this basement for accidentally discovering he's holding a hostage in the last bedroom at the end of the hall? Or does it mean that he wants to make things nice and clean and get rid of us both?*

Harry mentally shook off these speculations. Mr. Castillo wasn't going to kill her. Or Gabe. Probably.

Would he fire me if I said no? He might fire me even if he doesn't want to kill me. He might take offense.

But he was watching her intently, waiting for her answer.

"Um, sure. Or well, let me check with Gabe. He might have plans with his friends?"

"Wouldn't he speak to you about those plans before he made them?" Mr. Castillo asked.

There was a kind of judgment in his voice that Harry didn't like, especially coming from a man whose missing son was the primary suspect in a horrible murder. That tone put a little starch in her spine. Yes, she needed this job, but she was good at it, and she didn't need her employer judging her parenting skills. As a single mom she'd had enough of that in her life—people wondering what she did to drive Gabe's father away (*answer: nothing. The man didn't want to parent*) or why she didn't move back in with her parents so that Gabe would be more financially secure (*answer: my parents spent years trying to crush my spirit as a child and I wasn't going to give them a second chance as an adult*).

"Yes, he would speak to me," Harry said, her tone sharper than it had ever been with Mr. Castillo. "But he also makes tentative arrangements sometimes, contingent on my agreement. Which is fine and healthy and normal for a teenager."

Mr. Castillo's eyes reflected his surprise. She saw another emotion flicker after it, something she couldn't define. Then he nodded.

"You are right. It is normal."

Harry waited, but apparently that was all the apology she was going to get, because Mr. Castillo went back to dusting the puppet. They worked in silence for several minutes, then Mr. Castillo spoke again.

"Perhaps you could let me know for certain tomorrow? That would give me some time to plan."

"Oh, definitely," Harry said. "But you don't need to do anything fancy for us. With Gabe it's more quantity over quality. If you just ordered six pizzas that would do it."

"Yes," Mr. Castillo murmured. "Teenage boys do have huge appetites. One wonders where they put it all."

This was flirting dangerously close to talking about Mr. Castillo's own son, a thing that Harry definitely did not want to do.

"I bet we'll probably come, though," Harry said in a rush. "Because Gabe's a huge fan of your movies. I mean, so am I."

It was the first time she'd mentioned this fact in all the time she'd worked for him. He seemed startled by the revelation.

"You are? You never mentioned it before."

Harry shrugged, looking at her work instead of Javier Castillo's face, because he was looking at her like he'd just discovered a new species of insect. *Curious, and a little elated,* she thought. *He's glad that I'm a fan.*

"It didn't seem appropriate," Harry said.

"You didn't think playing up to my ego would have led me to hire you more quickly?" Javier Castillo asked, and his tone was wry now.

Harry said, "I thought it might work against me, actually. That you might worry that I'd somehow violate your privacy."

He gave her another measured look. Harry wished she could interpret his expressions better. It was hard when you only saw half of someone's face. She didn't know if she was on safe ground here, if she should be admitting all this. But she also thought it might be worse if Gabe said it for her, if he unwittingly stumbled into a land mine that caused her to lose her job.

Better to know now.

But if you lose your job, who will save the person in the last bedroom?
(there is no person in the last bedroom. You imagined that)

"You're right," Mr. Castillo said finally. "I likely would not have hired you if I'd known you were a fan. I moved here because I wanted to be away from prying eyes."

From the paparazzi. From the constant questions. From all the people who looked at him and wondered what had happened to him, where he'd gone wrong with his only child.

As Harry thought this, she realized something she hadn't noticed about Mr. Castillo before.

He was lonely.

He kept the guest bedrooms ready for guests that never came because he used to have guests in his house all the time. He had a large, beautifully appointed kitchen because he used to have dinner parties. But he'd given all that up when he'd moved from L.A. to Chicago, because that was the price he'd chosen to pay. He'd chosen to run from the cameras and the shouting, to hide away in a secret corridor of grief and regret. His wife and child were gone, seemingly disappeared into the ether, and he was far from his friends, far from his people. He hadn't made a new film since Michael was accused of murder.

And now he was alone in Bright Horses, surrounded by things, by facsimiles of life, and he wanted Harry and Gabe to eat dinner with him on Friday night.

Her ridiculous fears about a kidnap victim seemed just that then—ridiculous, the product of her overheated imagination and too much affection for *Jane Eyre*. Mr. Castillo didn't have an attic wife, or attic anything. He wasn't some secret serial killer. He was a lonely man, and the only person he seemed to have regular face-to-face contact with was his house cleaner.

Besides, she'd just watched *Hellraiser* and *Hellbound: Hellraiser II* with Gabe. One of the victims in the second movie said "Help me" right before she was flayed. That had probably been in Harry's head—that, and all her worry about their future housing. Her anxiety was making her imagine things that weren't there. The banging was just the sounds of an old house.

There was nothing wrong here. Nothing at all.

"Do you have a favorite?" Mr. Castillo asked suddenly. His tone was offhand, but Harry suspected that the answer was important to him. He suddenly reminded her of a child wanting attention from a parent, seeking validation in the form of a pat on the head for a job well done.

"Well, I know you've had bigger movies, but I really love *Blood and Roses*," Harry said. It was Mr. Castillo's first film, made on an extremely low budget, but Harry thought it featured some of his most inventive work. Plus, it had been shot in black-and-white, and Harry was a sucker for black-and-white films.

Mr. Castillo beamed at her, actually *beamed*. It was the first time she'd ever seen him smile—or at least, seen his eyes crinkle up in a way that indicated smiling. She could feel the joy radiating from him. He seemed more human in that moment than in all her previous interactions with him.

"That's my favorite, too," he said. And then, almost as if he couldn't help himself, added, "It was Lena's favorite as well."

Harry nodded, not sure what else to say, but Mr. Castillo's face shuttered then. He turned back to his work, and Harry did the same.

"SO I SHOULD PRETEND that I don't know anything about him," Gabe said as they walked from the bus stop toward Mr. Castillo's house.

Harry carried a tray of homemade brownies, because the one bit of her mother's teaching that had been ingrained in her was that you should never show up at someone's house empty-handed. Gabe carried a bag with a new, inexpensive pair of house slippers and they both wore disposable medical masks. Harry had never before taken off her mask around Mr. Castillo's treasures. It would be weird to do so tonight. Well, she'd assumed they would be taking their masks off in the dining room, but maybe they wouldn't. Maybe they would eat in the kitchen, which was the only place she'd ever been allowed to remove her mask before.

You are the help, after all.

Harry felt a little ashamed of herself. That was an ungenerous thought. Mr. Castillo had always been unfailingly professional around her. He'd never treated her like she was less than he was.

She directed her attention back to Gabe.

"No, you shouldn't pretend you don't know anything about him," Harry said. "It would be ridiculous if you did. I've been working in his house, and he knows you like his movies."

"But I shouldn't mention his son and the murder and all that," Gabe said.

"Obviously no," Harry said in her driest tone. "It doesn't make for the best dinner table conversation. If he mentions his son, or his wife for that matter, in some other context, then just follow his lead. Don't volunteer anything."

"It's weird, you know," Gabe said. "When you know all this stuff about someone you don't know personally. It makes you feel like you do have a personal connection when you really don't."

"It's called a parasocial relationship, and it's the bane of the twenty-first century, as far as I'm concerned," Harry said. "One person expending all of this energy and interest into another person who literally doesn't know they exist. It's not healthy."

Gabe rolled his eyes. "Please don't do the Social Media Is Destroying Society speech. Every time you say it, I feel like Laertes listening to Polonius' going-away-to-college lecture."

"Nice analogy. Just started *Hamlet*?" Harry asked.

Gabe rubbed the back of his neck a little sheepishly. "Last week. But I definitely thought of you when we read that part in class."

"Gee, thanks, I'm so glad that the blowhard of the play inspires thoughts of my parenting."

They turned down Mr. Castillo's street. Bright Horses was halfway down the block. Harry stopped in front of the gate and rang the bell.

"Come in." Mr. Castillo's voice came through the speaker, and a moment later he buzzed them in.

"Wow," Gabe said, looking up at the house. "This place is *huge*."

"Yeah, we could probably fit our whole apartment in the basement," Harry said. A little trickle of sweat had pooled at the base of her spine. She was nervous. Why was she nervous?

I never have any social interactions with people, she thought. She'd never made any real friends in Chicago, just acquaintances that had been the product of circumstances. Other parents at Gabe's elementary school, coworkers at her previous job—that was about it. People she hadn't bothered to keep in touch with when circumstances shifted, and frankly, they hadn't bothered with her, either. Harry wasn't upset about it. She knew she was the kind of person who came with walls—high, nigh-unscalable ones. She kept herself to herself. It was safer that way.

She wondered if tonight would make her see Mr. Castillo differently. She wondered if things would be weird when she came in to work on Monday, or if Mr. Castillo would just be his usual sober, professional self.

Then the front door swung open, and Mr. Castillo said, "Welcome."

He wasn't wearing his mask, as he usually did when Harry was in the house. And he looked a little unsure of himself, which was something Harry wasn't used to seeing from him.

Lonely, she thought again, and touched Gabe's arm. "This is my son, Gabe."

Gabe didn't appear nervous at all. He was staring up at the bottom of the first poster that lined the staircase.

"Gabe," Mr. Castillo said, shaking Gabe's hand. "For Gabriel?"

"Yeah. It's nice to meet you, Mr. Castillo," Gabe said. He made eye contact with Mr. Castillo for a moment, before his eyes drifted back to the poster. "Is that a *Cat People* poster?"

Mr. Castillo smiled. "Yes, it is."

"Cool," Gabe said, then he waved his arm at Harry. "My mom made brownies."

"How thoughtful," Mr. Castillo said, taking the tray from her, and it didn't sound like an empty platitude. It sounded like he really considered it thoughtful.

Harry was glad she'd taken the time to make the brownies.

Gabe had drifted to the end of the staircase, peering up at Mr. Castillo's movie posters. "Cool collection, Mr. Castillo. Are any of them originals?"

"Some of them are," Mr. Castillo said. "Please, call me Javier. Would you like to get a closer look?"

"Can I?" Gabe asked, looking from his mother to Mr. Castillo.

Harry nodded, and Mr. Castillo did, too, although Harry had the strange sense that he was nodding in approval because Gabe had checked with her first, because Gabe was a good son, unlike Michael.

It is terrible to know things about public figures. I'm putting all my own perceptions on him and they're probably not even true. Maybe he was just nodding yes like a polite host.

"I can put those in the kitchen," Harry said, indicating the tray that Mr. Castillo held. His eyes had followed her son up the stairs, watching as his sneakers disappeared. "If you want to go with Gabe."

"Thank you," Mr. Castillo said.

Sneakers, Harry thought in alarm as she took the tray. "Gabe, can you come back down and change your shoes before you go any farther?"

"It's all right," Mr. Castillo said, following after Gabe. "He can change when he's done on the staircase."

Harry stared after him in amazement. Entering Mr. Castillo's home was like entering a secure biolab—no outside germs allowed. She shook her head a little as she toed out of her own shoes and put on her work slippers. Maybe Mr. Castillo was just happy to have an enthusiastic fan appreciating his things. Harry, by design, never voiced her admiration for anything he owned. And as she'd already realized, nobody else came to visit.

That you know of. Maybe Mr. Castillo has a regular canasta game here on your days off.

Harry shook her head to herself as she pushed through the side door and went toward the kitchen. She heard Gabe's voice behind her expressing admiration for Mr. Castillo's (*I am* not *calling him "Javier," and Gabe won't either*) collection and the movies that they represented.

She passed through the library on her way to the dining room, which connected to the kitchen. As she entered she noted that the table had been set for three. They *were* eating in the dining room, and Harry again felt a little flush of shame at her earlier thought.

You always think the worst of people.

Harry entered the kitchen and placed the brownies on the counter next to the coffeepot. She smelled something good cooking—beef, maybe, and tomatoes?—and couldn't resist turning on the oven light to see. All the light revealed, though, was a large red cast-iron Dutch oven. A covered pot on the stove was on very low heat. It felt nosy to open it, so Harry didn't. Mr. Castillo had already tidily cleaned up his prep gear and put it away, so there were no clues to be gleaned from things air-drying on the sink rack.

Harry sniffed the air again, and her stomach rumbled. She and Gabe almost never ate beef, except for ground beef and only when it was on sale. She wasn't sure exactly what Mr. Castillo was cooking but it was obvious he'd taken her advice regarding quantity—the Dutch oven was twice the size of the one Harry used at home.

She went out into the dining room, expecting that Mr. Castillo and Gabe would be there, but the room was empty. Harry retraced her steps back to the entry hall, thinking they'd gotten caught up on the stairs discussing movies. Gabe's red sneakers, she noted, were in a cubby next to hers, and he'd hung his jacket up. At least he wasn't walking around in his outside shoes.

Harry heard the echo of an excited, younger voice and the rumble of an older one, and followed the sounds up the stairs to the blue room.

Gabe and Mr. Castillo stood in front of a costume, Mr. Castillo explaining the design process for the half-human/half-goat guardian from *A Messenger from Hell*. Harry wished they'd been examining literally any other figure in the room. She hated that costume with a passion, and was possessed by an almost irrational longing to grab Gabe and pull him away from that creation.

"Mom!" Gabe said excitedly. "Look! It's Sten from *A Messenger from Hell*. You love that movie."

"So do you," Harry said.

"Yeah, because it's beautiful. It's so weird to say a horror movie can be beautiful but this one is."

Mr. Castillo seemed to grow a centimeter with every compliment that Gabe gave him. Harry had never seen him like this before—not in person, that was. She remembered a similar kind of emotion on his face when he'd won the Best Director Oscar, though—a basking in the adulation, but underneath a sense that the adulation was also simply his right. Harry thought that Mr. Castillo was the kind of man who'd never doubted that he was a genius.

"Jordan Peele's *Us* is beautiful, too," Harry said.

"The pas de deux scene, I know," Gabe said, rolling his eyes. "You say that every time."

"I say it because it's true," Harry said. "That scene brought—"

"—tears to your eyes," Gabe finished.

"I guess I'm a broken record," Harry said to Mr. Castillo, smiling a little.

They were all still standing too close to the costume, as far as Harry was concerned. She smelled the scent that she always did—talcum powder and sweat—and wondered why the other two didn't seem to notice it. Gabe normally had a super-sensitive nose and complained if the slightest off-smells were anywhere in his vicinity.

"Your mother is right," Mr. Castillo said, surprising her. "It is a beautiful scene—the music, the cuts between the two opposing characters in the present and the past."

"Jordan Peele is a genius," Harry said, more than happy to discuss one of her favorite filmmakers. "I've loved all of his movies."

"Well, he doesn't always get the balance in his films exactly right—between intention and execution," Mr. Castillo said. Harry readied herself to defend Jordan Peele to the death when Mr. Castillo added, "But then, neither do I. He succeeds more than most. And he's young, so he'll be making films for many, many years to come."

Mr. Castillo looked broody, and Gabe jumped in.

"You're young, too, Mr. Castillo," Gabe said. "You've got a lot of movies left in you."

"I'm fifty-eight," Mr. Castillo said. "I don't know how many more I've got, especially considering how hard it is to get anything greenlit anymore. All the money is in prestige television and big-budget superhero movies."

"Ahh, don't talk about superheroes!" Gabe said, waving his hand. "Mom has a whole rant about mid-budget movies for adults disappearing and the infantilizing of American cinema through PG-13 tentpoles. If you get her started we'll never eat dinner."

Mr. Castillo grinned at her, and Harry was reminded again of how *weird* it was to see his whole face, not just his eyes above a medical mask.

"Apparently you have many secrets that you've been keeping while you silently dust," Mr. Castillo said. "I look forward to hearing your thoughts on this subject at dinner."

He looked a little startled then, hurrying to the staircase. "Dinner. I must go downstairs and double-check that everything is coming along as it should. Gabriel, please feel free to continue looking around this room with your mother if you're enjoying it."

"Thanks," Gabe said, wandering away from the *A Messenger from Hell* costume.

Harry blew out a breath of relief. As long as Gabe was out of the costume's reach . . .

What are you saying? That the costume is going to reach out and grab him?

Harry looked up at the mask—the distended chin, the oversized teeth, the icy blue eyes frozen in place.

The eyes moved.

They shifted in her direction, the pupils widening as they focused on her.

She gasped, stumbling backward. She wasn't imagining this. She wasn't. The costume was *looking* at her. This wasn't like the voice she'd imagined upstairs.

But what if you didn't imagine that voice?

(don't start that again and anyway this time it's real it's looking it's looking it's looking at me)

"Mom?" Gabe asked, turning toward her with a frown. "What's the matter?"

"The mask," she said, and she was shocked to hear that her voice didn't reflect the terror hammering in her blood. She wasn't imagining it—she stood right there and the mask was looking at her and there was *intent* in its eyes, intent she didn't understand but knew wasn't right.

Inanimate objects should not have *intent*.

"What about it?" Gabe asked, and Harry couldn't look away from the mask but she felt Gabe's movement toward her, the curiosity in his voice.

The eyes shifted toward Gabe.

No, she thought. *No, you will not have any intentions toward my son.*

"Nothing," she said, firmly turning away from the *A Messenger from Hell* prop and approaching Gabe before he could get another good look at the mask. "It just looked weird in the light for a second. Let's look at this corner of the room."

"It's cool to see all these props and stuff," Gabe said. "But it's a little creepy, too, isn't it? It's weird when they're disconnected from their performers. Like butterflies pinned on a board."

He's so much like me, Harry thought, a little startled to hear her own thoughts reflected back at her. But of course he was like her. His father hadn't stayed long enough to influence Gabe in any way, though now that he was older Gabe resembled his dad so much it sometimes hurt. She tried not to be bitter about his leaving—it had been so long ago, after all—and he was the one who'd lost out, really lost out, on the experience of parenting an amazing kid.

But sometimes, just sometimes, Harry looked at Gabe and remembered the boy she'd loved who hadn't loved her enough to stay. And it hurt.

She realized Gabe was watching her, waiting for an answer, but there was a patience on his face that she'd never seen before.

"What's that look?" Harry asked.

"Just waiting for the train to stop in the station," Gabe said. "You go someplace in your head sometimes, and you forget that I'm here."

Harry started to respond to this—to apologize, or something, she wasn't sure—and she felt strange and mixed-up and embarrassed that her *child*, her fourteen-year-old child, had noticed this behavior.

Gabe held up his hands. "Mom, no worries. Everybody's brain is different."

"Yeah, but I don't want to be standing here spacing out forever," Harry said.

Gabe's words made her realize how much she'd really lost the knack of being around people. When she had worked at the restaurant she was forced to be present, forced to stay in the moment every second of the day. But here, at Bright Horses, she could just quietly go about her physical tasks and let her brain drift away, let it follow whatever twisted track it wanted, tunnel inside her own thoughts until she couldn't see daylight.

"It's not forever," Gabe assured her. "More like a blip in the conversation, like you're a robot rebooting for a minute."

"Oh, that's great," Harry said. "Just what I always wanted. To be like a broken robot. Thanks, kid."

"No problem," Gabe said, grinning. "Can we see some of the other stuff in this house?"

"Let's go downstairs and see if we can help Mr. Castillo," Harry said. "He'll likely want to show you some of the other rooms himself."

"Okay," Gabe said, in that easy way he had. In that respect he was not like Harry at all. Harry didn't know how to be easy about anything, though she tried her best to hide it from him.

And I'm obviously failing, she thought as they went down the stairs. *The cracks are starting to show.*

She thought about the impending loss of their apartment, and the voice she definitely had imagined in the upstairs bedroom, and the mask that had shifted its eyes and stared at her.

Harry couldn't help it, even though she knew it was a horror movie cliché come to life. She glanced over her shoulder at the mask before she went down the stairs.

The eyes were right where they were supposed to be, but she

only knew that because the whole head of the costume had turned on the mannequin neck and watched her go.

Harry swallowed hard and turned away, knowing that when she looked back the costume would be back to normal.

And it was.

HARRY

b e f o r e

THE BURNING OF HARRY'S things was, for both Harry and her parents, a bright line in the sand. Mr. and Mrs. Schorr felt that by finding and destroying Harry's magazines and books they had rooted out Satan's hold on their daughter. They seemed to be under the impression that by simply ridding their house of those objects they could force Harry to lose interest in them, or that she would now willingly submit to their authority.

Harry was no longer allowed to go anywhere unsupervised by a member of her family. Margaret, despite being younger, was recruited as an appropriate chaperone, as she'd shown more-than-eager willingness to tattle. Harry was driven to work and home again, and not permitted to attend parties or gatherings unless her parents or Margaret also attended. The door was removed from her bedroom so that she would never be allowed any privacy, and when she was in her room her parents would check on her frequently, making sure that she hadn't managed to spirit a copy of *Carrie* under her Dairy Queen uniform and into the house. They supervised her morning and nightly prayers, and Harry had to submit to post-dinner Bible readings in which the temptation of earthly things was frequently alluded to. Mr. and Mrs. Schorr were certain that these measures would crush any spirit of rebellion that had been nurtured within their wayward daughter.

But the burning had thrown a spark inside Harry that ignited into a conflagration. She wasn't going to submit. She wasn't going to turn into her sister, whose personal piety was matched only by the breadth and depth of her personal judgment of others. She was going to run out into the world, where she'd be free to do and be whatever she wanted, and she wasn't going to wait any longer.

Harry turned seventeen in August, just before her senior year of high school. One night, well past midnight, when she was certain that her mother and father and sister all slept the sleep of the self-righteous, she packed some clothing and all of her savings from her summer job into a small backpack. She climbed out her bedroom window and onto the roof, carefully crossing to the eave that hung over their backyard. Then she swallowed the fear that threatened to overwhelm her—

(What if I break my leg? What if I land on my head?)

—crouched down, grabbed the eave in both hands, and swung her body down before she really thought about what she was doing. Harry was short, but this action still reduced the distance needed to fall to the ground. And fall she did, in an inelegant crumpled heap. There was a concrete walkway under the eave and her shins were scraped by the impact, but all in all she considered it a victory.

Harry stole out of the yard, climbing over the back fence. It bordered a country road that was rarely used in the middle of the night. The road led from Harry's backwater Indiana town to a larger town, one where there was a station to take the South Shore

Line into Chicago. The fare cost a little less than ten dollars, and she could mix in with the commuters who lived in Indiana but worked in the city. If anyone asked she could say she was going to Chicago to visit college campuses, a thing she had hoped to actually do during her senior year of high school.

No college for you now, not unless you get a GED at some point, she thought as she jogged lightly along the road. She knew all the statistics about the importance of education and future earnings. She also knew that her parents would never let her go to a college of her choice, would never let her go *period.* They would monitor and nag and preach until she broke, until she ended up screaming insane or a good little conformist doll.

She jogged and walked, jogged and walked, wanting to put as much distance between herself and her childhood home as possible. She passed the darkened houses of her neighbors, people who would happily call her parents and say, "It's so strange, but I thought I just saw Harry coming along the road. Is she at home?"

And then her father would clench his jaw and climb into his gray Ford Taurus and speed down the road, knowing that no police officer would ticket him because everyone knew Irv Schorr, he ran the hardware store in town and if he was in a hurry then there must be a good reason.

Harry would hear the car coming long before it reached her, and she would want to hide but there would be nowhere to go, nowhere to go because all the neighbors were on her parents' side. They would agree that Harry was a troublemaker and that she deserved anything she had coming to her.

Then she would start to run, and would feel her backpack slamming against her spine as she ran, and the muscles in her legs would burn but still her father's car would come, a relentless thing, and when it caught up to her he would cut the car across the road and block her way.

She would stop for a moment, calculating desperately, trying to figure out how to escape. But her father would climb out of the car and his jaw would be so tight now that she'd be able to see the muscle there ticking, ticking, ticking like a bomb. Then he would grab her arm and squeeze it in that way he had, that way that left finger marks on her skin and her bones feeling like crumbly powder. He would yank her toward the back of the car and she would scream and protest and fight but he was bigger than her and nobody would lift a finger to help her, nobody would come even though she screamed. They would all stand on their porches with their arms crossed or peek out from behind their curtains, shaking their heads, agreeing that Irv was only disciplining his wayward child, which he had a perfect right to do. Then he would toss her in the back of the car and slam the door, and she wouldn't be able to get out because he'd have activated the child safety locks—like she was a baby, like she was a prisoner.

Harry thought all this as the miles disappeared under her feet and the stars shifted their pattern across the sky and as her backpack slammed against her spine harder and harder as she ran faster and faster, running until she thought she could fly, like she could leap out into the night and grasp one of those stars and ride it all the way.

FIVE

HARRY TRIED VERY HARD not to think about the costume as they ate dinner. There was a thing that she felt was happening to her in Mr. Castillo's house—that the house itself was undermining her, that it was sapping all of the strength and certainty with which she'd conducted her life up to that point. More and more she wasn't sure if what she saw and heard was real, or if it was simply the manifestation of her deep-seated anxiety about her and Gabe's future.

Mr. Castillo had made short ribs braised in red wine with mashed potatoes on the side and rosemary olive oil bread. He'd taken Harry's warning about Gabe's appetite seriously, and had made a ton of food. Gabe was up to the challenge. It made Harry both happy and sad to see Gabe eat third helpings, knowing that he could eat as much as he wanted and also knowing she could never feed him like this at home. But she tried. She tried to give him as much as she could.

As they ate Mr. Castillo told them funny stories about the

various films he'd made. Gabe was an eager student, soaking everything up, and Harry would have been just as interested if the image of the mask-head turning toward her didn't keep popping into her brain.

She didn't know what to make of that, didn't know if it was actually haunted or if it was all in her head, didn't know if assorted life stresses had piled up on her until she'd lost her mind. She didn't know how to ask Mr. Castillo if maybe he'd noticed anything strange about the costume himself. If he thought she was nuts then he wouldn't want her to work for him, and "*must not lose job*" was her all-consuming priority. If she lost her job, then moving would be completely impossible, instead of the mostly impossible task she had now.

Will we end up living in a tent under Lake Shore Drive? She'd been homeless before, but that was when she first moved to Chicago. Despite all the fear and privation, it had in some ways been easier then. She hadn't had to worry about Gabe, just herself. If a squat had seemed too dirty or dangerous, she could just leave. Everything she owned was in one pack, and if she could get a bed at a teen shelter for the night then she would. She'd been sometimes scared, often hungry, but she'd been free and her circumstances were her own choice. It was not a life she'd ever choose for Gabe.

Sometimes she couldn't believe she was in this position. She had worked hard her whole life, done everything she could to provide stability for Gabe. But she had no backup, no support, no partner or family to fall back on, and now that disaster loomed she wasn't sure she could stop the inevitable tide.

"Earth to Mom," Gabe said.

Gabe and Mr. Castillo were watching her, wearing identical expressions of expectation.

"Sorry, I was woolgathering," Harry said. "What did you say?"

She noticed a brief flare of annoyance in Mr. Castillo's eyes, and she thought, with a little inward smirk, *I didn't give the genius his full due.* He clearly expected her to hang on his every word. She liked Mr. Castillo, but she'd seen hints of this arrogant streak before.

"I was speaking of *A Messenger from Hell*," Mr. Castillo said after clearing his throat, clearly about to hold forth. "The challenges we faced on that film were immense.".

Harry had liked *A Messenger from Hell* once, but she wasn't certain she liked it anymore. As soon as Mr. Castillo mentioned the movie Harry saw again the head of the Sten costume turned toward her, its eyes shifting in their sockets.

It wasn't real. You're cracking up.

Harry shoveled some food in her mouth, trying to look attentive, nodding and chewing, but she still zoned in and out, hearing Mr. Castillo's monologue like a radio that wouldn't stay tuned to the right station.

Gabe would mock me mercilessly if I said that out loud. The only thing he thinks is funnier than a compact disc is the whole notion of radio. But he didn't grow up in a backwater with parents who had Christian AM radio on all day.

"... and then Daniel got sick and the studio was pressuring us to not lose any shooting days. They argued that anyone could go inside the costume. I didn't think so."

"That's crazy!" Gabriel said. "It's not just a costume. Daniel Jensen created a whole *character*—the voice and the movements and everything."

Gabe's face was a little flushed, his eyes sparking. Harry loved seeing him like this, loved seeing him happy and interested and missing the little notch he got between his eyes when he worried. She'd been seeing that notch more often lately, she realized.

"Exactly right, Gabriel," Mr. Castillo said. "Exactly right. Daniel made a character underneath the costume and the mask and the makeup, and we couldn't just drop anyone into the role. I argued for taking a few days off so Daniel could recover—he was such an integral part of the shooting, as he's in so many scenes with Amina."

"It's really almost a two-hander," Gabe said. "Not completely, but it's got that quality."

Mr. Castillo gave Gabriel an admiring look. "Again, you're right. That was how I conceived the story—that the characters were partners but also adversaries. We'd spent time in rehearsal establishing the chemistry between Daniel and Amina, letting them build that relationship. And now the producer—representing the studio, of course—insisted that we forge on, completely disregarding this rehearsal. I decided that we could, perhaps, use a stand-in for Daniel, shooting scenes where the character would be seen only from behind or from the side, scenes without a lot of the motion that would draw attention to the fact that we were using someone other than Daniel."

"He's got a really distinct way of moving," Gabe said.

"And I didn't want to ask another actor to try to duplicate those movements," Mr. Castillo said. "But we had a second problem."

"Daniel is really, really tall and thin," Gabe said. "It's not easy to find a substitute for that."

"Again, exactly right," Mr. Castillo said. "You would have made a good production assistant on this film, Gabriel. You would have recognized so many problems."

Harry knew enough about movies to know that a production assistant was basically a jack-of-all-trades who ran errands, coordinated catering, and did a fair amount of script- and coffee-fetching. If Gabe had been the PA he wouldn't have been pointing out problems to the director, particularly ones of which Mr. Castillo would have been perfectly aware. Still, the compliment made Gabe glow, and Harry was grateful for that.

"So what did you end up doing?" Gabe said.

"Well, as it happens, my son . . . my son, Michael." Mr. Castillo's voice trembled only a little when he said Michael's name, so faintly that Harry was pretty sure Gabe didn't notice. "He was very tall for his age—he did not get that from me or my wife, so there must have been a latent tall gene somewhere—and also thin in the way that so many young people are. He wasn't quite as tall as Daniel."

"But who is? Besides professional basketball players," Gabe said.

"Exactly," Mr. Castillo said with a chuckle. "But Michael had almost the right proportions to stand in, and if he wasn't walking or moving about then we could put him on a platform so that the eyeline would be the same for Amina."

Gabe looked thoughtful for a moment. "The scene where Amina and Sten are in the alley, talking about the escalating curse. I always thought there was something a little different in that scene."

"Very good!" Mr. Castillo beamed. "You're correct. Even though the scene is shot mostly from behind the messenger, you can tell if you look closely that it is Michael, and not Daniel, under the costume."

"It's the hands," Gabe murmured, and Harry could almost see the film flickering behind Gabe's eyes, see him running the tape backward and forward in his mind. "Daniel had these little hand movements, almost flowy, like he was plucking the strings of an invisible guitar even when he was standing still. Michael didn't quite get that right. He was pretty close, though."

Gabe added this last bit almost as an afterthought, as if he suddenly realized that perhaps it wasn't politic to criticize the director's son.

"Yes, that is exactly it. Daniel was trained as a dancer, and he had a sense of his body that Michael did not." Mr. Castillo didn't seem to be bothered by any criticism of Michael.

Of course, what criticism could be worse than an accusation of murder?

"Mom, did you ever notice?" Gabe asked. "That it was a different actor in that scene?"

"Can't say I did," Harry said. She felt a little sting of disappointment emanating both from Mr. Castillo and her son at this, so she followed up with, "But it's such a beautiful film. It's hard for me to find fault."

Mr. Castillo puffed up a little at this. "It is very kind of you to say so."

"Mom never says anything unless she means it," Gabe said. "So she's not just making you feel good."

"Okay, Gabe," Harry said, which was her signal that he should stop talking. Every time Gabe had opened his mouth tonight it seemed like he'd revealed something about Harry, something that she didn't necessarily want revealed.

"'Stop talking, Gabe.' That's what she means," Gabe said.

Mr. Castillo laughed. "I recognize the signal. My wife used to do the same thing with Michael."

His smile abruptly disappeared as he stared into the middle distance.

"You miss them, don't you?" Gabe asked.

Harry sucked in her breath, hard. *What on earth is he thinking? I told him not to bring up Michael.*

The air seemed to go out of the room for a moment as Gabe waited for an answer and Harry waited for an explosion. She was sure that Mr. Castillo was going to start shouting, that he would scream at them to get out of his house and never come back, and then what would she do? She'd never find another job that paid as well as this one on short notice.

It wasn't too late to get her GED, maybe. Sure, she was thirty-four years old and George W. Bush had been president the last time she sat in a classroom, but she could do it. And work, and find a new place for her and Gabe. She'd figure it out. With her GED she'd be able to go to city college, get an associate's degree, apply for a job that wasn't dependent on the emotional whims of a reclusive movie director with a tragic past.

Then Mr. Castillo looked at Gabe, really looked at him, and said, "Yes. I do miss them. So much."

Harry watched in wonder as Gabe put his hand over Mr. Castillo's and said, "It's okay. It's okay to miss them."

Mr. Castillo's eyes welled with tears, and he let them fall.

HARRY WAS GRATEFUL THAT Saturday and Sunday existed, and that she didn't have to go in to work those two days. She wasn't certain how Mr. Castillo would feel after the dinner party, if he would feel embarrassed by his emotional outburst. She felt a little weird about it herself, if she was totally honest. For weeks they'd barely spoken except to discuss where she should dust and mop, and now she'd witnessed this big moment. It might make things awkward between them.

Well, it can't be any more awkward than only talking about the cleaning, she thought as she arrived at Bright Horses on Monday morning.

Mr. Castillo buzzed her in and she walked up the paving stones to the front door. There was a bite in the air, the first hint of fall weather to come, and she shivered. What if she and Gabe had to sleep outside all winter? She'd spent the whole weekend apartment hunting and hadn't found anything within her budget.

When Mr. Castillo opened the front door there was something different about him, and it took Harry a moment to realize what it was. He wasn't wearing his mask. While she'd expected him to be mask-free for the dinner party, she'd assumed he'd go back to his regular practice when she came in to work.

"Good morning," he said.

"Uh, good morning," she replied. That was new, too. He didn't usually greet her like this.

"How are you this morning?" he asked as she stepped inside and took off her sneakers.

"Doing well," she said.

"And Gabriel?"

"He's at school today," she said.

"Does he like school?" Mr. Castillo watched her take off her jacket, put on her slippers, tuck away her purse.

"Yeah, mostly," she said. "It's hard because they're doing half remote learning and half in person, and I think it would be a little better for him to be completely in person. Well, it would be better for most kids, really, but you know."

She gestured vaguely out at the world, as if to say, *You know, the pandemic and every other thing.*

"He's very bright. I imagine he's good at school," Mr. Castillo said.

"Mostly, I'd say. I think he might be struggling a little with math this year. I can't help him out, though. Math was never my best subject."

"Does the school offer tutoring?"

"Probably," Harry said. She tried not to feel annoyed at this sudden interest in her son's educational career. "I'll have to look into it. Gabe hasn't said anything to me, you know, specifically. It's just a sense that I have."

"Mm-hmm. Boys don't always speak up when they need help. Parents should follow their instincts when it comes to their children."

It was so hard for Harry not to say, *Like you did with Michael?* The little kernel of irritation inside her grew, like a pea under a princess's mattress. She knew that Mr. Castillo was projecting his feelings about his own son on hers in some way, and she needed to be patient, and she needed to remember that he was her boss and he held her short-term financial future in his hands.

"Anyway, you've obviously instilled in him a love of movies. Most teenagers don't have a working knowledge of Val Lewton's oeuvre."

Harry felt a little dizzy at the sudden change of subject, but said easily, "It was always just me and Gabe, so, you know, he was my pal. He still is."

Mr. Castillo nodded, and he got a faraway look in his eye. Harry stood there with her hands in the pockets of her jeans, not knowing what else to do. Never before had Mr. Castillo wanted to have a semi-personal conversation in his front hallway. Never before had he not barked a room assignment at her the second after she walked in the door.

"I enjoyed our dinner," Mr. Castillo finally said, coming back from wherever he'd gone. "We should do it again."

"Sure," Harry said automatically, although part of her was reluctant and she wasn't sure why. Maybe she didn't like all this camaraderie and interest. Maybe it was easier for her just to be Mr. Castillo's employee and not his friend. But she didn't feel she could say no. She thought he would be terribly offended if she did. "Me and Gabe would both like that."

"Wonderful," he said. "Let's get started in the blue room, as usual."

The blue room. Harry had almost—almost—forgotten what else had happened Friday night. She'd been hoping that they wouldn't go in the blue room at all today, even though they always cleaned that room on Mondays. Still, Mr. Castillo usually stayed with her while she was in there, so it wasn't like she would be alone with the Sten costume. And if it started behaving strangely, if it turned its head or anything else weird—well, at least there would be a witness. Maybe then she'd find out if it was all in her head or actually happening.

"What did you do this weekend?" Mr. Castillo asked as they climbed the stairs.

Harry still wasn't used to his small talk, and her mind was half on the costume that freaked her out, otherwise she wouldn't have been honest. "Apartment hunting."

Mr. Castillo stopped at the top of the stairs, stepped to one side, and frowned at her as she followed him up to the blue room. "Are you moving? Something Gabriel said made me think you'd been in the same place for a long time."

Stupid, stupid mouth, Harry thought furiously. She needed to wake up and pay total attention to her surroundings. She should have just said she and Gabe watched movies or went to the zoo or whatever. Mr. Castillo didn't need to know about their problems.

"Um, yeah. The landlord's son took over his properties and he—that is, the son—is selling the building so it can be developed into a single-family home. So we have to move."

"That's why you looked so worried that one day," he said. "I thought something must be wrong."

"It had just taken me by surprise," Harry said hurriedly, wanting to smooth over the moment. "But it's all good now. We're sure to find someplace."

"But will it be convenient for Gabriel's schooling? It would be difficult for him to travel a long way, or have to transfer to another school. Especially if he's having trouble with math, or any other subject. Consistency is important."

Harry bit back the retort that wanted to fly out. She'd been handling Gabe's schooling for his whole life. Of course she would put him first, prioritize his happiness and safety first. She always had. Mr. Castillo didn't have any right to imply that she wouldn't. Instead she kept a handle on her temper, remembered the importance of maintaining her current work situation and tried to tell herself that he was just being kind by asking. It still felt intrusive, though. It felt really damned intrusive.

"I think it will be okay no matter where we end up," she said, picking up the cleaning supplies needed and starting on the far edge of the room, away from the Sten costume. "Lots and lots of kids in Chicago go to high schools that are far from their home because of the selective enrollment system. In fact, Gabe is in a selective enrollment school already. We just happen to live at an easy distance from it."

"Selective enrollment—those are schools that students have to test to get into?"

"Yes, test scores and their subject grades in seventh grade. There's an application process."

"And Gabriel got into one of these schools?"

"Yes, he's a bright kid, as you noticed."

Mr. Castillo frowned. She thought he might be marshaling another argument or concern about the distance from the school, but he seemed to decide to let it go.

"Well, if you need assistance finding a tutor for Gabriel, let me know."

Harry privately thought that Mr. Castillo wouldn't know the first thing about finding a tutor in Chicago, since he didn't have a child who'd ever lived or been educated there, but she wanted this particular conversation line cut off, so she just nodded and went about her work.

As she worked she found herself glancing frequently at the Sten costume. It didn't move today (*maybe it had never moved at all*) but she still felt that some undefined menace emanated from the costume.

Just keep your head down and do your work and don't look at the thing. If you're lucky then Mr. Castillo will dust it and you won't have to.

Harry should have known she wouldn't be so lucky. When she was about a quarter done with the room Mr. Castillo glanced at his watch and said, "I have to make a few calls now that it's a decent hour in California. Can you finish this room and then go on to the guest rooms upstairs?"

"Sure," Harry said, though what she really wanted to say was, *Don't leave me.*

Mr. Castillo went downstairs. The stairs were old and despite Mr. Castillo's very light tread they squeaked as he walked. When he left the stairs and continued into another part of the house she felt vaguely abandoned, and told herself to get over it.

She cleaned the rest of the room, studiously avoiding the Sten costume. *I wonder if I can get away with not cleaning it at all. Maybe Mr. Castillo won't notice.*

Harry knew that wasn't possible. Mr. Castillo could spot a mote of dust at a thousand yards. He would definitely notice if she didn't clean the mask and costume from *A Messenger from Hell.*

When she'd finally dawdled around the room enough Harry

took a deep breath and approached the costume. The glass eyes stayed perfectly still as she approached. The smell that she hated, that talcum-powder-and-sweat reek, seemed to waft off the costume in waves.

How am I the only one who notices the smell? Is it really all in my head? Mr. Castillo never says anything about it, and Gabe didn't seem to be aware of it at all last week.

Harry hurriedly ran the duster over the face of the costume, avoiding looking directly at it. If the eyes moved to follow her, she didn't want to know. She started work on the costume itself, which required a bit more care. There were folds of cloth that needed to be pulled out and swiped so that dust didn't gather in the creases. Mr. Castillo had told Harry on her first day of work that dusty cloth creases were a pet peeve of his.

Harry finished dusting the cloth and stepped away, turning her back on the costume. *There. That's done. Now upstairs, where there are no creepy masks trying to communicate with you.*

(no, just disembodied voices)

Harry decided that if she heard any voices she was going to ignore them. They were probably stress manifestations, anyway. And even if they weren't, strange banging noises and whispers were easier to disregard than a mask that turned its head and looked at her.

She collected all of the cleaning supplies she needed to go upstairs, thinking that she would ask Mr. Castillo if she could wear headphones while she worked. If she was listening to a podcast then she wouldn't be worrying about ghostly voices.

Something rustled behind her.

Don't look. Don't look. Don't look.

But she had to look. She had to look because she'd read enough horror novels and watched enough horror movies to know that the

Thing, the Thing that Haunted/Stalked/Terrorized the characters always appeared behind them, in the audience's frame but not the character's. And the character always turned around a second too late, right before the knife fell or the axe swung or the specter reached out its arms for an embrace.

Harry turned, and she couldn't stifle the noise that came out of her throat. It wasn't a scream—it was something caught breathless before a scream, something that wanted to be a scream but was too terrified to be.

She'd expected to find the mask looking at her, but the mask hadn't really moved.

The entire *costume* had moved.

It had shifted a little off its frame somehow, even though the prosthetic feet weren't attached to falling folds of cloth. The long-fingered hands reached out for her, and the mouth stretched wide in a Joker grin.

Harry backed away, stumbling on her own feet, her hands held out in front to ward off what she was seeing. It couldn't be possible. It couldn't be.

She shut her eyes for a second, hoping for the human equivalent of a computer reboot, that when she opened them the problem would be wiped clean and everything would be back to normal.

The costume still reached for her. She saw the cloth rustling at the bottom, as if pushed by a localized wind.

Screw this, Harry thought. She wasn't going to stay and let this thing do whatever it was it wanted to do to her. She was going upstairs and she was going to shut the bedroom doors while she worked in them. She didn't think that the costume would be able to propel itself that far.

Then she thought, *Wait a second. Why the hell should I be afraid of this thing?*

Suddenly, in that moment, she remembered the girl she had been, the girl who'd run from her family home in the middle of the night, the girl who'd fought and clawed and done whatever she had to do to survive. And now she'd allowed all of her worry and stress pile up on her, had gaslit herself into believing what she was seeing didn't exist.

It existed. The costume was haunted, or possessed, or whatever. She'd never really contemplated the potential reality of ghosts except in the context of horror movies, but the evidence was right before her eyes.

And she would not be afraid of it. She would not be afraid of latex and glass and plastic, of fake claws and teeth. She'd always made fun of characters in the Chucky movies, laughing because they were terrorized by a doll. Why had she let herself be frightened of this false monster?

"Get back," Harry said through gritted teeth.

The lids around the glass eyes seemed to widen fractionally. The reaching fingers hesitated.

"Get back into your place or I will burn you," Harry said.

She would, too, even though it would probably break Mr. Castillo's heart and she would definitely, definitely lose her job. There were several fireplaces in the building—it was an old structure, after all, built just after the Great Chicago Fire of 1871, and central heating was not a thing then. She could drag the costume to one of them and set it alight, and that would be the end of that.

The costume seemed to shrink under her fierce gaze. Then she blinked, and the hands were back where they belonged. She blinked again, and the costume was settled on its stand. The whole thing happened so quickly that for a moment she really did doubt what she'd seen.

Stop that. You saw it. You told it off, and now you can finish your business without worrying about being terrorized by this damn costume.

The glassy eyes stared out, blank, no menace present at all.

This house is haunted, she thought. And then she thought, *I need to find a new job.*

"Something else to add to the to-do list," she murmured, thinking of the apartment she needed to find.

She carried her cleaning supplies upstairs and made sure not to look back as she left the room.

JAVIER CASTILLO

before

JAVIER TRIED NOT TO be angry when Lena told him she was pregnant. He'd always made clear to her that he loved her, loved her very much, but he had no intention of having children. The work was what mattered. How could he devote himself—his time, his energy, his gifts—to film if he had a child at home?

He asked her to get an abortion. She wept, promised to keep the child out from underfoot, swore that she'd spend all her time and energy taking care of it so that he wouldn't have to worry. He would never be inconvenienced. He could parent as much or as little as he wanted.

He said fine, because that was what it seemed to take to make her happy, and then went away for six months to make *The Devil Knows* in Chile, a film about a group of Americans on an adventure trip that goes horribly wrong. Javier didn't ignore Lena. He called her. He asked how she was feeling. He wrote letters. But he didn't ask about the baby, not even when she told him she'd learned that they were having a boy.

The film was plagued by problems. The weather wouldn't cooperate—there were days and days of torrential rainfall. The actors were miserable, stuck in a small town with little to do except, as one performer said, "watch the bugs crawling in the street." Half the crew got food poisoning at one point or another. They ran over time and over budget. The press started to describe the film as "Castillo's *Heaven's Gate*."

Lena told him she was getting bigger and bigger, that her mother had come to stay with her in their home. He listened, told her he loved her, told her that he wouldn't be home for another month or two. He pretended not to hear the tears in her voice when she said goodbye.

By the time he returned home, almost a full nine months after he'd left, he'd lost twenty pounds simply from the gnawing worry that the film would be a failure. Lena hadn't given birth yet. The baby was overdue, taking his own sweet time, and the obstetrician started to talk about inducing the birth.

Javier Castillo went away to edit his movie, a task he'd never leave to anyone else. He wrote his films, he produced them, he directed them, and he edited them. They would rise or fall on his vision alone, and he knew there was a great film hidden inside the mess of footage he'd brought home. The studio tried to interfere, to say that he needed a professional editor, but Castillo pointed to the terms in his contract. The studio waved lawyers with threatening faces in front of him, told him that things could be changed. He was not afraid, and went on editing his film.

On October 10th, Lena called him and said she'd given birth to their baby boy, and that she'd named him Michael, after the archangel. She said he was as beautiful as any seraphim, and she couldn't wait for Javier to meet his son.

Javier didn't hurry home. He finished editing his film, oversaw the final postproduction touches. When he finally showed the result to the studio executives they shifted in their seats and harrumphed and questioned whether their money had been well spent, but they set a release date, because they had to.

They scheduled the film for February, a place where movies are sent to die. Javier Castillo argued that his film would blow summer audiences away, that they were making a mistake, but they wouldn't budge.

Javier Castillo went home, furious at the lack of vision that had condemned his masterpiece to be seen by as few people as possible. He had no desire to meet the baby who seemed to scream in fury every time he telephoned Lena, the baby who took her attention away from him when he needed her comfort.

Then he walked into his house and she stood there, smiling tremulously, holding his two-month-old son. The boy was in striped footie pajamas and he had huge brown eyes and a shock of dark hair atop his head. Lena held the baby out toward him, and the baby smiled.

Javier Castillo fell in love, just for a moment.

"He's an angel," he said, taking Michael from his elated wife and holding the boy close to him. "An angel."

SIX

TWO WEEKS AFTER THEIR first dinner at Javier Castillo's house, Harry and Gabe found themselves at the front door again, this time bearing chocolate chip cookies. Harry had a pretty limited baking repertoire. She confined herself to things that weren't too expensive and that Gabriel could assist in making. It definitely helped to have a second pair of hands scooping out cookie dough.

I feel like I should have made an apple torte or something. Something fancy, she thought. *Although I don't even know what kind of pan such a thing would be baked in, and I probably can't afford the ingredients anyway, so the whole subject is moot.*

She had gone to look at a couple of apartments during the week while Gabe was at school. One of them seemed okay—a little smaller, a little more expensive than what they had now, but still— until she noticed an approximately eighteen-inch-wide hole in the floor in the corner of one of the bedrooms. The leasing agent hadn't seemed too concerned about it, saying the landlord would fix it "soon." Harry decided to take a pass. If the landlord didn't see the urgency in fixing a hole that someone could put their foot through then he probably wouldn't feel too pressed to fix, say, a broken refrigerator. And the refrigerator in that apartment had been old. Harry wasn't sure how old, but it was yellow, and not yellow because it had come out of the factory that way.

Mr. Castillo opened the door with a huge grin on his face. "Welcome, welcome," he said.

"We brought cookies," Gabe said, taking the plate from Harry and handing it to Mr. Castillo.

"Did you make these yourself?"

"Yeah," Gabe said, then added (after Harry gave him the side-eye), "well, Mom did. I helped."

As Mr. Castillo shut the front door Harry thought she heard the murmur of voices elsewhere in the house. For a moment she thought she was imagining it. Her next thought was that the ghost or whatever it was that had possessed the mask upstairs was trying to mess with her, make her hear things that no one else could hear.

She was surprised by her own equanimity in acknowledging the existence of the ghost (*or whatever*), but she felt better now that she'd confronted it head-on. Yes, it was weird. No, she'd never believed in ghosts before. But she wasn't going to Scully her way through this and pretend she couldn't see (or hear) what was before her.

The question of whose ghost it is, now, that's a whole other thing, she thought. The house was old. It could have been a spirit lingering from any time in the past—a previous owner, a servant who'd died, anything.

I wonder if anyone was murdered here and buried in the garden.

Gabe's voice interrupted this intriguing line of inquiry. "Is somebody else here?"

"Yes," Mr. Castillo said. His grin spread even wider, like he had a surprise for them.

Harry was already surprised. As far as she knew, only she and Gabe had ever entered the house during Mr. Castillo's entire residence there. She wondered who it could be.

She and Gabe quickly changed out of their shoes and followed Mr. Castillo into the library. A very tall, thin man with blond hair in a short ponytail faced away from them. A much smaller woman with the compact musculature of a gymnast and long black hair that spilled to the center of her back stood beside him. The two of them were examining an object on one of the shelves. As Harry and Gabe entered, the two people turned.

"Daniel Jensen and Amina Collucci!" Gabe said before Harry could.

The two stars of Javier Castillo's *A Messenger from Hell* smiled at Gabe's outburst. Amina came forward, her hand outstretched. Daniel followed a couple of steps behind. Harry noticed the fluid way that he walked, like he wasn't quite touching the ground. She also noticed that his head ducked a little, like he was embarrassed to be recognized.

That made sense. His body type was so unusual—about 6 foot 5, but extraordinarily thin. Harry bet he probably weighed maybe 170 pounds at the most.

"Harry Adams," she said as she shook their hands. "This is my son, Gabe."

"Oh my god," Gabe said. "I can't believe I'm actually meeting you. I'm such a huge, huge fan of both of you."

Mr. Castillo looked on with what Harry could only think of as a shit-eating grin. He looked so damned proud of himself for surprising them.

No, Harry thought as she followed his eyes. *Not me. Gabe. He wanted to surprise Gabe.*

She watched Gabe jabber for a few minutes, talking about how much he loved *A Messenger from Hell* and some of the actors' other movies. Mr. Castillo, she noted, watched him, too.

He misses his son so much, Harry thought. She could tell that he was delighted that Gabe was delighted.

"Well, everybody, let's move into the dining room. I've prepared some small bites for us to start."

They moved en masse into the next room, Gabe in the front talking excitedly to the two actors. Mr. Castillo followed, watching them raptly. Harry brought up the rear.

Just as she was about to cross the threshold into the dining room she heard a noise, like something heavy falling overhead. No one else seemed to hear it. Harry thought of the costume that had reached for her, the mask that had turned its head.

Did it try too hard to move off its post and fall down?

She wondered what everyone would say if she suggested such a thing. Gabe would look embarrassed, she was sure. He might not forgive her for making him appear foolish in front of his heroes.

It might not be the costume in any case, Harry reasoned. It might just be some books falling in the upstairs library or something. Or a picture frame.

Or a person locked in the bedroom at the end of the hallway.

No, she wasn't going to start thinking like that again. Any weird noises she heard upstairs were obviously linked to the same spirit in the Sten costume. It was too much to believe that there was more than one in the house.

Unless the bedroom at the end of the hallway is a doorway to hell or something.

She shook her head at herself. She clearly had missed her calling writing B movies. But just because she'd acknowledged the obvious truth that there was a ghost (*or something*) in the house didn't mean that she needed to let her imagination run wild. One weird supernatural event was enough for one person.

Harry thought again about looking for another job. It might be a little more awkward now to put in her notice, considering that Mr. Castillo suddenly seemed bent on pursuing a more personal relationship with Harry and Gabe.

Not me. Gabe.

Mr. Castillo, while polite and a little friendlier than he used to be, ultimately didn't seem that interested in Harry as a person. He did, however, seem interested in Gabe. And Gabe was definitely interested in him—excited to be in the proximity of one of his favorite filmmakers, thrilled to talk about movies and be heard. Harry wondered idly if she should stop the friendship before it went any further. She didn't know if it was necessarily a good thing for Mr. Castillo to use Gabe as a proxy for his own missing son.

Don't be hard-hearted, Harry. He's so lonely. And it doesn't seem to do Gabe any harm.

Indeed, as they nibbled on the various small treats that Mr. Castillo had set out—a bowl of warmed olives, a few select cheeses and cured meats, small toasts with peperonata and goat cheese—Gabe seemed to glow from within. He asked a million questions of Daniel and Amina, and Harry never saw them answer with anything but patience and good humor. She knew they both went on the convention circuit regularly, and she supposed that big panels and long lines with enthusiastic fans were far worse than one extremely eager fourteen-year-old.

"Remember the time you fell and the nose of the Sten mask completely ripped off?" Amina said, taking a sip of her wine.

Daniel grimaced. "It's not all fun and games, wearing a mask that limits your vision while trying to move around in long robes."

"The makeup department and the effects department were both upset with you," Mr. Castillo said.

"You weren't too happy, either," Daniel said, laughing. "Although you tried to hide it."

Mr. Castillo gave a rueful shrug. "We couldn't shoot with you for the rest of the day. The studio was not happy. All the shots that day were supposed to include you, and we fell behind again."

"There was only one mask?" Gabe asked. "I thought it was normal to have more than one, just in case of—well, stuff like that happening."

"There were two originally," Daniel said, then paused. His eyes darted toward Mr. Castillo, and Harry suspected a mention of Michael was in the offing. "But there was an incident with the other mask while I was ill, and then I had my accident soon after."

"Which is why the makeup and effects people were so annoyed," Amina said, smoothly skating around any awkwardness.

Harry hoped that Gabe wouldn't ask about the incident that happened while Daniel was ill. She hoped very much that he would take his smart brain and put two and two together, remembering that Michael Castillo had temporarily taken over for Daniel in the costume. She stared at the side of his head, trying to send a telepathic Mom warning to keep his mouth shut.

Gabe opened his mouth, but at the last second he seemed to feel Harry's energy, and glanced over at her. She gave her head the tiniest shake *no*, and he stuffed some Manchego in his mouth instead.

"Anyway, we wouldn't even use a full mask like that now," Daniel said. "Everything is latex pieces applied directly to the skin."

"Which do you like better?" Gabe asked.

"Well," Daniel said. "The mask was just one piece, and it slid pretty easily over my head. There was a little fiddling to attach it and hide the attachments under the wig, but no hours in the makeup chair. The drawback is that it had those big glass eyes, which weren't exactly easy to see through. The kinds of effects that are done now . . . well, you have to sit sometimes for five or six hours to have all the pieces applied, and then it's another couple hours at the end of the day to remove them. My skin is almost always irritated from the glue by the end of a shoot. But once everything is on it's generally easier to wear. You don't have to worry about breathing through a tiny hole. And they can fit me with contacts for eye effects. The Sten mask eye movement had to be remotely puppeted."

"Like, there was a radio control in there?" Gabe asked.

"Yes. If you've ever seen footage of the puppeteers that worked on Jabba the Hutt in *Return of the Jedi*, they use a similar radio-control effect for that puppet's eyes—to move them back and forth, to widen them, to dilate the pupils."

"And I bet that wasn't fun for you, either," Gabe said. "Especially when it's already hard to see through."

Daniel laughed. "I tried to walk around as little as possible when the mask was on, and created the character through hand and arm movements."

"What about the scenes when you're running?" Gabe asked.

"He didn't have the mask on," Amina said. "Javier would shoot a tiny bit of the two of us running together—maybe five or six feet of running. I'd have Daniel's hand and would guide him. Then Javier would switch to a rear view of us. Daniel would remove the mask so he could see while running."

"And put on my sneakers," Daniel said. "Those cloven hoof foot pieces were not meant for marathoning."

Mr. Castillo laughed. "What we go through for art."

Harry thought, *No, what you make others go through for* your *art.*

She considered that maybe she was being unreasonable. After all, a performer wanted to perform. If Daniel hadn't wanted to wear the mask and robes, she supposed he hadn't had to accept the part. Then again, how many parts were there available for an actor who had such a unique look? Maybe his only options were to get inside a mask or makeup, because film studios and casting agents refused to acknowledge that not everyone in the world looked like an Abercrombie & Fitch model.

Mr. Castillo stood and started clearing the appetizer platters and plates. Harry rose automatically to help him, following him into the kitchen with an armful of dishes. She noted that she was the only one who stood to help, but maybe she was the only one who felt like her job depended on it.

"Thank you, Harry," Mr. Castillo said. "You can just put them on the bottom rack of the dishwasher."

Harry started loading the dishes in as Mr. Castillo took two roasted chickens out of the oven.

"Smells good," she said as he placed the roasting pans on the kitchen island.

"Thank you," he said, transferring the first chicken to a cutting board. He carved the chicken expertly, placing the pieces on a serving platter. "Do you think Gabriel is having a good time?"

"Sure," Harry said. "He's really excited to meet Daniel and Amina. I can tell."

"Good. That is good," he said.

Harry finished with the plates and closed the dishwasher. She started toward the dining room but Mr. Castillo's voice stopped her.

"And how is the apartment hunt going?"

"It's going," she said, regretting for the five-hundredth time that she had ever mentioned it in front of him. "I'm sure we'll find the perfect place soon. There's lots of rentals out there."

This was the world's biggest lie, but Harry didn't want to discuss their housing troubles any longer than necessary.

Mr. Castillo gave her a hard look, like he suspected she wasn't being completely truthful, but then he said, "I'm sure you're right."

Harry slipped back into the dining room, relieved to have escaped.

Mr. Castillo carried out the chickens to great fanfare, followed by a platter of roasted root vegetables. He poured wine generously all around, although Harry was careful to only take a few sips while eating. She liked wine, but even a little of it went to her head. If alcohol loosened her tongue she might end up saying something she'd regret later, like mentioning the haunted mask.

Isn't that a Goosebumps book? she thought, a childhood memory resurfacing from the soup in the back of her mind. Harry's recollection was that a girl bought a Halloween mask that attached itself to her face. Her parents, of course, would have forbidden this book in the house, so Harry had read it in bits and pieces when her class went to the school library.

Maybe the Sten mask wants a face to attach itself to, like an alien face hugger.

Conversation flowed easily around the table, although Harry didn't participate much. She was preoccupied with staying on her guard and not revealing too much. Gabe was clearly having the time of his life, though, talking movies with three people who knew so much about the process of making them. This was the sort of conversation that Harry would normally have loved to have, because movies had been one of the constants in her life since she left home. But as the night wore on the air around them seemed to grow oppressive, like a heavy presence was pushing down on them. She was the only one who seemed to notice, though. Everyone else was having a wonderful time.

Amina, in particular, seemed to be drinking a lot. Mr. Castillo opened a third bottle of wine and gestured toward Harry's glass but she covered the top of it with her hand.

"Are you sure? This is a particularly good Tempranillo," he said.

"I'll have some," Amina said, guzzling the last of what was already in her glass.

"I'm good," Harry said.

"Mom can't have more than one glass of wine or else I'll have to carry her home," Gabe said.

Harry felt her cheeks heat as everyone at the table looked at her in varying states of amusement. "Yeah, I'm a lightweight," she said, covering up her embarrassment.

As soon as the conversation moved on she gave Gabe the Killer Mom Stare of Death and Also Lost Privileges. His eyes widened and he mouthed *Sorry* across the table.

She shook her head. *Not cutting it, kid.*

"What about dessert?" Mr. Castillo said. "Harry and Gabriel have made some wonderful cookies, and I also prepared flan for everyone."

Mr. Castillo set down a personal-sized flan in front of everyone. They were plated like desserts at fancy restaurants, with an artistic drizzle of caramel sauce over the empty side of the plate and a few neatly arranged berries.

Harry tried not to feel stupid when he carried out her plastic-wrapped tray of cookies and placed it in the center of the table. It was a thing she always fought against, the feeling that she was somehow inadequate by simply being poor. She constantly reminded herself that her character wasn't measured by the size of her bank account, but at that moment she felt very small. Mr. Castillo unwrapped the plastic and took a cookie from the tray, biting into it.

"These are delicious, Harry," he said.

It seemed like a kind thing. But the gesture somehow drew attention to the inadequacy of her basic Toll House chocolate chip cookies compared to the extremely fancy flan. Harry smiled tightly and took a small bite of flan, returning the compliment. Mr. Castillo beamed, and Harry wondered if his intention all along was to manipulate an accolade out of her. Amina, Daniel and Gabe all dug into their own desserts, exclaiming at the taste.

Harry knew if she dwelled on the incident she'd get broody, so she tried to push it out of her mind. Now that they were into dessert she and Gabe could probably leave soon. She felt exhausted and grumpy and a little headachy from the wine, despite having drunk such a small amount. She ate about half the flan. It was good but a little rich after all the food they'd already eaten. She noticed Mr. Castillo glancing at her plate as she set her fork down. His eyes hardened a little.

"I'm just saving half for Gabe," she said, knowing Gabe would bail her out. "He's always finishing my food."

"Oh yeah," Gabe said, pulling the plate toward him. He'd inhaled his own flan so fast Harry was unsure if he'd actually tasted it. "Whenever we go to Ann Sather I take half of Mom's cinnamon rolls."

Mr. Castillo smiled benignly, seemingly satisfied.

"What's Ann Sather?" Daniel asked.

"A Swedish restaurant on Belmont that has the best cinnamon

rolls in the whole world," Gabe said. "Mr. Castillo, you've been there, right?"

For the first time all evening, Mr. Castillo seemed a little uncomfortable. Harry knew it was because he was basically a shut-in. "Ah, no, I haven't."

"You gotta go," Gabe said. "It's sooo good. And they give you so much food. Me and Mom just go in there and stuff ourselves and then we sit on the couch the rest of the day holding our bellies and saying, 'I'm so full.'"

"Well, with the pandemic and everything it's still not a great idea to go to restaurants," Daniel said. "I know there are some half-capacity rules, correct? And patios. But it still seems unsafe to me." He'd seemed to pick up on the undercurrent of discomfort emanating from Mr. Castillo.

"Let's have a tour of the rest of the house," Amina said. She was slurring her words a little. "I only saw one room on the way up to the guest room. I want to know how you've arranged all your bits and bobs."

Harry did not want to take a tour of the house. She toured the house three times a week, meticulously dusting all of Mr. Castillo's "bits and bobs," as Amina put it. Harry wasn't certain Amina could climb and descend all of the stairs in any case. She was the kind of drunk that appeared to be staggering without even moving.

Harry opened her mouth to suggest that she and Gabe needed to get home, but before she said anything Mr. Castillo spoke.

"I need to get these dinner things cleaned and put away," Mr. Castillo said. "But Harry knows where everything is in the house. She can show you. Start in the basement, Harry. I don't think Gabriel got to see the very large props the last time he was here."

"No, I definitely didn't! Don't you have one of the ships from *Flight of the Navigator*? I read you bought it at auction."

Mr. Castillo smiled. "I'm surprised a young person like yourself would even know what that film is, never mind recognize the ship."

"Mom made me watch a lot of old movies when I was young," Gabe said.

"I hardly think a movie from 1986 is old," Harry muttered.

"It's older than you," Gabe said. "You were born in 1988."

Amina looked from Harry to Gabe and back again, and Harry could see Amina doing some sluggish, drunken math in her head. Harry stood up before Amina could comment on Harry's age at Gabe's birth. Yeah, she'd been young. But it was nothing she wanted to discuss at Mr. Castillo's dinner table.

"Let's head down to the basement," Harry said, waving her hands in the direction of the door.

Daniel seemed to pick up on Harry's cue. "Yeah, let's go look, Amina. Javier used to have an alien queen puppet from *Aliens*."

"Really?" Gabe said, even more excited. "I can't believe you never told me that, Mom. You know how much I love *Aliens*."

"Another ancient film from the dawn of time," Harry said, giving Gabe a look.

"Yeah, I know," he said. "Nineteen eighty-six, same as *Navigator*."

"Personally, I find I'd rather watch a lot of older films," Daniel said. "So many modern films just don't take enough time to develop characters and exposition."

"I'd settle for just one of those," Harry said. "I love movies, but I hate the fact that most studio films are two and a half hours long and two of those hours are just car chases and things blowing up. One-liners are not a substitute for actual characters."

It was the most she'd said all night, and she felt uncomfortable being the center of attention, if only for a moment. Particularly when she abruptly remembered that three of the five people in the room worked in the industry that she was slagging.

"One hundred percent agree," Daniel said. "And I say that as a person who's spent a lot of time in those studio films lately."

"Ah, I'm sorry," Harry said, her cheeks heating. "I forgot. You're doing a lot of motion-capture work now, right?"

Daniel shrugged. "Don't apologize. Motion capture for big films expands the number of roles I'm able to play, and all those giant CG budgets mean that pretty much every studio film can have a computer-generated monster for the action hero to fight. And if I can make money on those big films, then I can afford to do smaller films with directors like Javier."

Mr. Castillo nodded, but Harry saw him press his lips together in a way that showed he was irritated. She supposed that he didn't much care for his films being termed "smaller," even if that's exactly what they were.

Despite the financial success of most of Mr. Castillo's movies, his idiosyncratic vision and his constant public battles with studios over budgets meant that the big players didn't want to take him on. Almost every one of his films had financing from multiple sources, and when he did get a decent midsized budget like he had on *A Messenger from Hell* he'd spend all his time asking for more. Harry knew all this because Javier Castillo had given a ton of interviews over the years, and in nearly every one he'd complained about how lack of funds had limited his vision.

It was, honestly, the story of so many horror and horror-adjacent directors. Despite the fact that horror movies made a lot of money on small budgets, studios persisted in treating that success like a fluke. It didn't help when horror directors were given a crack at larger budgets and then, for whatever weird reasons, the films didn't do well.

Everyone except Mr. Castillo followed Harry out of the dining room and into the main hallway. There was a door under the main stairs and it opened onto another staircase that went down into the basement. Harry resisted the urge to look up the curving staircase to see if the Sten costume was peering down at them from the blue room. She'd be forced to take everyone upstairs after this in any case. Maybe, if she was lucky, the haunt (*or whatever it was*—she couldn't seem to stop herself from adding this adden-dum every time she thought of it) would act up while there were other witnesses present. Then, at least, she would be able to . . .

What, exactly? she wondered as she led the other three into the basement and turned on the lights. *Solicit their help in figuring out what it was? Document it so they could post it on the internet? What's your endgame here? Don't you want to just ignore it until you find a new job?*

But that new-job thing had to be pushed off until they found a new place. Harry hated the way her mind seemed to have become a running circle, or a treadmill with no sign of stopping. She had to find a new place for them to live. She had to find a new job. And she had to, she realized, get Gabe away from Mr. Castillo before he became any more attached.

"Wow!" Gabe said as they entered the room. Gabe's eyes were huge as he turned back to Harry. "Mom, this is the coolest job you've ever had for sure."

Although maybe that last part, about Gabe not getting attached—well, maybe that was easier said than done.

HARRY

before

HARRY WAS IN LOVE with Pete Ricciardo. She was so, so, so in love with him. She'd never felt this way about anyone in her life, and the only feeling that came close to the soaring joy she experienced when she looked at him was the same feeling she'd had watching *The Lost Boys* for the first time all those years ago.

She'd met Pete six months before when she'd been at the food bank picking up some snacks that she could carry in her pack. She'd still been shifting between sleeping on the lakefront and sleeping in shelters, and she thought she hadn't looked her best, considering it had been at least three days since she'd been able to shower.

But he'd said, "Hey, what's your name?" as they stood in line, and then he'd invited her to come and stay at the apartment where he and a few others lived. Harry had thought he was gorgeous, beyond gorgeous, all long limbs and dark eyes and black curly hair that fell over her forehead. But she'd been cautious still, so cautious. She didn't trust strangers not to hurt her.

Then he'd said, as if reading her feelings on her face, "No

pressure. Why don't you just come by and enjoy some of this delicious Hamburger Helper with us?"

And then he'd smiled, and his smile was a little shy, and she found herself smiling back and following him home.

It wasn't really an apartment, as it turned out. It was more of an informal arrangement, a squat in a building that was falling apart at the seams and had a super who looked the other way for a weekly bribe. There were ten of them, including Harry, crammed into a one-bedroom with an open living/dining space. There were bodies everywhere, it seemed—people making little nests for themselves of their stuff on the floor. Most of them were like Harry—they had one backpack and one blanket, and were ready to take all their things on their backs if they had to run somewhere suddenly.

One person, who preferred to be called Star for reasons Harry couldn't fully grasp, had blocked off a corner for himself by stacking piles of old used paperbacks up until he'd created a little wall that allowed him a modicum of privacy when he was stretched out on the floor. Harry didn't want to think about how long Star had lived in that place. He must have been there a while to have accrued that many books. Harry wanted to believe her circumstances were temporary, and that as soon as she got a job her life would turn around. She was quickly disabused of that notion when some of the other residents, including Pete, told her that they did have jobs. They worked in restaurants and fast-food joints and gas stations. They made money, just not enough to afford real housing in a city where the cost of housing kept going up more and more each day, where old two- and three-flats that used to house multiple families were getting converted into single-family dwellings that cost seven figures.

But it was indoors, and there was running water and gas for cooking, and everyone was welcoming because they were all in the same position as Harry—young runaways who just wanted to live their lives their own way, kids who'd been chased out of their homes because they'd been abused or because their parents found them unacceptable in some way, like Harry.

She'd eaten Hamburger Helper with them and used the shower. And then Pete had found an empty space for her to sleep, and she'd crashed on the floor. It had been the first time she slept through the night since she left home. She'd never slept that well even at the shelters, because she didn't trust the people who worked there. At the first shelter she ever tried to go to a guy who worked there had put his hand on her knee during the intake and she'd gotten up and left. She had a very clear idea of what he'd wanted from her and she wasn't going to give it.

Nobody seemed to want anything from her in the squat—not even Pete, who she'd half expected would try to make a move on her. He didn't, and she fell in love with him because he didn't.

He didn't even single her out for his attention until she'd been living there for a few weeks. He asked her to meet him after his shift at the gas station. He worked nights and asked if she would mind getting up early to have breakfast with him. They'd made their way to an IHOP in Boystown, where the waitress was about a million years old to Harry's young eyes and had the gravelly voice of a longtime smoker. They ordered pancakes and eggs and coffee and sat there talking for a long time, ignoring the waitress's eye rolls as they milked the free coffee refills long past the point of socially acceptable behavior.

But Harry couldn't stop looking at him, or talking to him. It was the first time in her life where she felt like someone was really listening to her. She knew it was love, real love, and that real love never died. The movies told her so.

SEVEN

AMINA SIDLED UP TO Harry as Gabe and Daniel walked around the basement. Harry heard Gabe's exclamations over each item, occasionally interspersed with Daniel's low murmurs.

"How did you meet Javier?" Amina asked, her eyes all innocence. "He's been very limited in his social contacts since . . ."

She trailed off, but Harry didn't think it had anything to do with delicacy. It seemed like she was trying to gauge Harry's appetite for discussing the scandal. It was also patently obvious that Amina knew exactly how Javier Castillo knew her and Gabe, and that Amina didn't think much of Harry's profession.

"I'm sure you know I'm his house cleaner," Harry said, staring straight forward. She didn't want to offend Amina, who might say something to Mr. Castillo about it. But she didn't want to encourage the other woman, either.

If Harry had known Mr. Castillo was going to invite Amina and Daniel to dinner she probably wouldn't have shown up. It put her in an awkward place, meeting his friends socially when she was his employee. Mr. Castillo obviously hadn't considered that it might potentially put Harry in a bad position.

All he thought about was pleasing Gabe, she thought, and sighed inwardly. It was hard for Harry to separate protecting herself and her son while also having compassion for Mr. Castillo's loneliness and his obvious desire to have his own son back.

Gabe is still my *son,* Harry thought, and she was surprised a little by her possessiveness. But Gabe *was* her child, not Mr. Castillo's. She should find a way to deflect from attending these kinds of dinners regularly, even if it disappointed a clearly dazzled Gabe.

"Javier would be a real step up if you're a house cleaner," Amina said, her eyes boring into the side of Harry's head.

Harry gave her a startled look. Apparently Amina was thinking that Harry had some kind of designs on Mr. Castillo. She felt anger burn its way up her throat.

"I don't know exactly what you're thinking, but whatever it is, you're wrong," Harry said firmly. "Mr. Castillo is my employer and that's it."

"What's he doing inviting you to these cozy little dinners, then?" Amina said, not bothering to hide her hostility anymore.

Harry didn't know if Amina was angry because she thought Harry was a gold digger, or because Amina had designs on Javier Castillo herself, or because she was an old friend who didn't want to see Mr. Castillo get hurt. Harry didn't really care about the reasoning, either. She had to nip this line of thought in the bud right now.

"If you're interested in why then you should ask Mr. Castillo," Harry said, ice dripping off her words.

"You're not his type, you know," Amina said, giving Harry the kind of look up and down that was meant to make her feel small and plain.

Well, Harry *was* small and plain, and she'd done nothing wrong. So she deliberately turned away from Amina and pretended she hadn't heard what the other woman said. It was ridiculous that she was being exposed to this kind of nonsense. She didn't know what Amina's problem was and she didn't need to engage with it. She was going to collect Gabe and head home.

"Mom!" Gabe called. "Come and look at this."

Harry gratefully took the opportunity to walk away from Amina. She called back to Gabe as she walked, "You know that whatever you're looking at, I've already seen it a hundred times. I dust down here on a regular basis."

Amina didn't follow Harry, which she appreciated. Harry caught up to Gabe and Daniel, who were carefully inspecting a motorcycle used in *Terminator 2*.

"Mom, look!" Gabe said, throwing both of his arms out at the cycle.

Harry couldn't help smiling at his response. This was the thing she loved so much about Gabe—his open heart, the way he responded to everything he experienced with so much of himself. He had none of Harry's natural caution or reserve.

"It's pretty cool," Harry said.

"Sometimes I can't believe you get to see all of this awesome stuff every day and you never talk about it," Gabe said, shaking his head. "You're the biggest movie fan in the world. You'd rather watch a movie than do almost anything."

Harry shrugged, feeling a little self-conscious because Daniel was watching her, his eyes curious. "I just wanted to respect Mr. Castillo's privacy."

"Because of the scandal?" Daniel asked.

Harry was surprised that Daniel asked it so baldly. He had seemed more circumspect than Amina.

"Kind of," Harry said. "Because he moved here so that people wouldn't bother him. But also because it just didn't seem like the right thing to do, to gossip about his possessions, even with my son. A home is a private place."

Daniel nodded. "You're right. It is."

"So what you're saying is I can't tell all of my friends about this cool stuff?" Gabe said, sighing.

"You know you can't," Harry said. "We already talked about this, after the last time."

"Yeah, I know," Gabe said. "I'm glad I got to see it all, though. Daniel, did you see the room upstairs? Your Sten costume is up there."

This was the part that Harry had been dreading. Despite coming to some kind of peace with the reality of the haunting, she still didn't want to spend any extra time in that room if she could avoid it. It wasn't the costume itself. It was the feeling that came from it.

"We just passed through it quickly when we arrived," Daniel said. "Because the guest rooms are on the next floor."

"Let's go up then," Gabe said.

Harry pointedly looked at her watch. "It's getting a little late for a fourteen-year old."

"Come on," Gabe said, throwing his arm around her shoulders. "I've got a chaperone. My mom is with me. Just a little bit longer."

"Alex Kintner said that in *Jaws*, and you know what happened to him," Harry said. "I bet his mom regretted it for the rest of her life."

"There are no sharks here," Gabe said, rolling his eyes. "Just another half hour."

"Twenty minutes," Harry said. "Counting down from now. We have to catch the bus, you know. And there aren't as many buses running this late."

"Okay," Gabe said, releasing Harry and tugging shyly at Daniel's sleeve. "Let's go quick, okay?"

Daniel smiled and let himself be tugged. Gabe started asking questions about *A Messenger from Hell* again. Amina waited in the spot where Harry had left her, tapping away on her phone. She gave Harry a dirty look when they reached her. Harry ignored it. She wished she knew what had set Amina off.

"We're going upstairs, Amina. To the blue room," Daniel said.

"Uggh, more stairs," Amina said, following Daniel and Gabe but making sure to shoulder in front of Harry. "There are so many stairs in this house. You'd think Javier would have an elevator installed or something."

"Climbing stairs is good for you," Daniel said.

"Don't give me one of your healthy-living lectures, Daniel," Amina said. "I hate sweating."

"All I'm saying is that if you exercised a little bit you would hate stairs less."

"Nothing in the universe can stop me from hating stairs as much as I want," Amina said.

Harry had thought Amina had the look of a gymnast when she'd first seen her, but apparently the actress came by her looks without effort. She'd also thought Amina seemed okay when they first arrived, but apparently wine brought out her real personality. Amina was a brat. If Harry remembered correctly, there was a ten-year age difference between Daniel and Amina. Amina had been about nineteen or twenty when they'd made *A Messenger from Hell* a few years before, so she was probably in her mid-twenties now. Their dynamic was very much like an older brother with a much younger sister.

Since Harry was walking behind her, she noticed that Amina was extremely unsteady on her feet, weaving from one side of a step to the other side of the next, gripping the banister with whitened knuckles. She managed to make it up the stairs from the basement without incident, but she brushed against the wall in the hallway as they made the turn for the next flight of stairs. Harry was certain the other woman would collapse at any moment.

Daniel and Gabe, wrapped up in their own conversation, were oblivious to Amina, so when Amina tripped on the second step, they didn't notice. Harry was right behind her, so she grabbed Amina's elbow to steady her.

"Get your hands off me," Amina snapped.

"I was just trying to make sure you didn't fall," Harry said.

"I don't need your help," Amina said, pulling away and marching up the stairs. Daniel and Gabe had disappeared onto the landing already.

Harry looked at her watch. She was holding Gabe to the twenty minutes she'd promised. She wasn't going to stay here a second longer than necessary.

When Harry arrived in the blue room the three of them stood in front of the Sten costume. She approached reluctantly, catching the usual whiff of talcum powder and sweat that no one else ever seemed to notice. The costume just hung there on its mannequin, an ostensibly inert and not at all menacing object. It was almost comical to think of what it had done, that it had turned its head and moved its eyes and tried to reach out to her like a special effect in a cheap horror movie.

It made her a little angry that the stupid thing only performed for her, only tried to terrorize her. What had she ever done to the ghost (*or whatever. I'm not committed to a ghost. There still could be a hell portal*) in this house? Her whole purpose here was to clean. There was nothing remotely threatening in that.

"The mask looks huge now," Daniel was saying. "It seemed big when I wore it but somehow it seems even bigger on this mannequin."

"I think this second version of the mask *is* bigger," Amina said.

"They used the same mold as the original one," Daniel said, shaking his head. "It's just your imagination that it's a different size. The perspective is different when it's not on a person."

Amina snorted. "The perspective was definitely different when that little shit Michael wore the other mask."

"Hey," Daniel said, giving Amina a sharp look.

"What?" Amina said, throwing out her hands dramatically. "He *was* a little shit. That was the reason why Javier slapped him in the first place."

Gabe's eyes were wide. "What?"

"Amina," Daniel said, his voice a warning that she didn't heed.

"Yeah, he might have been the only person Javier knew who could take your place temporarily, but the kid was an absolute monster. Never took direction, was always trying to do whatever he wanted when the camera was rolling. Contradicted Javier in front of the whole crew. Sneering at everything anyone said to him. He was such a goddamned nightmare. We had to do so many retakes of shots that he screwed up; I can't believe the studio thought it wasn't worthwhile just to wait for you to come back. I honestly don't know why Javier didn't lose it sooner."

"Amina," Daniel said, and this time he grabbed her wrist and shook it.

But Amina was on a roll, and Harry could tell she wasn't going to shut up unless Daniel taped her mouth closed.

"Anyway, I think it was day two or three of this, and I could tell Javier was starting to boil. It was his kid, his shitty little kid, messing things up, making everyone do the same setups over and over again because he wanted to showboat in the costume. All he was supposed to do was stand on a goddamned box so the sight line was correct and move his head and arms a little. But he kept trying to do these grand gestures that would block my face in coverage, and Javier was getting redder and redder with each new take. Finally he told everyone to take five except Michael. Well, we all kind of wandered away like we were going to give them privacy but most of us didn't *really* leave, you know? We were all sick to death of Michael already and we wanted to see Javier dress him down. Javier went right up to Michael and started telling him off, saying that he was slowing down the production when his whole purpose for being there was to keep it on schedule. And Michael told Javier to shove it up his ass, that he was doing Javier a favor. His own father. Can you imagine talking like that to your father? Then Michael took the Sten mask off—tearing the wig in the process, by the way—and threw the mask on the ground and stomped on it. It was ruined beyond all recognition. And Javier didn't say or do anything for a second. He just looked from the mask on the ground to Michael, and then he slapped him. Michael had this crazy light in his eyes when that happened. I thought he was going to strangle Javier. I've never seen a kid so young look so outright psychotic, I'm telling you. It was not a surprise to me at all when he was accused of murder. I'm sure he killed that girl. One hundred percent sure. That kid was out of his goddamned mind."

"Amina, stop," Daniel said. He threw a desperate glance from Harry to Gabe, and Harry took her cue.

"Well, we should go and thank Mr. Castillo for dinner," Harry said. She took Gabe's hand. His fingers were cold. He looked shocked, though Harry couldn't tell if it was because of Mr. Castillo's behavior or Michael's, or because Amina had been so indiscreet to tell the story in the first place.

"What, you don't want to hear any stories that put Javier in a bad light? Don't want your son to have the gloss taken off his hero?" Amina said, spittle flying from her mouth. "He's a genius, sure. He's a great artist. But his son was a bad seed, and a seed doesn't fall far from a tree."

"Amina, that's really enough," Daniel said. "I think you should go to bed. You're embarrassing yourself."

"I'm not the one who did anything wrong here," Amina said, poking her finger into Daniel's chest. "I'm not the one who ruined the shoot with my behavior."

"Oh, no, Saint Amina," Daniel said, turning away from Amina and crossing the room toward another costume, deliberately not facing her. "Like you've never acted like a diva on set. Running to Javier every time someone looked at you funny, making him feel sorry for you."

Harry was stunned at the amount of venom in Daniel's voice. It belied the all-good-friends-and-good-cheer vibe that Amina, Daniel and Mr. Castillo had projected at dinner. If she hadn't witnessed this outburst Harry would have thought Daniel and Amina were nothing but close. She'd even compared them to siblings in her own mind not a short time ago. Now she saw a hardness in Daniel that he'd carefully kept hidden before.

She also felt, more than ever, that she and Gabe should not be a part of this. If Mr. Castillo came upstairs and witnessed Amina and Daniel fighting—and discovered what they were fighting about—it would be awkward at best and terrifying at worst. Harry had a feeling that there was a grain of truth in what Amina had said—that a seed doesn't fall far from a tree. Harry had always had a sense that Javier Castillo had a bad temper that he kept hidden. Surely the mention of his long-lost and wayward son's bad behavior would bring that temper up to the surface. Harry didn't want to get caught in the cross fire.

She tugged at Gabe's frozen fingers, but her son wouldn't move. He stood there, staring from Amina to Daniel as their voices rose and rose, and as they began screaming accusations at each other.

"Of course. It's always me who's the problem, Daniel, never you. Mr. Nice Guy. Everyone always has nothing but good things to say about you. All those accolades from the makeup artists and the gaffers and the set decorators," Amina said. There was a sneer in her voice, like she didn't think much of Daniel's fan club.

"It's not hard to be kind to people, Amina. You should try it sometime. Maybe you would get more roles if you did," Daniel said, still not looking at her. It had to be making her crazy, the way he seemed to be ignoring her.

"I'm not going to kiss some producer's ass just because I'm a woman," Amina said.

"It's got nothing to do with being a woman," Daniel said. "And nobody's asking you to kiss anyone's ass. Just act like you're not the center of the universe for five minutes. That's all."

"You fucking asshole," Amina said.

Amina was shouting now, and Daniel's voice was raised beyond the socially acceptable level. Harry was sure that if Mr. Castillo came out of the kitchen he would be able to hear them. She pulled Gabe's hand again, and that was when she noticed the Sten costume.

The eyes of the costume had shifted to Amina. Its hands—those long-fingered hands tipped with claws—had shifted upward.

The upper body was bending forward, so microscopically slowly that no one would notice unless they were watching closely. And Harry was watching closely—the only one who was watching the costume at all. Daniel and Amina were too wrapped up in their argument to notice anything else. Gabe appeared capable only of staring at the two arguing.

The costume was trying to reach Amina. That was very, very clear. Its hands were level with Amina's neck. Surely it couldn't actually hurt her. Surely it was only trying to pose, or threaten, as it had done with Harry.

The fingers curled toward the back of Amina's neck, and Harry's eyes widened. That was when she knew, for the first time, that whatever was happening with the costume wasn't all in her mind.

"Amina!" she said, reaching for her to pull her away.

Amina reflexively jerked back, toward the costume. She wobbled on her feet, too drunk to have any kind of stability. Harry saw that Amina was about to fall into the costume. She didn't know what would happen then, and she didn't want to find out. She reached toward Amina, intending to pull her away from the costume—

—and then the costume *shoved* Amina hard, so much harder than Harry would have thought it could. She'd seen it move before but had assumed that the spirit inhabiting the costume had trouble moving solid objects. Suddenly it wasn't a silly bit of latex and cloth anymore. It was the physical manifestation of hate, hate that Harry could feel.

Amina flew in the direction of the banister/fence that separated the blue room from the stairs. Harry moved faster than she would have thought she could and grabbed the other woman's shoulders before she pitched headfirst over it and fell down the stairwell.

Harry tipped backward with Amina falling heavily on top of her. All the breath went out of her in a *whoosh* as Amina elbowed her hard in the stomach while trying to rise. Amina's long hair got caught under Harry's body and she screamed in pain.

"Sorry," Harry said breathlessly, trying to roll away, to get free of the shrieking, struggling Amina.

Daniel had turned when Amina started screaming and came over to help. He got Amina to her feet and reached toward Harry.

"Don't you help that fucking bitch!" Amina shouted, batting Daniel's hand away in fury. "She tried to throw me down the stairs."

"No, she tried to keep you from falling," Daniel said, extending his hand again and helping Harry up.

Harry did *not* mention that the costume had pushed Amina. The reason why she never said anything about the haunting was because she knew it would sound loopy.

"She did *not*. She pushed me. I felt her push me. And all because I'm onto her tricks." Amina said this with a distinct air of triumph.

"What tricks?" Daniel asked, bewildered. He glanced at Harry.

Harry had her back to the costume. She wanted to turn and look, to see what it was doing, but it seemed more important to divert Amina before she got up to full steam.

"Your friend," Harry said, emphasizing the word "friend," "seems to be under the mistaken impression that I am a gold digger with designs on Mr. Castillo. I can't explain what led her to this conclusion, but she seems quite convinced of it."

"Why else would Javier invite a *cleaner* to dinner with us?" Amina said.

"Christ, Amina," Daniel said in disgust. "This is exactly what

I was talking about before. You treat everyone who isn't exactly like you like garbage."

Suddenly Gabe spoke behind her, and Harry heard a coldness she'd never heard before in her child's voice. "My mom isn't less than you because she cleans houses. She's a better person than you'll ever be."

Harry felt warmth spread in her chest. A second later Gabe had grabbed her hand and tugged her around Daniel and Amina. Daniel threw Harry a quick glance of apology as Gabe hurried them down the stairs. Harry tried to see how much the Sten costume had moved, but Daniel and Amina blocked her view and Gabe was behind her, his sudden sense of urgency obvious.

"We should thank Mr. Castillo for dinner," Harry said. Despite everything else that had happened she knew her employer would be mortally offended if they didn't.

Gabe frowned. He looked very grown-up to Harry in that moment, and it hurt her heart a little to see this glimpse of the adult man he would become, the disappearance of her little boy. Then his brow cleared, and he nodded, and he looked like a teenager again.

"Yeah, we should," Gabe said. "It was a nice dinner, and a nice idea he had to let us meet Daniel and *her.*"

Harry rubbed her temples. The headachy feeling she'd had earlier had exploded into a full-blown conflagration. She didn't know how to begin to process everything she'd seen and experienced that night. She wondered, though, if Gabe had seen the costume push Amina.

They hurried into the kitchen, where Mr. Castillo was drying the last of the serving dishes and putting them away.

"Ah, I was just coming up to join you," he said. He gave no

indication that he had overheard any of the argument that had occurred upstairs.

"We're heading home," Harry said. "We just wanted to thank you for such a nice dinner."

Nice dinner, Harry thought. *It's not the biggest lie you've ever told, but there wasn't much nice about it.*

"Yeah, it was so cool of you to bring Daniel and A-Amina," Gabe said. Harry heard him stumble over Amina's name.

Mr. Castillo smiled at the compliment, but then his smile faded as he checked his watch. "Must you leave so early?"

"It's early for adults but not so early for a teenager," Harry said, her tone firm.

"Of course," he said. "Sleep is very important to adolescents. You sleep nearly as much as a teen as you do when you're a newborn."

Harry never knew what to do with these pronouncements of Mr. Castillo's. She was sure they were things he'd said to his own son, or wished he'd said.

"Yeah, and Mom makes the rules," Gabe said, giving Mr. Castillo a rueful smile. "I just follow them."

"You're a good boy, Gabriel. Very good. All children should listen to their parents the way you listen to yours."

The specter of Michael hung over the room again. Harry felt suddenly that she needed to get out of the house as soon as possible. She couldn't breathe. The spaces where things were left unsaid always filled up with Michael, with the son who was probably (definitely) a murderer on the run from justice.

"Anyway, thanks a lot, Mr. Castillo," Gabe said.

Mr. Castillo walked them through the dining room, obviously intending to escort them to the door. When they entered the hallway, however, the sound of Amina and Daniel shouting at each other on the next floor made him frown.

"What on earth are they doing?" he asked.

"I think Amina had a little too much to drink," Harry said. She figured this would cover a multitude of sins, especially if Amina started making accusations about Harry. She hoped that anything Amina might say would be dismissed as the ravings of a drunk person. Harry didn't think that Mr. Castillo would fire her just because Amina claimed Harry pushed her, but she didn't want a grilling over it, either.

How would I explain that something possessed the Sten costume and tried to shove Amina over the railing?

"I can't believe they're behaving like such children in front of other guests," Mr. Castillo said.

Harry hurriedly indicated to Gabe that he should put his shoes on. She did not want to linger if Mr. Castillo was going to wade into the argument.

"I'm sorry, I have to go and see. You're fine to drive home, correct? You didn't seem to have drunk as much as Amina."

"We're taking the bus," Harry said.

"Right, the bus." He glanced at his watch for the second time. "Isn't it dangerous to take the bus at this hour? Perhaps I should call you a cab."

Harry noted that it had seemed too early when they wanted to leave but suddenly too late when she mentioned the bus. She did not want to get stuck paying for a cab she really couldn't afford. "No, we're good. We're used to the bus, and it's really not bad at this hour. Thanks."

She practically pushed Gabe out the front door before Mr. Castillo could say anything else, but she didn't have to worry.

Mr. Castillo was already turning away from them, moving toward the stairs. A brief glimpse of his face made Harry gladder than ever that they were leaving.

As they walked down the path to the sidewalk, Harry thought of what Amina had said—"The seed doesn't fall far from the tree."

Mr. Castillo had looked like he wanted to murder somebody, anybody, who got in his way.

JAVIER CASTILLO

before

LENA GAVE JAVIER THE cold shoulder for weeks after he slapped Michael on the set of *A Messenger from Hell*. It didn't matter how he tried to explain that the boy had been willful and destructive and impossible to work with. It didn't matter how many times he expressed the pressure he was under from the studio to complete the film and that Michael had actively interfered in that. Lena felt that he was an adult and that hitting a child was beyond the pale.

"You should be old enough to control yourself," she said.

"He provoked me," Javier said, desperate to make her understand. "He deliberately pushed me until I broke. Ask anyone on set."

"And that makes it even worse," Lena said. "You hurt him, humiliated him, in front of all those people."

It was true that once the studio caught wind of the incident, lawyers had swooped in (*which cost more money*, as he was constantly reminded) and made sure any witnesses kept their mouths shut, signed NDAs and so on. It was easier then, because Javier never allowed anyone to keep their personal phone on-site. He didn't want any set photos or leaks. Without that clause Javier was sure that a video of him arguing with and hitting his son would have been on TikTok and Instagram and who knew where else.

Michael's behavior at home seemed to get worse and worse. Lena was inclined to sympathize with the boy, to treat him softly, to defend Michael when Javier tried to discipline him. It hurt Javier that Lena had become so blatantly partisan, that she always took Michael's side. And Javier knew that Michael knew the hurt he caused. He saw the gleam of satisfaction in the boy's eyes every time Lena told Javier not to be so hard on Michael.

Javier found that the little seed of love that had been planted on the day he first held Michael started to wither and die. He couldn't control his temper around the boy, especially when everything Michael did seemed designed to get a reaction out of his father. He felt he was constantly appealing to Lena for her approval, for her understanding, and she would not give it. All Lena would say was that it was a phase, that Javier should remember what it was like to be a child, that they shouldn't be too hard on Michael. He saw that he was losing her, losing her to the child he had never wanted in the first place.

He decided the solution was to bury himself in his work, to be at home as little as possible, to fill the house up with guests when he was home. In this way he kept a buffer between himself and his family, always forced them to be on their best behavior in front of others.

Soon enough Michael was leaving the house, going partying with other spoiled Hollywood children, and Javier was glad of it. If the boy wasn't at home then Javier and Lena argued less. They began to tentatively try to rebuild their relationship. They both pointedly ignored the tabloid reports of their son's behavior. As long as Michael wasn't home he could do whatever he wanted, as far as Javier Castillo was concerned.

He washed his hands of Michael.

EIGHT

"MOM, DID YOU SEE it?" Gabe asked the next morning at breakfast.

Harry had made pancakes for them from a big box of Bisquick. These were Gabe's favorite kind and she could make a zillion of them from one box. Which was good, because he shoveled them into his mouth almost as fast as they came off the griddle. She heated up some Brown 'N Serve sausage to go with them. This was the least expensive kind of breakfast meat in the store. Bacon cost way too much for her to buy regularly. Whenever they had BLTs for dinner Gabe would cheer because it was such a huge treat.

"Did I see what?" Harry asked, concentrating on pouring the mix in perfect four-inch circles on the griddle. She had to do more apartment hunting that day. She was starting to feel like their looming move date was an albatross pressing down on her.

"The costume," Gabe said. "You saw what the costume did, right? I saw your face right after it happened. I think you saw it."

Harry exhaled the breath she'd been holding. "Yes, I saw it. Why didn't you say anything last night?"

"Why didn't you?" Gabe countered.

"I wasn't completely sure you'd seen it move, and I didn't want you to think your mom was crazy."

"Too late," Gabe said.

"Smartass. Anyway, I can't believe you held on to this all night."

"I wanted to think about it," Gabe said.

"Okay, fair," Harry said. She'd been thinking about it herself for days.

"Anyway, what do you think it is?"

Harry was surprised by the eagerness in his voice. She'd become accustomed to thinking of the strange things happening at Bright Horses as frightening or menacing, but Gabe just seemed curious.

"I don't really know," Harry said slowly. "It was like the costume was sort of possessed, right?"

"Yeah, that's what I thought, too," he said. "Do you think there was a murder in that house or something? It's pretty old. We should look up the history. I bet we can find the information somewhere."

"Well, there's a research center at the Chicago History Museum," Harry said. "But I bet it's not open now, with the pandemic and all."

Gabe shrugged. "Google exists."

"Everything ever printed in the world isn't on Google, Gen Z," Harry said.

"Well it ought to be, Millennial," Gabe said. "Anyway, if anything completely crazy happened there, like a murder, I'm sure it would pop up in a Google search. We can at least eliminate the obvious."

He was already standing up and going for his phone. Harry had a strict no-phones-at-meals rule. She wanted to look at her son's face while she ate, not the reflected glow of his Instagram account.

"Just wait until you're finished eating," she said.

"But I want to know," Gabe said. "Don't you? I think we saw actual proof of a ghost, and you're acting like it wasn't that big a deal at all."

Harry finished cooking the last of the pancakes and carried them to the table, taking a few off the top for herself before Gabe grabbed any more.

"Well," she said, trying to decide how much to say. It was so important not to put any burden on Gabe. She was always conscious of the fact that he was a child and she was the parent, even if he was more and more adult every day. She didn't want him to worry about anything, ever. "It wasn't the first time I saw or heard something strange in that house."

"What? And you never said anything to me?"

"I wasn't sure at first that I was actually seeing or hearing what I thought I saw," she admitted. "I thought maybe I was having a stress response and hallucinating."

"Because you're worried about having to move out, and you don't want to lose your job," Gabe said.

"I never said that," Harry said, both annoyed and impressed that Gabe had gotten to the heart of the matter so quickly.

"You didn't have to," Gabe said. "It's all over your face all day long. Mr. Castillo even asked me about it."

"He did?"

"Yeah, he kind of asked on the down-low while he was showing me the blue room the first time. He wanted to know if we had found a place to live yet. He said you seemed preoccupied."

Harry didn't know how to feel about that. She wasn't sure if

Mr. Castillo was genuinely concerned about their futures or if he was worried that he might lose his house cleaner if they settled too far away.

"Well, anyway," Harry said. "Yes, I've been a little worried about stuff generally."

"A lot worried," Gabe interjected. "Stop trying to pretend you're not."

"*Anyway,*" Harry said, wanting to move away from this topic. She obviously needed to do a better job of covering up her thoughts at any given moment. "Back to the ghost or whatever it is. I kept hearing some strange sounds in one of the bedrooms. I thought I saw the eyes move on the Sten mask. But I'd convinced myself that it wasn't really happening, that it was all in my head."

"You gaslit yourself," Gabe said, shaking his head. "That's what happens when you keep everything to yourself instead of, you know, sharing with other people."

"What was I supposed to do? Tell Mr. Castillo that I heard someone saying 'Help me' through the wall of the upstairs bedroom?"

"Did you really?" Gabe asked, his eyes bright. "That definitely means there's a ghost in that house. Maybe more than one."

"It sounds completely ridiculous to say it out loud, to even be talking about it like it's a real thing and not something we saw in a movie. Especially the costume. I can't help thinking that if I saw a costume come to life in a movie that I would just laugh my ass off, that I would think it was stupid," Harry said.

"It is kind of stupid. But it doesn't mean it's not happening." Gabe shrugged. "Weird stuff happens in the world. We don't always witness it, but it still happens."

Harry reached across the table and ruffled his hair. "That sounds terribly wise and philosophical for a fourteen-year-old."

"I am terribly wise and philosophical. I spend all my time

marinating in my teenage hormones and thinking about the state of the world," Gabe said. "Also, your hoodie string is in your syrup."

Harry looked down and cursed. She was wearing her favorite hoodie, a black one with the pentagram and wolf from *The Wolf Man* on the front. "I'll have to change and wash it, otherwise I'll be sticky for the rest of the day."

"Might as well wait until you're done eating. Otherwise you could end up with syrup on two shirts instead of one."

"Really so wise today," Harry said.

"My mom taught me everything I know," Gabe said. "Can I have the last of these pancakes?"

"Sure," Harry said. She'd only eaten three of them, but the constant churn of worry in her belly made it hard to eat much of anything these days.

"So there's a ghost in Mr. Castillo's house," Gabe said. "And it tried to push Amina down the stairs last night."

"It might not be a ghost," Harry said. "It could be a demon, or something."

The words felt incredibly dumb coming out of her mouth. This was not something that happened in real life. This was a discussion that took place on *Buffy the Vampire Slayer*.

"Maybe," Gabe said, his eyes thoughtful. "What else have you seen or heard it do?"

"It banged on the wall of the upstairs bedroom for a long time. It sounded like someone trying to kick through."

"Ah, that's why you asked about the Catherine Keener movie," he said. "You thought that maybe Mr. Castillo was holding someone hostage. He doesn't seem like the type, really."

"That's what everyone says when they find out their neighbor was keeping someone in their basement or their attic or whatever.

'He was such a good neighbor. I can't believe he'd do something like this.'"

"But you have to agree that Mr. Castillo doesn't seem like the type. I can't see him, like, subduing someone and dragging them into the house. Or carting a body around. He gets out of breath walking up the stairs."

"Yeah," Harry said.

She didn't really think that Mr. Castillo was a kidnapper. And she certainly didn't think he'd keep a hostage in the locked bedroom at the end of the hall with Amina and Daniel staying at Bright Horses. It still seemed much more realistic that Mr. Castillo had a prisoner than that the house was haunted, despite the proof of her own eyes—and Gabe's. She'd thought she'd come to terms with what she'd seen and heard, but somehow the presence of other witnesses made her doubt return.

She did think that Mr. Castillo had a temper, one that he tried very hard to keep hidden. Temper didn't always equal violence, though Amina had told the story of Mr. Castillo hitting Michael in front of witnesses. If he was willing to do that, what would he do behind closed doors?

"And you *saw* it," Gabe said. "You saw the costume, which certainly should not have been able to do that, push Amina. Daniel saw it, too, I'm pretty sure. Mr. Castillo never said anything to you about strange things happening in the house?"

Harry shook her head. "Maybe he thinks he's the only one who sees paranormal stuff. Or maybe he bought the house because he knew it was haunted. It seems like the kind of thing a horror director would do."

"I think we should say something to him the next time we're there for dinner," Gabe said. "We need to know what he knows."

"I don't think that's a good idea," Harry said. "What if he thinks we're both loopy and fires me? I can't afford to lose my job right now."

"But if Daniel says something to him . . ."

"We don't know what Daniel saw, or what he'll say to Mr. Castillo," Harry said. "And it's not like we have Daniel's phone number and can ask him, 'Hey, did you happen to see the costume you wore in a film attack your friend last night?'"

"When you put it like that," Gabe said.

"Exactly. Let's just keep this to ourselves for the time being."

"Although Daniel did give me his phone number," Gabe said. It came out reluctantly, like it was a secret he wanted to keep to himself.

"He did?!?"

"Yeah, we exchanged numbers last night. He told me I could text him anytime."

"Why did he do that?" Harry asked carefully.

On the one hand, it might have just been a kind gesture on Daniel's part. On the other hand, Gabe was a minor and Daniel was an adult male. What motivation could Daniel possibly have for trading phone numbers with Gabe?

"Don't worry, Mom. He's not going to recruit me into his militia or pimp me out or anything like that," Gabe said, rolling his eyes.

"You don't need to act like I'm an idiot for being concerned," she said. "That is literally my job as your mom."

He finished the last of his meal and collected the dirty plates, carrying them to the dishwasher. "I just kind of mentioned that I might be interested in writing a screenplay. Not now. You know, someday. And he said he'd be happy to give me advice or whatever if I decided to do it."

Gabe said all this very fast, like he was hoping she wouldn't hear the words. Harry stared at him in surprise. "You want to write a screenplay?"

Gabe shrugged, putting the butter and syrup away. "Maybe."

"A horror movie screenplay?"

"Maybe."

"I didn't know you were interested in writing," Harry said. It felt like a flaw in her parenting, like she'd missed something important.

"It's just something I've been messing around with," Gabe said. "I like my English teacher this year. He's been giving us fun assignments, and some of the other students think my stuff is good."

Harry knew better than to ask to see anything Gabe wrote. If he'd wanted her to see it, he would have shown it to her already. But she wanted to make sure he knew she was receptive, whenever he was ready.

"That's amazing," she said, and she meant it. She'd never been good at anything creative in her life. She'd never been good at anything, really, except surviving. "I'm really proud of you. I think you should go for it. Try to write a screenplay, I mean."

Gabe scratched the back of his neck and looked at the floor. "Well, you know, I got a book from the library about screenwriting. I'm going to try. I need a real good idea, something that's different from everyone else's ideas."

"It's your first try. It doesn't have to be perfect," Harry said. "In fact, maybe you should just think of it as practice. Like practicing the piano or practicing pitching a baseball or whatever. You're just practicing now. Just because you write words down doesn't mean they're carved in stone, that they can't be changed later."

"Yeah," Gabe said, his face clearing. "Yeah, I'm sure you're right. Anyway, Daniel said I could bounce some things off him if I wanted."

"That was very kind of him," Harry said. "But why didn't you ask Mr. Castillo? He's written or cowritten all of his movies."

Gabe looked scandalized. "I couldn't ask Mr. Castillo. He won an Oscar."

"That seems like it would make him pretty qualified to answer any of your questions," Harry said.

"Overly qualified," Gabe said. "And he probably would be, I don't know, pretty critical. Like he wouldn't see it as practice, like you do."

"It would be a sign that he took your writing seriously, though."

"I'm not sure how serious I am myself yet. When I am serious, he's the one I'd go to. Until then, I think I'll just stick to messing around. And maybe asking Daniel. If *he's* actually serious about looking at it."

"I don't think he'd give you his phone number otherwise. Unless he really does have a hidden agenda. Let me know if any of his messages make you uncomfortable."

"You always think the worst of people."

"I don't," Harry said.

"You definitely do. You always act like everyone is about to pull the rug out from under you. It's why you don't have any close friends, why you take so much worry on yourself."

"All right, that's enough for today, Mr. Therapist."

"I'm just saying that maybe you could share stuff with me. Even if I'm a kid still. You should have told me about the ghost. Or demon. Or whatever's going on in Mr. Castillo's house."

"Let me sing a song you have heard before. I am the parent. You are the child. Your responsibility is to learn stuff at school and do your chores and have fun with your friends and learn to navigate the world—gradually. My responsibility is to feed and clothe and guide you, and generally take on all the adulting."

"But it's so hard for you," Gabe said, and Harry was surprised to see his eyes welling up. "You can't do everything yourself."

"Oh, Gabe," she said, and went to him and hugged him hard. He was her little boy, he'd always be her little boy, even though she had to reach up to hug him now. "I just don't want you to worry. It's not your job to do that. And I can definitely, one hundred percent do everything. I've been doing it your whole life. Look."

She pointed at an old drawing of his that she'd never taken off the refrigerator. On it Gabe had drawn her—wild yellow-crayon hair, blue eyes peeking out of a red mask, a blue bodysuit and a red cape. In her left hand she held a red sword. Underneath he'd written "supur momm."

"You *are* a supermom," he said. "But you don't have to be. People should reach out to people, ask for help when they need it. Otherwise you'll end up like Mr. Castillo, all alone in a house full of stuff with nobody to love you. You don't even try to date, or, like, go out for cocktails with other moms you meet at school."

Harry thought that Mr. Castillo's case was a lot different from her own. But she felt the justice of what Gabe said. She'd held herself apart from people ever since Pete had left her. She'd always expected that others would leave when life got hard. And she'd never, ever wanted to expose Gabe to a series of temporary "fathers," to let him get attached to someone who might hurt or disappoint him.

"Who can afford cocktails?" Harry said, smiling.

"Don't try to make a joke when I'm being serious," Gabe said, pushing away from her. "You always do that. You always try to deflect."

"Hey," Harry said, touching his shoulder. "I'm sorry. I really am. I take you seriously, you know. I really do."

"You take *me* seriously," he said. "You don't take yourself seriously. You act like you're not as important as I am, or like your life is on pause until I go to college."

She felt a little scared then, scared of how much he'd observed and noticed, how long he must have been thinking about these things to have it all come out now.

"Listen," she said. "I'm being serious now, too. I'm sorry I made you worry. I'm sorry that you think I take too much on myself. But it's the way that I've been for a long time. I've only been able to rely on myself, and it's hard to change."

"Try," he said.

"Okay," Harry said, holding up her hands in surrender. "I'll try to make some friends. But after this move is done. I have too many things to think about right now. The logistics of a move are not small."

"And we don't actually have a place to move to at the moment," Gabe said.

"But I will find something. Apartments always pop up, sometimes at the last minute. People are moving a lot right now because of the pandemic, buying houses because they want more space or whatever. Something will turn up. I'll keep looking."

"What will happen if you can't find a decent place?"

"I will," Harry said again. "I promise to make some friends if you promise not to worry about this."

"Pinkie promise?" Gabe asked, holding up his hand with the pinkie extended.

Harry mirrored him and they wrapped their pinkies together. "Stamp it," she said, and they touched thumbs.

"I expect to see you going out on Fridays," Gabe said in a warning tone.

"Not *every* Friday," Harry said.

"At least two per month," Gabe said. "Join a bowling league or something."

"Don't try to pressure me into doing something that involves coordination," Harry said. "We seem to have gotten pretty far off the topic of what happened last night."

"I'm going to Google the house right now," Gabe said.

Harry got out cleaning spray and cleaned off the table while Gabe grabbed his phone. He came back with his head bent over the screen, fingers tapping away.

"Listen," she said. "Next time you go to Mr. Castillo's house— if there is a next time—"

"There'll be a next time," Gabe said, not looking up. "He likes showing off, and I'm a good audience."

Harry frowned. "Do you mean that you're pretending?"

"Oh, no," Gabe said, looking up. "I really do like all the stuff he shows us, and I did like meeting Daniel. Amina, too, at first. But it's not like Mr. Castillo really wants to be friends or whatever. He's lonely, and he's used to having lots of people around who look up to him."

Harry shook her head. "You're just a fountain of perception all of a sudden. Anyway, if you go back into the house I want you to stay away from that costume."

"But you said that you heard noises upstairs, too. Whatever is happening can't be confined to that one costume. Besides, if I'm going to stay away from it, you should, too."

"I can't," Harry said. "I have to dust the stupid thing or else explain to Mr. Castillo why I didn't. But I don't see any reason why you should take a risk."

"It doesn't move very fast," Gabe said, his eyes distant. "It seemed like it was moving really slowly right up until it actually pushed Amina."

"I thought that, too," Harry said. "It makes sense, right? A spirit would have trouble trying to move a physical object. That's how it always is in the movies."

"So I'm probably not at any risk," Gabe said. "Besides, up until it attacked Amina it only moved for you."

"Maybe the ghost doesn't like women," Harry said.

"Maybe it doesn't," Gabe said, looking concerned.

"That was a joke."

"I'd like to see if it would move for me," Gabe said. "If no one else was around."

"No way," Harry said. "You think I'd let you risk yourself like that?"

"I wouldn't go close to it. I just want to, I don't know, provoke it and see what happens."

Harry reached out and knocked her knuckles against his head. "Hello in there! Have I not spent all these years educating you in the Ways of the Horror Film? Do not provoke the monster. Those that do get eaten. Or possessed. Or whatever. Besides, I didn't do anything to provoke it in the first place."

"Nothing?" Gabe asked.

"No, what could I possibly do? My entire purpose is to run a duster over it. Me and Mr. Castillo hardly even talk when we're in that room. He's very serious about cleaning."

"I had this idea," Gabe said slowly, "that it was feeding off Amina's energy last night. That she somehow gave it the power to move the way it did. But if you're saying that never happened when you were in there before . . ."

"Believe me," Harry said. "I didn't do anything to piss off a ghost. When I'm at work I keep my head down and get my jobs done."

"Maybe it wants your attention," Gabe said. "Maybe it's trying to get you to do something for it."

Harry rubbed her forehead. "I don't have enough time in the day to worry about posthumous requests for assistance."

"But what if it hurts Mr. Castillo when you're not there?" Gabe asked. "Because you didn't do what it wanted?"

"How am I supposed to know what it wants?"

"Well, if we can figure out who it was in real life—if it's a ghost, that is." Gabe returned his attention to his phone. "There's lots of articles about Bright Horses here, but almost all of them are about its architecture."

"Who designed it?"

"It wasn't Ivo Shandor, if that's what you're wondering," Gabe said.

"Things would be a lot easier if it were. Then we could just call the Ghostbusters and that would be the end of the story."

"The Ghostbusters would completely, one hundred percent wreck Mr. Castillo's house trying to catch the ghost. He wouldn't even let them in the door."

"So who designed it?" Harry asked again.

"Well, that's the weird thing, according to this article I found. There's no record of the architect, only that the building went up right after the Chicago Fire."

"Probably explains the burning horse imagery," Harry said. "What else?"

"The first person that lived there was a wealthy widow named Anna Schultz," Gabe said. "There's not a lot of information about her. It just says her husband was a big lumber magnate and that he died in the fire."

"That also makes sense. There were a lot of lumberyards along the river at that time."

"And that she was very reclusive once her husband passed away," Gabe said. "Apparently the house only attracts recluses."

"She and Mr. Castillo can't have been the only people to have ever lived there," Harry said. "The Chicago Fire was in 1871."

Gabe scanned the article he was reading. "Anna Schultz lived at Bright Horses until 1924."

"The year of her death, I assume."

"You assume correctly. No children and no close living relatives came forward to claim the property and it was auctioned by the city."

"Who bought it? Another recluse?"

"You're not wrong," Gabe said. "One Harry Long purchased the property. He was a doctor who'd apparently made a lot of money on medical patents. He had a wife, but she died young, and their son died in World War I."

"Well, that's sad."

"He lived there until 1948. After his death the property passed to his cousin, Sarah Long Halliwell. And before you ask, yes, she was another recluse."

"It's a gothic monstrosity on a double lot," Harry said philosophically. "It's pretty much only going to attract wealthy weirdos. They're the only ones that can afford the property taxes."

"The thing is," Gabe said. "I don't see anything about murder, or strange events that might cause the place to be haunted."

"Maybe it's built on top of a cemetery. But to find that out you'd have to look somewhere besides Google. I can't believe there's no record of the architect. That seems really strange."

"You mean given the way Chicagoans absolutely worship architects?"

"Exactly. Adler and Sullivan, Burnham and Root, Frank Lloyd Wright, Jeanne Gang. We all have such a crazy chip on our shoulder for anything that originated in this city. And Bright Horses is a really unusual house. It's enormous. It's old, for a Chicago structure. And it's got significant architectural features. Why isn't it always being photographed and tagged on Instagram?"

Gabe shook his head. "Instagram is not cool anymore, Mom."

"People my age and older still exist, Gabriel. We use Instagram."

"Which is why it is not cool. Obviously."

"Okay, well, the point is that for some reason this building has flown under the radar for a long time. And only single people seem to live there."

"Maybe you can't actually take a picture of the house," Gabe said. "Maybe if you try you'll be cursed."

Gabe collapsed onto the couch and kept tapping around and scrolling on his phone. Harry finished cleaning up their breakfast and got her laptop out, ready to do a serious apartment search.

"Hey, Mom? Something just popped up when I refreshed the search for Bright Horses," Gabe said. His voice sounded weird, and Harry looked over.

"What is it?"

"It says that Amina Collucci died at Bright Horses last night."

HARRY

before

PETE WANTED HER TO get an abortion or give the baby up for adoption.

"We've worked too hard to get established," he said. "It's not time for us to have a child."

Harry knew he was right. She'd legally changed her name as soon as she turned eighteen, making sure Harriet Anne Schorr disappeared forever. Not that she thought her parents would come looking for her. They were afraid of the big bad evil city. They'd never set foot into such a den of vice, and they'd never let her sister do so, either. She'd gotten jobs—crummy ones at first, washing dishes and busing tables, and worked her way up to a server position in a semi-fancy restaurant. She and Pete had moved out of the squat and gotten their own place and filled it with IKEA furniture that they'd bought with their own money. They were doing better. They were outrunning the runaway life.

And then Harry's period didn't come.

At first they were both just scared. Harry was only nineteen;

Pete was twenty-one. The concept of a baby, a little person who'd be completely dependent on them, seemed a huge and impossible thing to grasp. But when the time came to go to the clinic Harry found she couldn't do it. She wanted that little person growing inside her, wanted to hold that person and help them grow. She didn't have stars in her eyes. She knew it would be difficult, knew that their income wasn't exactly stable. But she wanted to try.

Pete didn't want to try.

They fought—just a little, at first. Then the fights got bigger and more frequent, until they could barely look at each other and speak a civil word. Pete kept telling her that she was being selfish by having a baby she might not be able to care for. Harry said *he* was the selfish one, that he was only thinking about how his freedom would be curtailed.

After a while they stopped shouting, and the silence became a living, pulsing thing stuffed with all their unsaid resentments.

Pete left before eight months were up. He took half of the IKEA furniture and left behind two hundred dollars, the only child support payment Harry would ever get from him.

Harry was tiny and Pete was tall, and the baby took after his father. That meant that by the time Pete left Harry's stomach was measuring much bigger than expected, and her obstetrician was making noises about a C-section. Harry feared a C-section. She didn't want the surgery and knew that women who got them needed a lot of help to recover. Harry didn't have anyone who could help her. She could just imagine calling her parents, asking them to assist her with their out-of-wedlock (which would be unforgivable in their eyes) grandchild.

Harry's son took away the worry about the C-section. He couldn't wait to get out of his tiny prison, and Harry's water broke in her sleep a few nights after Pete left.

She calmly changed her clothes, called a cab, prayed she had enough money to pay for it and threw a few items in a bag for the hospital. She thought she'd have more time to pack it, but she didn't forget the little yellow onesie she'd bought at Target. It had an embroidered giraffe on the front, and it matched the small stuffed giraffe she'd bought for the baby.

The labor was less than six hours long. The labor and delivery nurse held her hand and spoke soothing words. Harry gritted her teeth and got through it, refusing the epidural because she was afraid of both a needle in her spine and the subsequent medical bills.

When her son finally emerged he was long and skinny and wrinkly. He was four and a half weeks premature but already twenty-one inches long. He had no fat under his skin because babies get their fat deposits the last couple of weeks of gestation, and he had a full head of dark hair that was the exact same shade as Pete's.

Harry loved him instantly.

"My Gabriel," she said, as the nurse placed her baby in her arms. "My angel."

NINE

"WHAT?" HARRY SAID, HURRYING over to Gabe to peer over his shoulder at the phone. "How can Amina be dead?"

"It doesn't say." Gabe's shoulders were hunched and tense.

"Can I see the article?" Harry asked.

Gabe handed her his phone. His face was pale. "I can't believe she's dead. I never knew anybody who died before."

Harry scrolled up to the top of the article. The headline said **TRAGEDY AT RECLUSIVE FILM DIRECTOR'S HOME**. Harry read the copy underneath aloud.

"'Amina Collucci, the young star of director Javier Castillo's cult horror hit *A Messenger from Hell*, is reportedly dead after an accident at the director's Chicago home. Representatives for Collucci and Castillo did not give any further details at this time. Representatives from the Chicago Police Department would not comment on an ongoing investigation.

"'Javier Castillo has been living in Chicago since the mysterious disappearance of his wife, Lena, and their son, Michael.

Michael Castillo is considered a suspect in the murder of model and actress Adelaide Walker. Castillo has claimed not to know the whereabouts of his family since their disappearance. This is a breaking story.'"

"'Investigation' makes it sound like they suspect foul play," Gabe said. "Do you think Mr. Castillo might get in trouble?"

"Not necessarily," Harry said. "If someone dies suddenly I'm sure the police have to make sure it really is an accident."

"But what if it isn't an accident?" Gabe persisted. "What if the ghost went after Amina because it didn't take care of her the first time?"

"I don't think we have any evidence of that," Harry said, handing Gabe's phone back to him. "We don't know what happened. She could have died in her sleep but it was reported as an accident."

"Why would such a young woman die in her sleep?"

"Any reason," Harry said. "She could have had a health condition we don't know about. She might have drunk too much."

"I'm going to ask Daniel."

Harry grabbed the phone out of his hand before he could open the text app.

"You most certainly will not," she said. "That was his colleague. You can't just ask him how she died like some car-crash rubbernecker."

"I'm not rubbernecking."

Harry raised her eyebrow at him.

"I'm not. I just want to know how she died so we can figure out if it was, you know, paranormal."

"It's not appropriate," Harry said. "And I'm not giving your phone back until you swear that you won't ask Daniel about Amina."

Gabe gave her a sulky look.

"Promise," she said. She knew if he promised that would be it, because the one unbreakable law of their household was "no lying."

His mouth took on a mulish line.

"Okay, no phone at all then," she said. "If I can't trust you with it then you can't have it."

"Fine," Gabe said, throwing up his hands. "I promise."

"Promise what?"

"I won't text Daniel about Amina's death."

Harry held out the phone to him and he snatched it from her hands like it was a trick.

"I can still use Google, right?" Gabe asked, in a slightly smarmy tone that put Harry's back up. "That's not off-limits?"

"Searching the web for more information is not the same as texting Daniel, yes," Harry said, deliberately keeping her tone mild. She felt like she'd just had a taste of Gabe's adolescent attitude and decided she was not looking forward to sixteen.

Harry's phone was still on her nightstand. When she went in to get it she discovered that there were several missed calls from Mr. Castillo. Only one voicemail, though, and Harry pressed the play button to listen.

"Harry," Mr. Castillo said. He sounded tired. "There's been a terrible accident and Amina—"

His voice hitched, like he was swallowing a sob. "Amina fell out the window of her bedroom. I don't know how it could have happened, although she did have a lot of alcohol last night. I blame myself. I wanted to let you know before you or Gabriel discover this news elsewhere."

He hung up the phone then without a goodbye. Harry stared at the wall in shock. *Amina fell out the window? The third-floor window?*

Harry cleaned those guest bedrooms. The windows were kind of small, and had old-fashioned sashes with rope weights on them. There were screens, too. Had Amina fallen through a screen? Was it just that she was drunk and messing around and lost her balance while opening the window?

Or did something push her, the way Gabe thought?

Harry shook her head. The ghost, or whatever, was able to move the costume. She'd seen it, and so had Gabriel, and probably Daniel, too. But Harry found it highly unlikely that the costume would have made its way up the stairs and into Amina's bedroom. The thing could not move that fast.

She'd seen no evidence that the haunt in the locked room could directly touch someone. It surely would have tried to do so with Harry. It had banged on the wall and spoken (*maybe*). But it hadn't tried to touch her shoulder or anything. No, Amina's death seemed to be exactly what Mr. Castillo had said—a terrible accident.

When Harry came out of the bedroom Gabe was watching something on TikTok. Harry could hear a bit of ominous-sounding music with someone talking over it.

"How do we know that Javier Castillo didn't kill Amina Collucci? The media are saying it's an accident, but we know his son is a killer. Why not the father, too?" the voice said, sounding slightly tinny as it came out of the phone speaker.

"What are you watching?" Harry asked, more sharply than she intended. She wasn't Mr. Castillo's biggest fan, but she didn't think Gabe should be watching videos full of unfounded speculation.

"Nothing," Gabe said, looking guilty and turning his phone over on his lap. "I was just looking for, you know, more information."

"You're not going to get accurate information from TikTok. That's practically their motto."

"I know."

"Anyway, I know what happened, so you can stop scouring the darkest corners of the internet. Mr. Castillo left me a message."

Harry explained that Amina had fallen out of her window in the night.

"Do you think—" Gabe began.

"No, I don't think that the costume pushed her out the window. Or Mr. Castillo, either."

"I didn't think Mr. Castillo did it," Gabe said. "I wouldn't think that, really."

Harry looked pointedly at his phone. "Then don't listen to that kind of nonsense. How can some rando on the internet speak with any authority less than an hour after the death was reported?"

"But the costume, or rather the ghost, I guess," Gabe said. "It seemed like it went after her specifically. How do you know it didn't kill her?"

"Remember how slowly it moved? Can you imagine it going up the stairs, into Amina's bedroom, tossing her out the window and then getting back into place before Mr. Castillo or Daniel noticed what was going on?"

"I guess not," Gabe said. "But what if—"

"All right," Harry said. "Enough of this. It was an awful thing that happened, but we're not going to spend the whole day speculating. And no more ghost talk today, either. I'm imposing an embargo until tomorrow. I can't look for apartments and think about this at the same time."

"I'm going to keep looking for stuff about Bright Horses, though, okay?" Gabe said.

"Fine," Harry said. "Historical data only, not social media videos. And you can tell me if you collected anything interesting tomorrow."

Harry went back to her laptop and started scrolling through

Craigslist, looking for apartment listings. Small owners who owned one or two buildings usually posted there. She didn't want to rent from a big real estate corporation if she could avoid it.

Despite what she'd said to Gabe, though, she couldn't stop thinking about Amina, standing at the window. Harry could almost see her there, pulling up the sash for some night air, and then *something*, some force Amina wouldn't have suspected was present at all, suddenly shoved between her shoulder blades.

Amina's face pressed against the screen for a moment, then the force of her body broke through, and she fell, and fell, and fell. Harry could almost hear her scream.

HARRY WASN'T SURE WHAT to expect when she went in to work on Monday. She figured Mr. Castillo would be upset, but she assumed he would want the house cleaned anyway. He hadn't called her to say she couldn't come in. She thought that maybe he would just isolate himself if he was grieving, leave the work to her.

Leave me alone with that goddamned costume.

Harry rounded the corner to Mr. Castillo's block and paused. Bright Horses was about halfway down the street, and there was a massive crowd in front of the gates. Several reporters stood in front of cameras on tripods, and there were news vans blocking most of the parked cars.

Oh, no, I'm not messing with that. Harry most definitely did *not* want to be caught on camera walking up to the front gate. She was sure the reporters would try to ask her questions, and if Mr. Castillo tried to buzz her in she wasn't confident that they wouldn't try to run across the lawn to the front door.

She stood there for a moment, then walked back the way she'd come. There was an alley that ran behind Mr. Castillo's house, parallel to the street where the reporters were encamped. Maybe she could enter that way, through the garage.

Harry peeked down the alley. She didn't see anyone lurking about. She called Mr. Castillo's number.

"Hello?" an unfamiliar voice said.

"Um, I'm looking for Mr. Castillo?"

"It's Daniel, Harry. He's not answering the phone right now. I only picked up because I saw your name."

"Oh, okay. Listen, I can't come in the front because there are a million reporters. Can somebody let me in through the garage?"

"Is there anybody back there? Media, I mean."

"Not that I can see, but I'm still on the sidewalk. I didn't want to come down that way unless I knew someone would be there to open the side door. I don't want to get caught standing around back there if one of the crowd up front decides to go investigate."

"Understandable," Daniel said. "I'll meet you by the door in a few minutes."

Harry put away her phone, looked around to make certain she hadn't been observed by anyone, and hurried down the alley. She was nearly there when she saw the door open a crack and Daniel peeked out.

"Daniel Jensen!" a man's voice shouted. "Can you comment on the death of your costar?"

The man sprang from between two garage buildings, waving a microphone and followed by a cameraman, clearly hoping for this exact scenario. Harry rushed toward the door, wanting more than anything to be inside before her face, hair or any part of her ended up as a clip on the news or on TMZ or whatever. Daniel turned his body so that his back was to the inside of the door and she could duck under his arm. A second later Harry stood inside the garage, panting a little. Daniel yanked the door shut and locked it. The reporter outside actually went so far as to bang on the door with his fist and call Daniel's name again.

"Christ. What a nightmare." Daniel scrubbed his hands over his face. He moved them away from the door so they wouldn't be overheard by the still-lurking journalist.

"I didn't expect you to still be here," Harry said. "I guess I had the impression you were only staying for the weekend?"

"I couldn't leave Javier right now. This has been terrible for him."

Isn't it also terrible for you? Harry thought, but she didn't say anything. Daniel and Mr. Castillo were obviously closer friends than Harry had realized. Or perhaps Daniel felt some kind of loyalty to Mr. Castillo because of their long working relationship. She already liked Daniel, but his obvious kindness made her like him more.

That kindness was causing a strain, though. He looked exceptionally pale to Harry. His face practically glowed in the murky light of the garage. She had never been in here before, never had any reason to be. Mr. Castillo only let her into the parts of the house that she needed to see.

There was a sleek black BMW with tinted windows parked in the exact center of the room. Two walls held shelves with the kind of varied detritus that accrues in garages—cases of paper towels and bottled water, canned and boxed food, a toolbox, beach chairs, camping equipment. Everything was neatly stacked and labeled, which was exactly as Harry would have expected.

The camping gear seemed pretty incongruous to Harry— somehow she couldn't imagine Mr. Castillo in a tent. She wondered if Michael had enjoyed camping, and if that was why Mr. Castillo kept the stuff.

Not that his son will be doing much camping if he's ever found. Murderers aren't usually allowed to go on outdoor excursions.

Harry marveled a little that Lena had managed to hide herself and Michael so thoroughly. She imagined them in a non-extradition country, far from the prying eyes of both governments and people with cameras.

"I'm glad you're here. Maybe you can get him to move around a little. He's done almost nothing except stare at the wall in his office since Amina's body was taken away. And with the reporters outside it feels like the place is under siege. It's like when Michael . . ." Daniel trailed off, his voice faltering a little. "Well, anyway, I think that he's upset about Amina but also about other things."

"I understand," Harry said.

"He's worked really hard to keep a low profile here. He bought the house under an LLC so he could outrun the wolf pack in L.A. He had all the furniture and props first shipped to Toronto, where everything was stored in a warehouse for a while, and then he had it shipped here. He's done so much to try and rid himself of the constant press of reporters. He thought Chicago would be safe. Chicagoans, well, you guys seem to keep yourselves to yourselves, mostly, and don't dig around in other people's business. I mean, he hired you and you never said a word to anybody about who you were working for, and you could have."

"I would have lost my job," Harry said.

"Sure, but you could have made a ton of money giving an interview somewhere. Even just describing the inside of the house and the state of Javier's emotional health . . . you would have lost your job but you'd have gotten a tidy payout." He gave her a searching look.

Harry frowned. "That would have been a violation of his privacy. I'm not a total asshole, you know."

"I know. I could tell that Javier trusted you, and that was why. He told me that you knew who he was but you never mentioned it, not even during your first interview."

"I needed the job," Harry said. She didn't know where Daniel was going with all this. He was kind of interrogating her and kind of giving a backhanded compliment at the same time. "And I should get to it. Mr. Castillo is very particular about my start time."

Harry started around the rear bumper of the car, toward the few steps in the far corner of the room that led up to the main part of the house. The door was open there and she could see the hardwood floor of the short hallway beyond. The hallway ran into the back of the kitchen.

She realized that she'd taken her mask off after she'd gotten off the bus and reached into her pocket to put it back on. She didn't want to assume that the no-mask protocols that were allowed during meals would always apply.

"Wait," Daniel said, following her and grabbing her arm. "I can tell by the look on your face that you don't understand why I'm bringing all this up. It's because Javier—he's been through a lot. And I know he's not always demonstrative, but it means something to him that you would keep his secrets."

"Okay," Harry said. She didn't really feel comfortable getting complimented for being a decent human being.

"It really unmoored him when Lena and Michael left," Daniel went on. "He's the kind of person who likes to have a big group of people around him all the time. He likes that support system. But Michael's actions, and the disappearance—well, it sort of made him a pariah. He told me how much he's enjoyed having you and your son come to dinner here, that it made him feel normal. And now this."

Daniel gestured vaguely toward the outside world in general.

"Okay," Harry said again.

"The point I'm trying to make here is that he's going to need that connection, that grounding, more than ever. I'm not sure who alerted the media but once Amina was identified to the police and paramedics his location could have leaked out from anywhere. Someone could have been listening to the police scanner and discovered it, even. It doesn't have to be malicious. But this means that all the stuff with Michael, with the murder, everything is going to get dredged up and rehashed again. There will be reporters outside every day for the next month at least. I'll stay with him as long as I can, but the more people who can help him out, the better."

Harry was not thrilled about the direction this conversation was going. "Listen, I appreciate that Mr. Castillo is in a tough spot. And it's been really kind of him to consider Gabe and myself as friends. But ultimately I'm just his house cleaner. We don't really have a relationship of any kind. And I'm about to get evicted. The new owner of our building is converting our apartments into a single-family. I have to look for a new place to live or else my son and I will be illegally living in a storage area. I don't have the time or the resources to be here constantly, making Mr. Castillo feel better."

She'd stated it a little baldly, but she wanted to manage expectations. Harry wasn't about to accept the role of Mr. Castillo's caretaker, which was what Daniel obviously wanted her to do. She was sorry, extremely sorry, about Amina and the situation Mr. Castillo was in. But she had her own life, her own concerns, and

Gabe had to be her priority. She couldn't have her son living the life she'd lived when she first came to Chicago. She'd worked so hard to ensure that would never happen to him.

Disappointment flickered in Daniel's eyes, but he shuttered it quickly. "I understand. But, whatever support you can give him—"

"Of course," Harry said. "I'm not unfeeling. Just—"

She hesitated, not sure what she wanted to say here. She didn't want to commit herself to more than she intended to do, to accidentally say something that would make Daniel think she would spend extra time looking after Mr. Castillo.

"It's just that you have your own life. I get it," he said, and this time he sounded more sincere. "I sometimes forget that Javier isn't the center of everyone's orbit."

"The two of you are very close, then," Harry said. It was a question but it came out like a statement, inviting a confidence.

"I wouldn't even have a career if it wasn't for Javier. I mean, look at me," Daniel said, gesturing toward his body. "I'm not exactly leading man material."

"Why not?" Harry said, and she meant it. "I think Hollywood—and audiences in general—could stand to broaden their idea of what it means to be a leading man."

To her surprise she saw a flush climbing up his neck toward his jaw.

"That's very kind of you," he said. "Really very, very kind. I don't think I'll be changing the world anytime soon, though. In any case, playing monsters and creatures is so much more rewarding, in its own way. I get to create people's ideas of these characters whole cloth. There's no template for how to be."

"I didn't get a chance to say it because Gabe was in full fan mode, but I've always enjoyed your work."

"Thank you," he said. "I appreciate that. I get the feeling that you give compliments sparingly."

"Guilty," Harry said, and laughed a little. "Except when I'm talking about my son. Then there aren't enough superlatives in the English language."

"Like any parent," Daniel said, also laughing. He glanced at his watch. "I don't want to leave Javier alone for too long, and I know you have a schedule to keep. But can I speak to you later, perhaps when you have a break?"

Harry felt a little pull of dread in her stomach. She had a feeling she knew what Daniel wanted to talk about. He was going to try to give her the hard sell on looking after Mr. Castillo, maybe after Daniel finally packed up to return to the place from whence he came.

"Uh, sure," she said. "We can speak later. I need to see what Mr. Castillo wants me to do today, though."

Daniel gestured for her to follow him. They both removed their shoes at the door. Daniel left his shoes on the mat there, but Harry wasn't sure what to do with her things.

"I need to put these in my cubby," she said, holding up her bag and phone. "I can't have my phone with me inside the building."

"What if Gabe has an emergency at school? If he's sick or something?"

"I can check it during my lunch break," Harry said. "Luckily there have been no emergencies thus far."

"I think you've shown you can be trusted," Daniel said, frowning. "You can probably keep it with you."

"It's all right," Harry said, because she was not at all sure that Mr. Castillo would approve such a thing. She still felt very much in an "employee" space and not in a "friends" space. A friend might be able to keep their phone but an employee would not. "Just let me put all of these in the front hall."

Daniel trailed behind her as she passed through the kitchen, the dining room and into the hallway. She felt him watching her as she put her coat and bag and phone and shoes in her cubby, and put on her house slippers and mask.

"You do this every time you come in?"

"Yes, Mr. Castillo is very particular," Harry said.

"It seems a little—" Daniel hesitated, obviously not wanting to criticize his friend.

"Particular," Harry said firmly.

"Okay, if you want to use that word," Daniel said. "I'll speak to Javier. I don't think it's necessary for you to go through all of this rigmarole."

"I'd rather you didn't," Harry said. "Mr. Castillo has enough on his plate right now. I don't mind it, and following routine is probably best at a time like this."

"If you say so," Daniel said.

"I work for him," Harry said. "It's his house. His rules."

Daniel looked like he wanted to say more, but decided against it. Harry followed him to Mr. Castillo's office, a place Harry had only ever seen from outside in the hallway. She considered it something akin to the Batcave or the Fortress of Solitude, a place where Mr. Castillo went to brood. If ever she knocked on the door Mr. Castillo would always come to the doorway and block her view of what was inside, so she didn't have a real sense of the space at all. Daniel knocked on the door and Mr. Castillo's voice called, "Enter."

He sounded tired. Harry lurked in the hallway while Daniel entered.

"Yes?" Mr. Castillo said. His voice seemed to be coming from the right. Harry could see a wall in front of her, covered in bookshelves. The bookshelves were filled with objects, like the rest of the house, but these objects were arranged much less tidily and they seemed to be random. There were stacks of what looked like bound scripts. The number of these far exceeded the actual number of films Mr. Castillo had shot, so Harry assumed they were early drafts or films that never got made. There were baseball caps piled messily together. Most of these had the names of various Castillo movies on them, so Harry figured they were crew gear, but there were also two San Francisco Giants hats placed carefully next to each other—one larger, one smaller. There was also a collection of child's toys—stuffed animals, board games, constructed Lego sets.

Michael's toys? she wondered. Michael hadn't been so small when he went missing, certainly not small enough for toys. Though Harry supposed that any parents might keep some of their child's possessions from their young years—she had a few things of Gabe's that she prized still.

"Harry?" Daniel said, popping back into the doorframe. "Are you coming?"

She shook her head. "Mr. Castillo doesn't like me in his office."

Daniel gave her a disbelieving look.

Mr. Castillo called out then, "It's all right, Harry. You can come in."

Harry felt like she was stepping over some magic threshold. Mr. Castillo sat at a large desk at the back of the room, the desk facing outward. The desk was made of some heavy dark wood, scratched and scarred, unlike every other carefully preserved piece of furniture in the house. There were notebooks and papers stacked on the desk, and an open sketchbook with a black fine-point marker resting on a half-finished sketch of some creature Mr. Castillo had imagined. The walls that weren't hidden by book-shelves were papered with film posters of '70s and '80s films—*The Texas Chain Saw Massacre, The Hills Have Eyes, The Evil Dead, The Thing, A Nightmare on Elm Street.* The floor had deep, thick carpeting that looked like it needed a vacuum. It was a little off, considering how clean and organized Mr. Castillo kept the rest of the house. Harry thought maybe this room was just for him, where he could release the hard grip of control.

Mr. Castillo sat slumped over, his forehead resting in his hands. His eyes were on the surface of the desk. Harry stood there for a moment, hesitating, wanting to fly back to the doorway where she felt she belonged. Her presence felt intrusive in this sanctum. Daniel hovered at the edge of the desk.

"Javier?" Daniel said.

Mr. Castillo didn't respond for a moment. Daniel reached over the desk and touched his shoulder. When Mr. Castillo lifted his head Harry just stopped herself from gasping. He looked like a ghoul—pale, dark circles rimming red eyes, his face drawn. Harry would not be surprised to find he hadn't slept since Friday.

"Harry," he said. "Of course. It's Monday."

"I'm sorry about Amina." She hadn't liked Amina, but she hadn't wanted her to die, and certainly not in Mr. Castillo's house, with all the attendant problems that came with that.

"Thank you. It was a terrible thing that occurred. So terrible." His eyes were faraway, unfocused. "She fell, you know. Her head—there was so much blood. So much blood."

"I don't think you should talk about that right now," Daniel said. "Don't you think you should lie down for a while? You need rest."

"I don't deserve rest," he said. "She died. She died in my house."

"But it wasn't your fault," Daniel said.

"Yes, it was. It's always my fault," Mr. Castillo said, and Harry had a feeling he was talking about more than just Amina's death. It was about Adelaide Walker's death, too.

Michael, she thought. *Always Michael.*

JAVIER CASTILLO

before

JAVIER CASTILLO PRESSED THE button to end the call on his cell phone and threw it on his desk with unnecessary force. The boy. Always, the boy. He'd told Lena to rein him in, that it was unseemly for a child his age to be caught on film partying with older women in clubs that he should not have even been able to enter.

And now Michael's behavior was preventing Javier from getting funding for his next film. He knew it could be a great work, a masterpiece, if only Lena would stop the boy. Every moment of affection he'd given to the child now seemed fruitless, wasted. The boy would barely speak to him. Punishments had no effect on his behavior. He grew more and more wild, more and more willful, every single day.

Javier went out into the house, locking his office door behind him. He found Lena in the kitchen, making a salad for lunch.

"You don't need to eat that," he said. "You're getting too thin as it is."

She gave him a mildly reproving look and went on with what she was doing. "Did you want something?"

He hated this. He hated that the child he hadn't even wanted had driven a wedge between him and Lena, that he was losing his wife more every day. But she'd chosen Michael. Over and over she'd chosen Michael, had acted like Michael needed to be protected from his own father. She'd petted and indulged the child and now he was a spoiled little monster.

"You need to speak with Michael," he said. "I just spoke to an executive who passed on the new project because he was afraid that Michael's behavior would be bad publicity for the film."

Lena lifted up the cutting board and slid the half avocado she'd just diced on top of her salad greens. "Why don't you speak with him? He is, in fact, also your son. As long as you can keep your temper."

Javier slammed his fist on the counter, the temper she'd just reproved him for rising to the surface like a spiraling tornado. Lena looked at his hand and then at him, her brown eyes full of disappointment.

"He *provokes* my temper," Javier said. "Just like you do every time you imply that I would physically harm him."

"You slapped him."

"Three years ago, Lena. Three years ago. When are you going to forgive me for that? When are you going to see that he was behaving badly as well?"

"It doesn't matter how he was behaving," she said, a line of reasoning that always maddened him. "He was a child and you are an adult. You're supposed to be the better person."

"Am I supposed to be perfect, Lena? Am I never allowed to be human?"

"You only expect perfection of others, so why should you be permitted to be deficient?"

"When have I ever expected perfection?" he asked, stung.

"Please," Lena said, putting her knife down next to the cutting board. "I've been on your film sets. I know how you are."

"Whatever I expect there is in service of the movie, and I hold myself to the same standard as the rest of the crew."

"Yes, everything is in service of your vision, your *genius*." She practically spat the last word. "Even your family is expected to change so that your way might be eased, so that you never experience any hardship whatsoever."

"You think I've never experienced hardship? Do you think it's easy to make movies on tiny budgets, to beg for financing from people who don't even watch movies?"

"Yes, I know the story of the young Javier Castillo, valiantly struggling to fulfill his dream of becoming a great filmmaker," she said.

Javier had never heard Lena express such contempt for his work, for *himself* before. He loved this woman, loved her with all of his heart, loved her one thousand times more than he ever had Michael. She sounded like she hated him, like she hated her own husband.

"I never even wanted a son," he muttered.

She looked stricken, and he wanted to take the words back the second he said them. Not because he didn't mean them, but because he didn't want to hurt Lena. He never wanted to hurt Lena.

Michael, however, was a different story.

TEN

HARRY DIDN'T WANT TO linger in Mr. Castillo's office. The atmosphere felt crushing, the weight of his guilt emanating like a poisonous fog.

"Should I start in the blue room?" Harry asked. "Or would you rather I go up to the third floor and tackle the bedrooms first?"

"The bedrooms," Mr. Castillo said, but it didn't sound like a directive, more like a sigh. "The police dusted Amina's room, searched it for any sign of foul play. They found nothing, of course."

Harry noticed Daniel shifting his weight from one foot to the other. His eyes were shuttered, though, giving nothing away. Did he know something about Amina's death, something he wasn't telling?

And does it have anything to do with that goddamned costume?

The costume shouldn't be scary at all without a person in it. It should be comical when it moves. But Harry—and Gabe—had seen it try to push Amina down the stairs. It couldn't be funny anymore, or even merely creepy. It was dangerous.

Or was it? Did we really see the costume actually push Amina? Maybe it moved, maybe it gestured toward her but didn't actually push her. Harry didn't know what to think. She knew if Gabe were there he'd tell her she was gaslighting herself again, but she couldn't help it. A haunted costume in a horror director's house . . . if she was writing this script she'd cross out her own work and start again.

"I think it would be a good idea for Harry to start in the bedrooms," Daniel said, agreeing with Mr. Castillo. "I'm sure it would be better to have all the dust cleaned away."

"Did the police say it was all right?" Mr. Castillo asked.

Harry hated the way he sounded, like a child looking to its parents for guidance. He was normally so commanding, so in control of everything around him.

"Yes, they said it was all right." Daniel patted Mr. Castillo on the shoulder.

"I'll just get to work then," Harry said.

She hurried out of the room and collected the cleaning supplies from the hall closet.

To reach the third floor she had to go through the blue room. She felt acid rising in her throat as she climbed the stairs to the second floor.

Get yourself together. You have to work in this room later.

She resolved not to look at the stupid Sten costume. Still, her eyes were drawn to it almost the second she cleared the landing. It was on its frame, innocuous, a nonliving object, not threatening in any way. She stepped closer to it, careful to stay out of reach.

The eyes did not move. The hands did not reach.

"I know you're playing possum," she said. Her heart pounded hard in her chest, making her words sound thick and uncertain.

The costume just hung there, a costume.

This is so stupid. The ghost (or whatever, but Gabe seems pretty convinced it's a ghost) doesn't have to stay in the costume all the time. Sometimes it pounds on the walls upstairs, trying to send me messages.

(and sometimes it speaks sometimes it says "Help me" and you didn't help)

Harry deliberately turned away, crossed the room and climbed up to the third floor, careful not to look back. She wasn't going to give it the satisfaction. Assuming it was even there. Assuming it could even see and interact with the world the same way a living human could.

She should probably do some actual research on the previous inhabitants of Bright Horses. Gabe's Google search was hardly enough. There was something at work in this house, and she couldn't pretend it wasn't there anymore. Forewarned was forearmed.

Mr. Castillo had put Amina in the second guest bedroom on the right. There was no crime-scene tape to melodramatically rip away, and Harry was grateful for that. The window was pulled shut but the curtains were open and she could see the broken screen on the other side. Amina had fallen through that window, through that screen. She'd fallen screaming to her death and her body broke, the bones cracking, the soft tissue and liquid inside her spilling out until whatever had made up Amina was gone and there was nothing left but an obscene mess to clean.

Harry went to the window, pulled by some irresistible force. She stared at the hole in the screen, felt her eyes drawn to the ground below. The lawn, always impeccably groomed (*and when does that happen? Does the landscaping crew only show up on my off days?*), was tramped down by the soles of many shoes. Harry thought she could see the faint dark stain of blood in the grass.

She pushed away from the sill, sickened by herself. Why was

she staring down at the place Amina had died like some gross rubbernecker? She was there to do a job. The only reason she had come in that day was specifically to do that job, and she needed to get to it.

Every hard surface was coated in thick fingerprint dust. The bed was a mess, the sheets pulled up and off the mattress, the blanket rolled in a ball. Harry didn't know if Amina had been a messy sleeper or if that was the investigators' work.

She wondered why no one from the police department had called her. She figured that if they went so far as to dust for fingerprints then they should have contacted her to eliminate hers from the room. At least, that was how it worked on TV crime shows. Maybe it didn't matter. Maybe Mr. Castillo had just told them to assume any fingerprints that weren't Amina's belonged to the house cleaner.

Harry started with the regular duster on the dresser. She soon found it didn't pick up the fingerprint dust very well—there was a shadow left behind. She had some microfiber towels in the bucket that she normally used for drying the floors after washing and those seemed to work better, but the surfaces still didn't appear quite as clean as they normally did.

Harry was certain that when Mr. Castillo was back to his normal, gimlet-eyed self that he would notice if all surfaces weren't spotless. She went back around everything again with another microfiber towel, checking and rechecking that she'd picked up all the dust. It seemed like it had gotten in every crevice, intended or not. Lots of it had spilled onto the floor, as well. She wasn't entirely certain it would all go up into the vacuum cleaner, and she didn't want any of it to be blown around the room.

After an hour of this she had several blackened microfiber cloths and a 99 percent clean room. She couldn't see any obvious dust, but she ran the regular duster over all the surfaces one more time, and sure enough, there was still some debris. Then she stripped off the sheets and blanket and dropped them into a laundry basket and put the dirty cloths on top. She'd have to wash the microfiber cloths before she mopped the hardwood floor in the hallway so she decided to bring everything down to the laundry room off the kitchen to get started while she vacuumed Amina's bedroom and then continued on with the regular cleaning in the other rooms.

She bent to lift up the basket. And then she heard it.

A rhythmic bang that seemed to be coming from the room next door, the one she'd never been permitted to enter.

No, Harry thought, *not this again.*

But she was frozen, half-crouched over the basket, watching the wall in the corner of the room as if it might suddenly bow outward, might burst open like Kane's chest in *Alien,* revealing something bloodied and horrible.

"No," she said aloud. She left the basket behind, went to the place on the wall where the banging seemed loudest. "I know what you're doing, and it's not going to work."

She was certain that whatever entity inhabited the costume downstairs was responsible for the noise in the wall. She was also certain that it wanted her attention, had been trying to get her attention for weeks, but she didn't know why.

Harry abruptly decided that she didn't care why. She wanted it to stop. She was tired of feeling uncertain, tired of feeling off-balance. She was going to look for another job as soon as she got the new apartment squared away. Mr. Castillo could stay here and deal with his haunted props and assorted bangs and everything else.

A whisper seemed to drift in from nowhere, everywhere.

"Help me. Help me."

Harry put her hand against the wall, ready to tell the ghost (*or whatever*) to take a long walk off a short pier.

And then something happened.

Harry couldn't describe it later, not even to herself. She *went somewhere.* Her body stayed exactly where it was, staring at the blank bit of wall and her hand pressed against the cream-colored paint (*tastefully neutral, like all of the bedrooms*), but her brain and blood and heart went away, went someplace she couldn't even recognize, only feel.

He's killing me.

He's killing me.

He's killing me.

Harry felt the air struggling to enter her lungs, felt the squeezing pressure on her windpipe, heard her own chokes and sobs struggling to break out of her throat. A scream rose inside her, a long desperate thing, a scream like the wail of a siren, a scream that would send help running to her but it wouldn't come out, she couldn't get it out, he was choking her and his eyes were wild and she was dying.

He's killing me.

He's killing me.

He's killing me.

Somehow Harry pulled her hand away from the wall and everything inside her went blank suddenly, like a TV disconnecting from its socket. She sucked in air like she'd just risen from the bottom of a pool, desperate to breathe. Her hand came up to her throat, which felt soft and bruised.

"Harry?"

Harry jumped, spinning toward the door, her hands out in a

defensive push. Daniel stood there, the hairs on his head just touching the top of the doorframe. He frowned at her.

"Are you all right?"

No I am not all right I just saw a vision of whatever is haunting this goddamned house and I don't want to work here anymore thank you very much I'm going to go home and never come back

She didn't say any of that, didn't speak the run-on babble that was loose inside her head.

"Yes," she said, flapping her hand at him. "You just startled me."

Daniel raised his eyebrows, like he didn't believe her. "Are you sure that was all?"

"Yes, why?" Harry said, letting her irritation show. She wasn't in the mood for dealing with Daniel at the moment. The vision, or possession, or whatever had just happened to her was still coursing in her blood. She'd been able to both feel the hands on her own throat and see the hands around the throat of a woman—large, masculine hands. There had been no faces, though—not the woman nor her attacker.

Unhelpful, Harry thought. *How am I supposed to put this thing to bed if I still don't know who it is, or what exactly happened?*

Harry blew her hair out of her eyes and waited for Daniel to say whatever he'd come to say. She'd knocked her mask askew in her panic and she fixed it, fussing with the metal nosepiece. She had a feeling that he wanted to renew his request for her to look out for Mr. Castillo once he left town again.

"You just looked like . . ." He trailed off, his expression unsure.

"Like what?"

"Like you were having a panic attack or something."

"I'm not having a panic attack," Harry said. She wasn't lying. What had just happened to her most definitely wasn't a panic attack.

There was no panic in her. Fear, yes, fear and frustration and a lot of other feelings, but no panic.

"Okay," he said. He stood there, his eyes running all over her face, looking for the truth in her words. There was nothing to see except Harry's eyes above the mask, and she kept them deliberately blank.

"Did you want something?" Harry asked. "Because I have a lot more work to finish, and I need to get on with it."

"Well," he said, and he looked at the tips of his socks. They were red and black plaid with gold stitching. His feet were very long and thin, just like the rest of him, and his ankle bones stuck out under the hem of his jeans. Harry thought it must be difficult to near impossible to find pants that fit him. "I was hoping I could talk to you. You know, like I mentioned earlier, when we were in the garage?"

Harry remembered. She thought, with a sudden bell-ring of dread in her mind, that he wanted to talk about Amina's behavior on the night of the dinner party. It didn't seem like a good idea to do that in this room, not with the presence so close, close enough to reach out and grab Harry in the metaphysical sense if not the literal one.

"Uh, okay," Harry said. "But not in here. In the little library."

Harry pointed Daniel toward her favorite room in the house, the one that was stuffed full of used paperbacks and had comfy chairs for reading. It always surprised her a little, how much she liked this room, when she'd traditionally considered herself more of a movie watcher than a reader. The props that Mr. Castillo had scattered throughout the house should have been more impressive. Harry supposed that this was her favorite room because it was the only one that really felt like someone's home and not a part of a museum.

Daniel led the way into the other room. He sat heavily in one of the chairs, his shoulders bowing under some internal weight. Harry didn't feel comfortable sitting down when it wasn't her break time, so she perched on one of the armrests. Since she was so short and he was so tall, this practically put them at eye level.

"So," Daniel said.

There was a long pause, like he wasn't sure what came after the "so." Harry wasn't going to help him out. He was a nice man, but she wasn't in the mood for this conversation at all. What she wanted to do was go away and try to process what she'd seen and heard in the guest bedroom.

"On Friday, on the night of the party." He stopped again, his eyes searching hers.

"Yes," Harry said, prompting him to continue.

"What happened in the blue room? With Amina?"

Harry said, "What do you mean?"

"It's just," Daniel said carefully, not looking right at Harry, "she seemed really convinced someone had pushed her. She kept telling Javier about it later."

"You know I didn't. You know Gabe didn't," Harry said. She was not going to point the finger at the costume he'd worn in a movie once.

"I don't think you did, or Gabe. It's just that . . ."

"What?" she asked, her tone sharp. "Amina was so insistent? She did not like me, in case you didn't notice."

A flush rose in his cheeks. "I know. I know. And I definitely don't think you have designs on Javier. But she was so sure something had touched her. I wasn't looking, because I was so aggravated at the time. Then I turned around, and I thought I saw—"

"Saw what?" Harry asked. They were skirting very close to it now, dancing on the edge of something that could not be unsaid.

"I thought I saw something else move in the room," he said.

Harry wasn't going to say it if he wasn't. Daniel Jensen had already tried to drag her further into Mr. Castillo's life because of a terrible accident. What would he want her to do if he realized the house was haunted?

She waited, and after a few moments he seemed to change his mind.

"Nothing," he said, and looked down at his lap. "It was a trick of the light, I guess. Amina was drunk and probably bumped into one of the costumes."

"Exactly," Harry said. "Look, I'm really sorry about your friend."

"Right." Daniel seemed at a loss for words again.

"Was there something else you wanted to talk about?" Harry noticed a fine trembling in her hands, the aftereffects of shock. Her body was acknowledging that she'd just been through something terrible in the guest bedroom, even if her mind wasn't. She wanted to be away from Daniel so she could collapse for a minute, let her horror shake out.

He's killing me.

"There's something else. I don't know. Maybe. It might have been a nightmare."

"Okay," Harry said, even though she really wanted to escape this room as soon as possible. If Daniel had been having visions of a woman being strangled, too, then maybe she would tell him what just happened to her. Maybe.

"Maybe" seems to be the word of the day, she thought a little ruefully.

"I think someone pushed Amina out that window."

Harry stared at him. Of all the things he could have said to her, this was the absolute last statement she'd expected.

"Someone? Mr. Castillo?"

Daniel shook his head no, several times. "Of course not. You saw how devasted he is. I can't imagine Javier hurting Amina, or anyone else."

"And you didn't push her out the window," Harry said.

"No!" He scrubbed his face with his hands. Harry waited. Harry was good at waiting, good at masking the expression in her eyes. "But I heard something. I thought I heard someone running through the house after Amina fell."

The pitter-patter of cloven hooves? Harry thought, but she only said, "The only people in the house were you and Mr. Castillo, though."

"Well, I don't know. After you left on Friday Amina completely lost it, started screaming at me that I hadn't defended her when you'd pushed her. I know you didn't, not even close. I knew it then. She was so drunk I don't know if I could have gotten through to her in any case. Then Javier came upstairs, and tried to do his stern father thing."

Harry glanced at the door. Mr. Castillo had a habit of appearing suddenly and silently, and she didn't want him to hear this conversation.

"Don't worry," Daniel said. "He's downstairs in his office, doing the exact same thing he's done since Amina died. Staring into space like a broken robot."

"Okay," Harry said, but she shifted uncomfortably. She hoped Daniel would get to his point soon.

"He told Amina she was being ridiculous, that he knew your character and that you would never do such a thing. But she was just, well . . ."

"Drunk," Harry said flatly. "Drunk and fixated, for some reason. Does she—*did* she have a crush on Mr. Castillo or something?"

Daniel looked thoughtful. "You know, maybe she did. She always hero-worshiped him, thought he hung the moon because he cast her in her first big role. She was never anything but nasty to Lena, no matter how the woman tried to be kind to Amina. And she hated the whole concept of Michael. It was like she resented the fact that Javier had a child to take his attention away from her."

"He never encouraged her, though?"

"Javier would never. He loved Lena so much. Still does. It absolutely broke his heart when she left him and took Michael with her."

"She was probably just thinking about protecting her son," Harry said. She knew the feeling, knew how she longed to keep Gabe safe from everything.

"From the consequences of his actions?"

Harry gave Daniel a startled look, and he waved his hand dismissively.

"Come on. You know and I know and everyone knows that Michael killed that girl. But money and influence can go a long way, and I think Lena and Javier used theirs to keep the charges away from Michael for as long as possible. I suspect that the police were on the verge of arresting him and Lena just panicked and ran. She always doted on Michael. Probably half the reason the kid turned out the way he did."

"It's not always the mother's fault," Harry said, her tone sharper than she'd intended.

Daniel gave her a long look. "No, you're right. We're too quick, as a society, to blame parents. To blame mothers, specifically. Kids aren't programmable robots. They make their own choices, no matter how much parents try to control their actions. But Lena did indulge Michael, always. That's just a plain fact. And it's also a plain fact that Amina really wanted Javier to fire you. She wanted to get you out of this house."

"Why, so she could come here and be his cleaning lady instead? Somehow I don't see her on her hands and knees scrubbing the floor. Or didn't see her. Sorry." It was awkward, because she'd only met Amina once, and her death still didn't seem real somehow, despite the broken screen and the stains on the lawn and the crowds of reporters outside the building.

"Anyway, Javier told her enough was enough, that she was making a fool of herself and that she was to apologize to you the next day."

"I bet she didn't take that very well."

"She had an absolute temper tantrum. I think that since Lena has been gone for so long, Amina had been thinking she'd be asked to come and take Lena's place. But the way Javier spoke to her—well, it was pretty clear that he didn't think of her that way at all. He thought of her as a child, as the young woman he'd cast in his film so many years ago. And Amina hated being treated like a child."

Daniel sighed. "Things really escalated then. Amina started saying awful things about Michael, about Lena, and Javier screamed back at her. You don't need every single detail, but suffice it to say they said terrible things to one another, possibly unforgivable things. Then Amina finally stormed off to her room in tears, leaving me to try to calm Javier. That was the last time they spoke."

"That's why Mr. Castillo is so upset. Because the last time they spoke he shouted at her, and he thinks—what? That she committed suicide?"

Daniel nodded. "He's been saying it's an accident to the police, but yes, he privately confided to me that he thought Amina threw herself out the window because of their argument. He feels responsible.

"Everyone went to bed, including me. I lay awake for a long time, thinking about the argument. I was angry with Amina for ruining the evening, especially when I knew that Javier has been so isolated here. It seemed so selfish, but also, in a way, so Amina. Everything is—was—about her.

"I was tossing and turning, tossing and turning, staring at the ceiling. I thought about turning on the light to read for a while but then decided against it. I must have finally started dozing off, because I had this sense that I was dreaming and then I would think, in a half-awake state, that I'd heard something in the house."

Harry thought warily of the voice that had spoken to her, more than once now. "What something?"

"Knocks and bangs, and loud talking, like Amina was on the phone bitching to one of her friends and slamming around her bedroom while she was doing it. I know she has a couple of friends here in Chicago, so I thought maybe she was packing up, planning on melodramatically walking out in the middle of the night."

"Mmm," Harry said. She wasn't so sure the knocks and bangs were all Amina, but she had to allow for the possibility that not everything was malign, or related to whatever entity was at work in the house.

"I was drifting in and out. I thought I heard someone walking in the hall, and a man's voice."

Harry tensed. The only voice she'd heard had been a woman's voice. Did that mean there was more than one ghost at work here? Or did it have nothing to do with the haunting at all?

"Did you recognize the voice?" Harry asked.

"It didn't sound like Javier, if that's what you're asking. I thought it might be one of Amina's friends."

"Did you check the time?" Harry asked. She wondered if it had been too late for a friend to come over, but more importantly, she couldn't imagine Mr. Castillo letting a stranger into his sanctum. Anyone who'd come to pick up Amina—if such a person existed—surely would have been asked to wait outside.

Daniel shook his head. "I didn't notice the time. Then I fell asleep again for a bit, and I thought I heard two people yelling. But it might have been my memory of Amina and Javier, because I kept dreaming about it, about the two of them shouting.

"The next thing I remember is sitting up in bed, sure that I'd heard footsteps in the hall. My heart was pounding, and for a second I was sure there was a burglar in the house. Then I heard Amina scream."

"I jumped out of bed, and as I went into the hallway I saw Javier coming out of his bedroom, pulling on his robe. He asked me if I'd heard Amina, and I said yes. Then he pushed open the door and we saw the window."

His voice broke a little on the last word, and Harry felt sorry for him. Whatever his conflicts with Amina, it wasn't the way you wanted a relationship to end.

"So," she said, deliberately brisk to get him back on track, "Mr. Castillo thinks Amina committed suicide because of their argument. You think someone was in the house and that person pushed Amina out the window. But you're not completely sure of this because you were basically asleep at the time."

"Yes," Daniel said.

"And neither of you think that she was just drunk and that it was an actual accident?"

"When you put it like that," Daniel said.

"Look, I understand this situation is incredibly upsetting. And I'll also admit that this house has a certain . . . atmosphere."

Daniel gave her a sharp look at that but he didn't say anything.

"It's easy to imagine you heard things you didn't actually hear, and it's natural for Mr. Castillo to want to blame himself. But the truth is, this entire building is surrounded with security cameras. If anyone came in during the night, it would be recorded. I don't think anyone could have been here, running around and pushing Amina out a window."

"Right. The cameras," Daniel said, leaning back in the chair and closing his eyes. "I forgot about them. I'll ask Javier if I can view the footage."

"Didn't the police already do that with him?"

"I wasn't there when they spoke to him, but probably," he said. He seemed to admit this with great reluctance. Daniel reminded Harry of Gabe, unwilling to let go of a pet theory once he'd formed it.

"I think we're just going to have to accept that Amina drank a little too much that night," Harry said.

Harry didn't want to think that the haunt had somehow pushed Amina out the window, but it wasn't beyond the realm of possibility that it had spoken to her, startled or frightened her in some way. Still, Harry wasn't about to present that possibility to Daniel. She wasn't going to be the one who mentioned a ghost in the house if he wasn't.

"I suppose," Daniel said, sighing. "It just seems so dumb and pointless, getting drunk and falling out a goddamn window."

"Dumb and pointless and sad things happen, unfortunately."

"Yeah. It's good you're here, Harry. I was well on my way down a rabbit hole."

"That happens, too," she said.

"I'm glad that you'll be here for Javier, too. He needs someone like you to keep him from getting lost in his own head."

Harry didn't think she had any power to influence Mr. Castillo. Not that she was going to try. She had no intention of staying in this job any longer than she had to. But she wasn't going to tell Daniel that.

HARRY

before

HARRY WASN'T ABOVE APPLYING for assistance if she
needed it, or going to food banks. Things were hard when Pete
left, and they were even harder when Gabe was born. Her pride
meant nothing if she couldn't provide for her baby.

She wasn't able to nurse him—he wouldn't latch on, and no
matter how many times the lactation consultant grabbed her
breast and tried to squish it into Gabe's mouth he would just fuss
and cry and turn his tiny head away. She felt like she was failing
him, like she should try harder somehow, and the consultant definitely reinforced that feeling.

But Harry finally had to acknowledge that Gabe only wanted
a bottle, and that meant either (1) pumping her own milk with an
expensive breast pump she couldn't afford, or (2) buying expensive
formula that she couldn't afford. The breast pump wasn't even a
realistic option. She needed to work, and working as a server in a
restaurant meant that she wouldn't be able to take long stretches
of time to pump out her milk. Plus, there was nowhere for her to

do it. There was no break room for the staff, who usually just ate their meals in the back of the kitchen.

She went to every food pantry she could looking for formula. She signed up for coupons. She asked her pediatrician for samples. No matter what it took, Harry was going to make sure that her son had all the food he needed, especially since she had to pay someone to watch him while she worked. The cost of childcare was almost equal to her take-home pay some days, and she despaired of ever getting ahead. She wished, sometimes, that her parents hadn't been terrible, that she could drop Gabe off at his grandparents' house like so many other moms.

Then she would shake off that feeling, and figure things out, no matter how hard it seemed or how much she would cry, late at night, when she wished Pete had loved her enough to stay. Harry had made her choices, and Gabe shouldn't have to pay for them. Some months it meant getting creative with her bill-paying, knowing that she could skip the power bill one month in order to pay the gas bill. She'd go to thrift stores and buy baby clothes for cheap, because Gabe just kept growing and growing—she knew, even when he was an infant, that he would have his father's height when he got older.

When Gabe was five and entered kindergarten Harry was finally able to breathe a little. She could work when he was at school and not worry about having to pay someone else. Of course, school brought its own problems—kids who had the latest sneakers and brand-name backpacks, kids who would brag about the PlayStation they'd received for their birthday. Gabe would ask for these things, and Harry would try to explain that it wasn't within their means, and her heart would break when she saw that look of longing on his face when she passed the toy aisle in Target. She wanted to give him everything. She wanted so much better for him than she'd ever had.

Once, she was downtown taking Gabe to a doctor's appointment at Northwestern and she spotted Pete. Gabe must have been four or five, and his regular pediatrician had sent him to the hospital for some lab tests. Gabe was fussing as they left the building because he didn't like needles and was putting on a whiny voice that worked her last nerve. As she pushed out of the revolving glass door, Gabe squished into the space in front of her, she saw Pete coming in on the other side.

Her heart had slammed in her chest, wondering if he would notice her and his son, wondering what she would say to Gabe if Gabe asked who Pete was. But Pete didn't notice her, or pretended not to. He looked prosperous, Harry realized. He wore a much nicer coat and shoes than Harry's own. *It's easy to spend money on yourself when you don't have to worry about child support.* She thought bitterly of the last twenty dollars in her pocket and how it had to last two more days, until her next shift at the restaurant.

Harry had mechanically continued out onto the sidewalk and into the chill of a Chicago winter. She forced Gabe's woolly hat down over his ears as they walked to the L.

Harry steered Gabe up Michigan to Chicago Avenue so they could catch the Red Line north. He looked across the little park with the water tower and saw the Ghirardelli shop on Pearson.

"Mom, can we have a sundae?" He gave her his best pleading, cute-puppy-dog look.

Sundaes at Ghirardelli were expensive. One sundae shared between the two of them would eat up most of the twenty dollars in her pocket.

"Pleeeeeeeease," he said, and held up his arm, covered by a cheap puffy coat from Old Navy. "I had so many needles today."

Harry thought of Pete's shiny leather shoes. He'd clearly moved on with his life, moved up in the world, while Harry was still in the same place, still grinding on the same hamster wheel.

"Mom?" Gabe asked again.

She looked down at his face. She didn't have what Pete had. But she had Gabe. Gabe, the best kid in the world.

"A small sundae," she said, and pretended that the choice didn't make the acid in her stomach churn. She wondered if she had enough milk at home to make it through the next couple of days. She could always use some of her laundry quarters if need be to pick up a pint. Laundry could be put off for a little bit. Laundry wasn't more important than an ice cream sundae after a blood draw.

"Yes!" he said, and pumped his fist in the air. "I wonder what sample they'll have. I like the caramel ones the best. You know those are my favorite, Mom."

Gabe always liked going places where he got food samples. At Ghirardelli they handed out free little wrapped chocolates at the door. Harry never ate hers. She always saved it for later and gave it to Gabe as an extra treat.

She couldn't count the number of times she'd pushed a cart that held only a large package of toilet paper around Costco just so Gabe could try all the foods they gave out as samples in the store. Sometimes he ate enough that he didn't even want lunch, and that saved food for another day.

Harry kept working, and she got older, even though she was still a young mom, and she saw her own little dreams for her life slipping away—the possibility of a home of her own, maybe a chance to go back to school and get a better job. Everything she was, everything she had, was bent toward the arc of Gabe's life.

And that was as it should be, she thought. She was his mother.

It was her job to provide the foundation for his life so that he could go out and fly, so that his life would be better than hers. Every night she would pray for this, speak out into the universe even if no one was listening.

And nothing ever got easier, not really, but she kept asking, and hoping. Someday, Gabe's life had to be better. It had to be more than scrimping and saving and living off free samples in stores. It just had to be.

ELEVEN

ON HER THIRD WORKDAY after Amina's death, Harry found that the other journalists camped outside Bright Horses had cottoned on to the alleyway entrance. She was honestly surprised that they hadn't figured it out sooner, but maybe they just didn't enjoy rats. *To be fair,* Harry thought, *the rats just run wherever the hell they want. They don't confine themselves to alleys, although they seem to prefer them.* Harry couldn't even count the number of times she'd been startled by a rat the size of a small dog while bringing the trash out to the dumpster behind her building.

Sometimes the rats just sat inside the garbage can, like they were waiting for the trash to fall on them like a rain of winning lottery tickets. This was always the most disconcerting, to push open the dumpster lid and see the gleaming eyes inside. Harry always hastily threw her bag inside and ran-walked back into the house. Gabe could tell if she'd encountered a rat because she'd be breathless when she came back in. Harry didn't like rats. Gabe thought she was silly, but then Gabe had never had to sleep outside under bridges where rats liked to run at night.

Harry halted at the end of the alley, spotting the crowd milling around the garage, and wondered what to do. Daniel had been sneaking her in that way—usually past the one reporter who'd been there on the first day, though it was easy enough to ignore one person—but there was no sneaking now. The back entrance was just as crowded as the front one.

Harry ducked back onto the sidewalk, out of sight. There was no way that she would be able to get inside the house without having to run the gauntlet. There were nearly as many reporters hanging around the back as there were in the front.

Damn Michael, she thought. People were here because of Amina's accident, but Adelaide Walker's murder made the whole situation a sundae with a great big cherry on top. She didn't understand what these reporters thought they would get out of this, though. Did they really think that Mr. Castillo would suddenly relent and give a statement or answer their questions when he'd gone to such lengths to hide himself?

And if it wasn't for him opening up some, opening his house to Amina and Daniel, they still wouldn't know that he lived here. She wondered if he regretted trying to take back some part of his old life, even beyond the tragedy of Amina's death. This incident must have taught him that he should snuggle even deeper into his cocoon and never come out.

Not that the constant press of reporters would even allow for that now, Harry thought in despair as she took out her phone to text Daniel and ask what she should do.

Harry had asked Daniel if it was legal for these crowds to hang around outside Bright Horses day after day. He'd explained that as long as they weren't on private property they had a right to be in the public way.

"But isn't it, like, harassment?" she'd asked, windblown and aggravated from running past the persistently shouting reporter who always stood in the alley. She'd never been so thankful for her mask. It allowed her to get past him without him getting a glimpse of her face.

"Have you ever seen pictures or video of paparazzi around some noteworthy starlet?" Daniel asked.

Harry shook her head. "I'm not a celebrity gossip person."

"No wonder Javier likes you so much," Daniel said. "Anyway, celebrities will go to clubs or restaurants, places like that, and paparazzi will hover around outside, hoping to get a photo or video that they can sell to TMZ. And when these actors and singers and whatever get out of the car they are literally surrounded by people with cameras. Surrounded. They can't move, they can't walk. Half the reason most of them have security is not to protect them from overeager fans but to push the photographers out of the way."

"That sounds terrible," Harry said, and she meant it.

"It is extremely terrible. I dated a very famous actress once—we were on a film together, and there was that constant-proximity chemistry—and it was impossible to go anywhere with her. Somehow the paparazzi always had her schedule, always knew where she would be. And if they didn't know in advance then someone at the café or whatever would call a photographer they knew, and that person would be waiting outside with a camera. It was a real strain on our relationship. Well, that and the fact that I look like Jack Sprat."

"You mean, people thought that you weren't attractive enough for her?"

Daniel rolled his eyes. "That's the understatement of the

century. And if you're constantly being told, 'You can do better,' I guess you start to believe it."

Harry wrinkled her nose. "That's not the kind of person I'd want to be with. You're the one who can do better."

He smiled. "Don't worry. She didn't break my heart or anything. The point is that it's perfectly fine for a hundred reporters to stand on the sidewalk outside Bright Horses. As long as they don't impede the public then it's fine."

But they were impeding Harry, stopping her from going to her job. For the millionth time she thought she should look for something new. Some restaurants were starting to hire back staff as things slowly reopened. From what she'd heard there weren't that many people eating out yet, and those people who did were not tipping well. Servers relied on tips to live. Harry couldn't afford to take a job with uncertain income at the moment.

Besides, it all seemed too much—to try to find a new job and a new place to live, and quitting on Mr. Castillo right after this horrific tragedy seemed downright cruel. She sent a message to Daniel and then shoved her phone in her pocket, rubbing her temples where a headache had suddenly sprung up. *Why can't anything ever be easy?* she thought, the lament of the single mother.

Her phone vibrated in her pocket. It was Daniel, responding to her text.

"Harry, just wait a few moments. All the reporters will go to the front in a minute." Daniel sounded absolutely grim.

"Why? Is Mr. Castillo going to set off fireworks or something?"

"Something like that," Daniel said. "He's going to make a statement. I'm going to go to the back and tell anyone out there that they should go to the front of the house. They'll probably sprint past you. When they do, you can come in the garage door as you've been doing."

"He's going to make a statement?"

Harry was beyond stunned. Mr. Castillo had never made a statement of any kind—not when his underage son was seen partying in clubs, not when Michael was accused (publicly, if not legally) of killing his girlfriend. Mr. Castillo hadn't made a statement when his wife and son had disappeared. Mr. Castillo didn't make statements. That was just a fact. His personal philosophy seemed to be, "Ignore it and it will go away." But reporters never went away, not all of them. They stayed and sniffed around and waited with the patience of Job for that moment when a person of interest slipped up, lost their temper, acted out of character.

"Yes," Daniel said. "I'm going to the garage door now. Just hold on."

Harry kept the phone to her ear as she peered around the corner of the alley toward the back of Mr. Castillo's house. The cluster of reporters looked like any workers without a purpose, milling about, chatting with each other. The cameramen had their cameras resting on the ground beside them. Clearly nobody actually expected something noteworthy to happen. It had been a week since Amina's death, and Mr. Castillo never spoke to reporters, unless it was about his movies. She genuinely wondered why they bothered.

They bothered because of the hope of a moment like this, when Mr. Castillo finally spoke to them.

Harry heard the rustle of fabric and the sound of Daniel's breathing.

"Okay, opening the door," he whispered.

Harry watched covertly from the end of the alley. As soon as the door opened an inch there was a kind of frenzy. All the cameras were picked up and the cameramen jostled to get the best view of their network's correspondent. Harry heard the echo of shouts and questions drift down the alley and also through the speaker of Daniel's phone.

"Mr. Jensen! Mr. Jensen! Do you have anything to say about the death of your costar, Amina Collucci?"

"Javier Castillo is going to give a prepared statement from the front lawn of this house in ten minutes. I have nothing further to add."

Harry heard the exclamations that followed this. She casually crossed the alley so that she would be on the west side of the entry and went a little farther down the sidewalk. The reporters would have to turn toward the east side and then north to get to the front lawn of Bright Horses. She didn't want to be in their path. She didn't want anyone to notice her at all, not even by accident. She heard the sound of the door closing through the phone she still held up to her ear.

"Okay, I think that got them out of the way," Daniel said in a low whisper. "Just give it a few minutes and then come back. They've all been hanging around waiting for Javier to appear. I can't imagine any of them would think it's more valuable to talk to me."

Harry heard a rush of talk and noise behind her. She moved a few more steps down the sidewalk, murmuring into the phone, "They're going past now. I'll let you know when I'm heading down the alley."

Someone tapped her on the shoulder. "Excuse me, miss?"

She whirled around, her shoulders hunched, her fight-or-flight reaction kicked into high gear. The reporter that had been lurking around outside the garage on the first day was standing there, wearing a fake half smile that didn't touch his eyes. He was about 5 foot 8—taller than Harry, everyone was taller than Harry, it seemed—and had a slim build and curly brown hair. He wore a tan trench coat that made him look a little pretentious, like an aspirational Columbo. His cameraman stood behind the reporter with the camera on his shoulder.

Harry was grateful for the mask she wore and the hat that covered her bright gold hair. "Yes?" she said. She sounded pretty aggressive.

"What is it?" Daniel asked.

"You're that girl who's been going into Javier Castillo's house, right? What's your relationship with Mr. Castillo?" the reporter asked, thrusting his microphone into Harry's face.

She pushed the microphone out of the way and stalked away from the alley, calling out, "I don't know what you're talking about."

Daniel's voice was frantic in her ear. "What's happening? Is someone bothering you?"

"Some guy with a microphone," Harry said, trying for a mix of casual and annoyed, since she was sure the reporter could still hear her. "I don't know what he wants."

"Hey, miss, I know it's you," the reporter said, following her down the sidewalk.

"Fuck off," Harry said, not turning around. She walked faster. She never swore, not anything worse than *damn* and *hell*, anyway. She thought that a more innocuous-sounding statement wouldn't be effective, though.

She heard the cameraman saying, "Hey, I don't think she's who you think she is, and anyway, isn't it more important to get Castillo's statement?"

"Everyone is going to have that," the reporter said dismissively. "I want the word from someone who's been inside his house."

"Well, I'm going back," the cameraman said. "I'm not getting fired just because I missed the first statement that this man has ever given in public. What if he talks about his son?"

Harry felt the acid churning in her stomach, rising up her throat. She didn't want this. She didn't deserve to be harassed just because she happened to be Javier Castillo's house cleaner. The panic inside her felt like it was rooted in something deep, a panic that she'd felt before.

"Go, then," the reporter said.

"Harry, should I come out and help you?" Daniel asked.

"I don't think that's wise. They might get the wrong idea," Harry said. She was walking faster and faster. The corner was in sight. She'd turn and go around the block and come in on the other side of the alley. "I'll be there in a few minutes."

Harry kept her head resolutely forward, refusing to look back. She was afraid if she did look that the reporter would take this as an invitation and chase her down. It was a policy she used with people downtown, people who were shouting through megaphones for Jesus or drumming buckets for change or handing out beaded bracelets that they would try to slip on your wrist. Head up, eyes forward, do not acknowledge. Acknowledgment was weakness.

"Miss, miss!" the reporter called behind her.

"I'm coming out," Daniel said. "He sounds like he's not giving up."

"No," Harry said. "I don't think that's necessary." She just needed to get to the corner. She felt that if she turned the corner the reporter would stop, see that it was fruitless to keep following her.

She heard his feet pounding on the sidewalk behind her, the sound of his breath, and she remembered the feeling she had the night she'd left home, the night she'd run into the darkness, terrified every moment that her father would appear and drag her back where she would be a prisoner forever. She'd run so she could be free, so she could live the life she wanted.

She turned around, suddenly furious. The reporter was much closer than she expected, and he halted, his face surprised. He had a smartphone out in front of him now that his cameraman had bolted, and the way he held it told Harry that he had the camera running.

"Fuck. Off," Harry said, each word clear and distinct.

The guy's face hardened, but Harry had already turned and walked away.

"Is he still following you?" Daniel asked. "God, I can't believe anyone would when Javier never talks to the press."

"I can't explain it," Harry said. She'd been keeping her responses deliberately neutral on the off chance that he was following and recording her. She turned the corner, and she used the opportunity to give a quick look back down the block.

The reporter stood there, the phone down by his side. He had a dark look that Harry didn't like. She had a feeling it wasn't the last she'd seen of that guy.

She made it around to the other side of the alley without incident, saw no one in the back, and told Daniel she would be at the door in a minute.

"Good. Javier has been waiting to go out front until you're safely inside."

A few moments later Harry was in the garage, windblown and irritated. Daniel's face was a mask of anxiety as he pulled the door shut behind her. He tapped out a quick text and Harry heard the answering ping of Mr. Castillo's phone in the front hall, followed by the opening of the front door.

"Let's go into Javier's office. He has a television in there," Daniel said.

"I don't think I should—" Harry began. It felt like a violation of Mr. Castillo's privacy to go into his office when he wasn't present. She'd felt weird standing in there even when he *was* present.

"I think we should see his statement," Daniel said, tugging her hand so that she had to follow.

Harry slipped out of her shoes at the door into the house, but that was all Daniel permitted her to do. She felt tangled up inside, sick with the knowledge that Mr. Castillo was doing this for her and worried about the persistent reporter who'd chased her down the street.

Daniel led Harry to the office, where the television was already on a local channel, as if in anticipation of this moment. Harry saw the exterior of Bright Horses on-screen. The house looked unreal somehow, its huge size and strange, eye-closing windows exaggerated on film. Then the cameraman focused on the front door, and Harry saw Mr. Castillo standing on the front porch, his silhouette framed by pillars on either side. He had a strange look on his face, resolute but also something else that Harry couldn't put her finger on.

A local reporter who looked vaguely familiar to Harry appeared in the frame. Her face looked unnaturally lacquered, all of her wrinkles and freckles and any other normal human features buffed and colored over. She was using that robot newsreader voice that made Harry crazy. Daniel turned up the volume.

". . . Javier Castillo, who's been virtually a recluse since the disappearance of his wife and son, is about to give a formal statement. It will likely be related to the death of Amina Collucci, the young star of Castillo's film *A Messenger from Hell*, who apparently plummeted to her death outside this very house. A spokesperson for CPD has stated that there is no indication of foul play in Collucci's death and that alcohol may have factored into the accident. Mr. Castillo is approaching now."

Harry watched Mr. Castillo move slowly down the long walk. The camera followed every step. It was hard not to feel like she was watching a man approaching his doom.

"It's all right, Javier, just say a few words and come back inside," Daniel murmured to the television.

"Why doesn't he ever talk to the media?" Harry asked. "If he would speak to them maybe they wouldn't act so insane. These crowds around the house are far beyond what I would have thought the interest would be for an accident, even of a well-known actress."

"Well, the crowds are there because he's linked to an unsolved murder. There's nothing more beloved in this country than true crime. As for Javier, he thinks that his personal life is personal. Discussing his art is one thing, but anything else is off-limits."

"I understand that. But when your son is . . ." She trailed off, unsure what to say.

"Openly and credibly accused of a murder, yes," Daniel said. "You'd think he'd say something then. But he always felt that speaking would add more fuel to the fire. And Lena felt the same. It was out of the question for Michael to make any kind of statement, of course. I can't imagine that kid saying anything that would help him."

Mr. Castillo stopped a few feet away from the front gate. Harry thought about all the days she'd stopped before that gate, rung the bell for Mr. Castillo to buzz her in. The bars of the gate and the fence were very high, so Mr. Castillo appeared in the camera frame with black bars in front of him, like a prisoner.

He looks exactly *like a prisoner,* Harry thought. *And he acts like one, too—a person given a life sentence for a crime he didn't commit.*

All the reporters immediately started shouting and jostling for position. The camera wobbled, jerked, refocused back on Mr. Castillo.

He didn't respond to any of the questions. He didn't acknowledge the scrum going on in front of him. He simply waited, his hands folded in front of him like a professor waiting for the class to settle down. His expression was one of mild reproof, as if he couldn't believe they would behave so childishly.

The reporters continued to shout for a few moments longer, but Mr. Castillo just stood and stared. Slowly, a hush spread over the crowd. Right on cue, the camera zoomed in on Mr. Castillo's grave expression.

"Thank you for your attention. I am going to make a brief statement. I will not be taking questions regarding this statement, today or in the future.

"Amina Collucci was a bright and beautiful young star who had her whole life ahead of her. During our time working together on *A Messenger from Hell*, she proved time and again to have the unerring instincts of a much more experienced actress. Sometimes it was almost startling to remember that it was her first major role. I watched her career grow and blossom with the pride of a father. The terrible accident that happened here last week will haunt my heart forever. My abundant, and more than abundant, sympathies go out to Amina's family and her many, many friends. We will miss her, always."

His voice cracked and broke, and Harry saw him take a deep breath.

Daniel watched all of this with a peculiar intensity, his body taut, nearly vibrating. "All right, Javier, that's great. Just come back inside now before they realize they should try to scare an answer out of you."

"He won't be tricked into speaking if he doesn't want to be," Harry said. "Don't worry about that."

"He's always been so completely in control of himself," Daniel said. "Even to see him trying to collect himself now is unusual."

Harry thought of the one time she'd really seen Mr. Castillo emotional—the first night Gabe had come to dinner and they'd been speaking of Michael and Lena. She realized then what Daniel meant, how out of character it was for him to speak this way in public, for any part of the mask to slip.

She thought of the other mask, the mask and costume upstairs, the one that moved and smiled and maybe had killed Amina.

"As for the other reason you are here—" He paused, and in that pause Harry heard a little gasp from someone off-camera, possibly the lacquered reporter. "I know that many of you, as well as the authorities, wish to know where my son Michael has gone. I must tell you once and for all that I don't know where he is. His disappearance, and that of my beloved wife, has been the greatest heartache I have ever experienced. As a father, I would like to believe that my son could not possibly have committed the crime associated with his name. As an intelligent human being, I must acknowledge that it is very likely that Michael did, in fact, murder that poor girl."

The stunned silence held for a second. Then there was a cacophony of shouting and jostling again.

"Oh, Jesus Christ, Javier, what are you doing?" Daniel said. He had both hands in his hair and gripped tight to his scalp. "They're not going to go away after you've said that. They're going to stay, and more of them will come."

"He should have said her name," Harry said.

"What?" Daniel said, his eyes glazed over with confusion.

"He made a mistake," Harry said. "He should have said Adelaide

Walker's name. It makes him seem like he doesn't care about her as a person if he just calls her 'that poor girl.' It makes her an object."

"Well, I don't know what the hell he's thinking at all," Daniel said, and this was the angriest Harry had seen him over the course of their short relationship. "He was supposed to say something to send them away. Michael shouldn't have come into this."

Mr. Castillo stood still and silent on the television screen, waiting for the reporters to cease their shouting as he'd done before. It took longer for the message to sink in this time, though. Harry could hear some of the reporters commenting on what they'd just heard to their audiences, giving context to the statement.

". . . Castillo's son Michael was never formally charged in the murder of model Adelaide Walker. However, sources indicate that the Los Angeles Police Department was on the verge of arresting and charging Michael Castillo, and that this was the reason for his mysterious disappearance, as well as that of his mother Lena Castillo."

The reporter for the channel Harry and Daniel watched didn't jump in front of the camera, perhaps partly because the cameraman had zoomed in on Mr. Castillo's solemn face. After about five minutes or so, when it became clear that Mr. Castillo wouldn't respond to any of their shouted questions, the noise died down again.

"This will be the only report you will gain from me, so please, after today, stop bothering my landscapers and house cleaners and the various delivery people trying to drop off groceries or packages. They know nothing of these matters and don't deserve to be harassed in the course of doing their jobs."

There was an irritated murmur at this, as if some of the journalists present didn't think much of the word "harassed." But Harry remembered the man who'd followed her down the sidewalk, and thought it captured the feeling pretty well.

"That is all," he said, and turned away, striding back up the front walk toward Bright Horses.

TWELVE

DANIEL SNAPPED THE TELEVISION off and went into the hall to meet Mr. Castillo. Harry hurriedly followed him, hoping to get her jacket and shoes in her cubby before Mr. Castillo came into the house. She felt a little like a child trying to hide naughty behavior from a parent. Whatever Daniel had said, Harry didn't feel right about entering Mr. Castillo's personal space without permission.

I'm always that sixteen-year-old girl, furious that my parents poked around in my room while I was out, she thought, putting away her things. She tried to give other people the same kind of respect she wanted for herself. She disappeared around the corner and into the kitchen closet to collect the cleaning supplies just as the front door opened.

Harry didn't stay to hear what Daniel said to Mr. Castillo. Her simple cleaning job had gotten much more complicated than she wanted it to be. The statement that was meant to drive off the press would instead, if Daniel was correct, only whet their appetite more.

I'm going to have to get a new job. That's it. No more of this nonsense.

As she dusted the downstairs library, she resolved that she would spend the whole upcoming weekend looking for a new position—preferably not in a haunted house owned by a film director whose son was a murderer. People were super-paranoid about germs these days because of COVID. Surely there was another cleaning job for her.

But will it pay as well as this one? she wondered, and then decided not to borrow trouble. There was plenty of trouble right in front of her.

Harry heard Daniel and Mr. Castillo talking in the hallway, both of their voices pitched low. She wished she could wear headphones while she worked. She didn't want to hear their argument. Her shoulders hunched as she methodically moved the duster over the rows of books, like she could keep the noise out if she only made herself small enough.

". . . appreciate your concern, Daniel, but it was my decision to make," Mr. Castillo said.

"But they'll never stop," Daniel said. "You think it's bad now? Harry was followed around the block by a reporter today who knew she's been inside the house."

"I'm not worried about Harry," Mr. Castillo said dismissively. "She won't betray me."

Harry's hand slowed. The phrase was strange, old-fashioned. It implied a kind of fealty that Harry didn't possess. She wouldn't knowingly hurt Mr. Castillo, wouldn't speak to the press for any amount of money, but "betray"? It made it seem that she owed him something beyond a job.

She shouldn't have taken him up on any offers of dinner, shouldn't have allowed Mr. Castillo to blur the lines between employer and employee. But she'd felt sorry for him. He'd seemed so lonely.

She'd have to be firm in the future, let Mr. Castillo know that she didn't think it appropriate for her and Gabe to socialize with him.

"It's not about what Harry might do," she heard Daniel saying. "It's about what *they* might do. She doesn't deserve to be followed or shouted at. How long do you think she'll put up with this?"

There was a long silence at this, then Mr. Castillo said, "What do you mean?"

"Why would she keep coming to this house to clean your props when she can get a job elsewhere and not have questions pelted at her every time she tries to enter the building?"

Harry could almost see the expression on Mr. Castillo's face, the frown pulling his eyebrows close together. She shouldn't be listening to this. She moved across the room, farther away from the doorway, in hopes that the conversation would recede.

It wasn't far enough. She heard Mr. Castillo say, in an even softer voice than before, "But if she goes, what will I do without them?"

IT WAS OVERCAST AND windy when Harry left work that night. Gabe had already texted her that he was home from school and starting his homework. He'd joined the cross-country team, which was good for him in more ways than one, but they usually practiced early in the morning. That meant he was back before Harry most days.

She'd felt unsettled and slightly sick to her stomach all day, although the haunt in the house hadn't done anything for a change. No ethereal voices, no moving props, no banging sounds. It was a combination of the overheard conversation and the determined reporter that was upsetting her. She was done for the week, but she dreaded returning on Monday, dreaded encountering the man again.

The comment that Mr. Castillo made had plagued her all day, too. *But if she goes, what will I do without them?* It made her feel guilty about wanting a new job, about wanting to cut off any budding social relationship.

You don't owe him anything other than your work, she reminded herself as she slipped out the garage door. She was a single mom who'd left home as a runaway and survived on the streets of Chicago. Surely she could handle Mr. Castillo. There was no movement in the alley other than a squirrel on the fence across the way. Harry went down the alley and then turned onto the sidewalk. As she approached the intersection she looked down the street toward the front of Mr. Castillo's house.

The reporters had not left, as Daniel had predicted. In fact, the crowd in front of Bright Horses had swelled to twice its previous size. But everyone seemed to be staying in front now, perhaps in hopes that Mr. Castillo would appear again. There was no interest in the garage entry, which was good for Harry.

Harry darted past the intersection, not looking at the mass of people halfway down the block. She felt like a prey animal trying to slip away from a herd of predators. She knew she shouldn't think so, that these people were just doing their jobs and that journalism performed a vital function in a healthy society. She just didn't think titillating gossip about a murder was "journalism." It felt like content for the news churn machine, something for people to click on in their Apple News feed, look at for a second and then move on to the next thing.

She hurried toward the bus stop, the sound of leaves skittering across the sidewalk making her think someone was behind her. When she looked back, the street was empty. For a second Harry thought that someone was standing on a lawn a few houses away looking at her, but then she realized it was a Halloween display that she'd passed a few moments before—two witches around a cauldron and a skeleton wearing a superhero cape. Still, a sense of unease lingered. Given everything that happened on a daily basis at work, that wasn't unexpected.

Halloween was normally her favorite holiday, particularly because her parents never celebrated it. They'd believed it was the work of the devil. Harry had never trick-or-treated as a child. At school the other kids would talk excitedly about their costumes and the candy they hoped to receive, and Harry would only have a gloomy prayer meeting to anticipate. Since she'd established her own home Harry would spend the entire month of October trying to celebrate Halloween in some way—putting up decorations, watching lots of scary movies, eating as much candy as she could afford.

This year her special month had begun without her notice. Of course, she had been preoccupied with the weird happenings at Bright Horses, with their impending eviction, with Amina's death, with the fleet of reporters. She had excuses, but she didn't want to excuse herself.

My life doesn't revolve around Bright Horses, she told herself firmly, and vowed to unpack the Halloween decorations when she got home that night.

As she walked along she made herself pay attention to her surroundings, to notice all the fun (and sometimes scary) displays, to appreciate the bite of cold air and the crackling of leaves under her sneakers.

More than once, though, she was sure she heard someone

walking behind her, or felt someone's eyes on the back of her neck. Harry had spent enough time on darkened streets to trust her instincts. Someone might be following, looking for an opportunity to rob or assault her.

She walked faster, turned a block earlier than she normally did for the bus stop, and jogged to Ashland. Ashland was a busy main road, with four lanes of traffic and a popular bus route. She breathed a little easier once she was under the bright streetlights. Then she walked the extra block up to the bus stop and pulled out her phone to use the CTA tracker to see when the next bus would arrive.

The tracker said only three minutes, so she looked down the road to see if the bus was approaching. As she did, she saw a man exit the side street she'd just come from. He looked up and down the sidewalk in both directions. Harry got a good, clear look at him—the slim build, the curly brown hair, the slightly pretentious trench coat—and realized it was the reporter who'd chased her down the block that morning.

He's following me, she thought. The bus wasn't in sight, so the tracker wasn't correct, which was not unusual. There was no chance she'd be able to jump on the bus before he reached her. She debated with herself for a moment, wondered if it would be better to keep moving, decided to walk quickly to the next stop a couple of blocks away in hopes that he hadn't seen her yet and had lost track of her. Harry could imagine nothing worse than this man discovering where she lived. He'd be crouched outside her building day and night.

Why are men such absolute assholes when they don't get their way? Harry thought furiously. There was no reason for him to follow her except that she'd told him *no* when he wanted her to say *yes*. And he hadn't *seemed* dangerous, but that didn't mean he wasn't.

She risked a quick glance over her shoulder and saw that he

was onto her, his stride long and determined as he followed her down the walk. She reached an intersection where the green light would allow her to cross immediately to the southbound side of Ashland. This would take her away from her bus, which was northbound, but she didn't care. The reporter was still a block behind her and by the time he reached the intersection the light would have changed. The pedestrian crossing sign was already blinking a warning when Harry was halfway across.

.Luck was on her side, because a southbound bus pulled up just as Harry reached the opposite corner. She joined the queue, hidden from the reporter by the size of the bus, and climbed aboard in time to see him skittering down the walk on the other side, trying to catch a glimpse of her. He clearly thought that she was going to emerge on the other side of the bus, walking north. She tucked herself in the back of the bus and decided to ride several blocks south. By then he'd have given up the chase. She hoped.

She texted Gabe that she was going to be a little later than expected.

I thought you left work already? he messaged back.

**I did. I'll explain when
I get home.**

**Can I make a grilled cheese?
I'm starving.**

Harry normally didn't like it when Gabe ate shortly before she got home, because she would prepare their dinner almost the second she walked in the door. But with the nonsense spy routine necessitated by the jackass following her she realized that Gabe would gnaw his own arm off by the time she got in.

Yes, let's just have grilled cheese for dinner, Harry typed back.

Can I have two??? Gabe typed.

Yes, she replied, and got a heart emoji in response. Sliced American cheese had been on sale at the deli that week, and she'd bought a pound. It always made her feel good when she could let Gabe eat as much as he wanted.

Harry rode south for a while, then hopped off the bus when she spotted a northbound bus a couple of blocks away. She crossed the street and managed to grab her actual bus home without a wait.

When she got home she found that Gabe had washed the pan and put it in the drying rack, although he gave her a slightly guilty look when she kissed his cheek hello.

"What?" she asked.

"I made three sandwiches," he said. "But I ate an apple, too."

"So we have successfully fended off scurvy for another day," Harry said. "Don't worry. There's an extra loaf of bread in the freezer."

That, too, had been on sale. Harry was a professional sale-follower and coupon-clipper.

"So what happened?" Gabe asked, following her into the kitchen to watch her prepare her own dinner.

"This guy was following me," Harry said, and she explained about the reporter and her evasive maneuvers.

"What a dick," he said.

She gave him a sharp look.

"Sorry," he said.

"You're not wrong, but I'd rather you not get in the habit of swearing," she said. "I'm sure you and your friends do it amongst yourselves, and you should keep it there."

"Is this some moral habit left over from your super-Christian upbringing?"

"Not really. I mean, we could never swear in our house, of course. But I just think it's polite not to swear, generally," Harry said as she buttered two slices of bread and put them in the cold pan. She didn't mention her own use of profanity earlier in the day. It had certainly felt justified at the time.

She placed a piece of cheese on each side and turned the pan on medium-low heat. This, she'd discovered, was the best way to make a perfectly melted grilled cheese. The heat slowly caramelized the bread and the cheese melted at the same pace, so one didn't end up with scorched bread and undercooked cheese. Harry hated burnt bread. She also hated the burnt edges of lasagna and the corner pieces from a tray of brownies.

"I always hear people swearing up a storm on the bus," Gabe said. "Eff this, eff that. They'll be on the phone shouting into the receiver saying all kinds of things."

"And it's annoying and uncomfortable for everyone around them, right?"

"Yeah," Gabe said.

"So you won't be one of those people. I hope," Harry said. "Because you won't develop a bad habit."

"I guess," Gabe said. "So what happened at work today besides the stupid reporter? Any more weird occurrences?"

Gabe had been determinedly researching the history of Bright Horses, especially after Harry told him about the memory she'd experienced the other day, the one of the woman being choked. She'd hesitated at first to tell him, because she didn't want him to worry about her. Then she figured out a way to tell him without it seeming like she was actually being possessed (*or whatever had happened*) and more like she'd just had a vision. It was a lie of omission, she knew, and she hated lying to Gabe. But he was just a kid, and he was already much more involved than she wanted him to be.

Despite Gabe's dogged Google searching, he hadn't come up with any records of assault or murder at Bright Horses. It was just a weird-looking house that always seemed to be occupied by one individual at a time. But Gabe wouldn't give up. He'd seen proof that there was something supernatural occurring at the house, and he wanted to know why.

"Nothing especially weird today," Harry said, thinking of Mr. Castillo's whispered comment.

What will I do without them?

Gabe didn't need to know that Mr. Castillo thought of Harry as some kind of emotional crutch. Her son already felt sorry enough for Mr. Castillo. If he knew about that remark then he would want to visit more, try to comfort Mr. Castillo in his time of need. Harry didn't want that. All of her internal alarms were telling her that they needed to get farther away from Bright Horses, not closer.

"What are you going to do if you find out where this ghost came from?" Harry asked as she plated her sandwich. They'd agreed to refer to it as a ghost unless they were given evidence otherwise.

It just had better not be a demon, Harry thought, and resisted the out-of-nowhere urge to say a little prayer. Demons were the province of her parents, dark things from the deep that tempted the pure-hearted. They weren't real. And prayers were useless. She'd prayed more times than she could count for a better life for her son, and they were still stuck in the same place.

"I've been doing a little research. Don't freak out," Gabe said.

"That's usually a cue to freak out," Harry said as she carried her sandwich and a bag of pretzels to the table. "What have you been researching, witchcraft or something?"

Gabe blushed. "Sort of. I've been reading about ghost hunters and paranormal researchers, trying to figure out how we can clear a house even if we don't ever find out why this is happening."

"You want we should hire a medium, like in *Poltergeist*?" Harry asked, her eyebrow raised.

"Well, we might need a professional at some point," Gabe said. "I don't think this is a problem that we can solve on our own."

"I don't think it's our problem to solve in the first place," Harry said.

"But we're the only ones who know about it," Gabe said. "Therefore it's our responsibility to fix it."

Harry did not agree, but it didn't seem like it was worth it to argue about personal responsibility at the moment. She was worn-out and not up to fighting on more than one front.

"And just how are we supposed to explain a medium to Mr. Castillo? Never mind the expense or the fact that a lot of these people are just con artists preying on the grieving and the vulnerable," Harry said.

"I'm not sure how we'd weed out a real psychic from the fake ones," Gabe said. "And Mr. Castillo could pay for it. After all, it's his house and he's rich."

"The trouble is that he doesn't seem to have had any paranormal encounters. He acts like the house is perfectly fine and normal. And maybe it is, for him," Harry said. "Before you ask, this is not a subject I'm going to broach with him. I don't think I'll be working there for that much longer anyway."

Gabe looked stricken. "What do you mean?"

"I just don't think it's a very good work environment. First the ghost, now all these reporters harassing me every time I come and go. It's not worth it. I'm going to try to find a new place to work."

"But you can't leave!" Gabe said. "If you leave we'll never get the ghost out of the house for Mr. Castillo. And he'll be super-lonely."

This was exactly what Harry had been afraid of—Gabe getting attached to Mr. Castillo. Gabe hero-worshiped the man—loved his movies and all the cool objects in his house. Thanks to Pete's abandonment and Harry's nonrelationship with her father, there were no adult men in Gabe's home life. It made sense that he'd look up to Mr. Castillo, and his natural compassion made him worried about the man's well-being. Harry needed to start cutting the cord now, gently, before Gabe became any more involved in Mr. Castillo's life.

"Gabe—" Harry said, but he cut her off.

"No," he said, and she was surprised to see that he was really angry, his face twisted up with emotion. "You're always like this. Any time anyone gets a little bit close to you, you push them away. All those moms at school pickup—they'd invite you to coffee or whatever and you'd always say no. You never let anyone near you that might hurt you. Just because my dad left doesn't mean that everyone will."

"That's enough," Harry said, her own temper rising. She had a long fuse, but it wasn't Gabe's place to criticize the way she lived her life. If she was protective of herself, that was her business, and Pete walking out never really stopped being a sore spot, though she kept the bruise well hidden. Besides, Harry had never had the extra money to spend on four-dollar coffees nor the leisure to sit in a café for hours chatting. "How I do or do not conduct my relationships is not your concern. However, my concern *is* your safety and well-being. Nothing good can come of continuing to associate with Bright Horses or Mr. Castillo."

"You just don't want to deal with Mr. Castillo's problems," Gabe said.

"No, I don't," Harry snapped. "And that's not unreasonable. He's not a relative, or even a friend. He's my employer. We have plenty of problems of our own. We don't need to take on his troubles, too."

"But what if the ghost is dangerous and he doesn't know? You're so selfish," Gabe said.

Harry stared at him, stung by the profound unfairness of this comment. Selfish was the absolute last thing she was. Every decision she made put Gabe first, always. But she couldn't tell him that, couldn't enumerate all the times she'd given up something to make him happy. She wasn't going to be a martyr, and her choices weren't his burden to bear.

She took a deep breath and reminded herself that teenagers lashed out at their parents, that it was part of their growing process, and that she shouldn't take it personally. She ignored the place in her chest were it felt like her breath snagged, like it was caught on a thorn.

You're so selfish.

Gabe took her silence for assent. "You're the one who always tells me we should be compassionate to others, that we don't know their circumstances, that people are dealing with all sorts of things on a daily basis."

"Yes, we should," Harry said. "But that doesn't mean we need to personally solve Mr. Castillo's problems. He's lonely, but at least some of his loneliness stems from a complicated crime that occurred long before we met him. Some of his loneliness appears to be a choice that he's made to protect himself."

"Yeah, and he chose us to help him out of it. He chose *us*, because he trusts us. And you want to betray that trust by leaving him."

"Gabe, enough," Harry said, suddenly exhausted. "I'm not going to have a back-and-forth with you all night about this. I'm going to make the decision that is best for our family because I am the adult."

"Yeah, I'm just a kid so my opinions don't count," Gabe said bitterly, storming out of the room.

Harry heard his bedroom door slam. She picked up her sandwich, took a bite, put it down again. She wasn't hungry anymore.

FOR THE NEXT WEEK Harry followed the same routine on workdays—sneak in the back of the house on the way in and take a circuitous route home. More than once she caught the asshole reporter trying to tail her. She'd walk far out of her way, take different bus routes, switch buses unexpectedly. Every time she saw him her fury would spike, but since he didn't approach her directly she felt she couldn't confront him. Each occasion that she lost him felt like a massive victory.

Gabe got used to her arriving home late and harried. It didn't matter anyway, because overnight Gabe had gone from being her pal to giving her the silent treatment. He'd speak when he was spoken to, provide the bare minimum of information. He'd do his chores and homework, come home on time from school. There was no outward sign of rebellion beyond the fact that he didn't want to talk to her.

It hurt. It hurt terribly, a deep-seated ache in her stomach. It was hard not to feel like her son had somehow chosen Mr. Castillo, a man he barely knew, over his mother.

This is just a speed bump, she'd tell herself, as he shoveled food into his mouth at dinner, avoiding her eyes. *He'll come back. Things will be the way they were before, once I find a new job, once I get him out of Mr. Castillo's orbit.*

But the job search and the apartment search were not going well. August and September tended to be the best time to look for apartments, and Harry was about a month late. The apartments she did view were often cramped and dingy or in areas far from convenient public transit. She was reluctant to have Gabe make multiple bus transfers to get to school, so while they didn't have to stay right in the same area they were currently located, there was a geographic limit to their choices.

As for a job, forget it. There were lots of delivery jobs, but you needed a car and Harry didn't have one. There were lots of positions available if you had a degree or computer skills. Harry didn't have computer skills. She didn't know how to use a spreadsheet or make a PowerPoint presentation. She didn't have a high school diploma or a GED. Basically, she knew how to carry food trays, smile at people and clean things. Maybe once the pandemic ended and restaurants reopened at full capacity indoors there would be more of those jobs. But at the moment, nothing.

Harry tried not to panic. She convinced herself that things would work out, sooner or later. But the day when they would have to leave their apartment crept closer and closer.

At least the haunt has kept to itself, Harry thought as she walked quickly down the alley to the garage. There had been no activity of any kind since the day that Harry had seen the vision of the woman being strangled. She'd almost—*almost*—begun to relax when cleaning the Sten costume in the blue room. Maybe whatever force was at work in the house had overdone it when it killed Amina—for Harry did believe it had somehow been responsible for Amina's death.

Daniel seemed to grow thinner and more translucent with each passing day. He never said so, but Harry thought he must be plagued by constant thoughts of Amina falling. She could practically see the accident hovering around his head like a cloud. And Mr. Castillo's conviction that he'd caused Amina to jump made the very air at Bright Horses taste like guilt.

Harry knew it, because she felt it every time she looked at Gabe. Guilt that she couldn't do more for him, guilt that he'd been dragged into Mr. Castillo's life drama. Guilt that seeped into her mouth and throat, that coated her stomach, that made her constantly sick and sorry. Daniel and Mr. Castillo and Harry all had the same disease, and they weren't getting any better.

THIRTEEN

SHE EXPECTED TO SEE Daniel but Mr. Castillo opened the door instead. Harry quickly put on her mask even though Mr. Castillo wasn't wearing one. She slipped past him into the garage.

"Daniel is resting," Mr. Castillo said, by way of explanation. His voice was croaky, like he'd been up all night talking.

"Right," Harry said. *He probably needs it.*

The crowds of reporters outside Bright Horses had swollen, then receded a little, then swollen again. Daniel hovered over Mr. Castillo practically every second of the day, and on days when Harry came to clean she often didn't see Mr. Castillo at all. He stayed in his office with the door shut and relayed all of his instructions through Daniel. He was functioning full-time as stressed-out caretaker to Mr. Castillo. Daniel didn't need a rest. Daniel needed a trip to an all-inclusive resort on a tropical island.

Harry had a good look at Mr. Castillo for the first time since the day he'd made his statement from the front walk. The circles under his eyes were so deep and dark that they looked like purple bruises spreading from his nose. The skin of his cheeks was loose and saggy and his eyes were bloodshot.

He noticed her scrutiny and said, "I look terrible, don't I?"

Harry shook her head no, was about to lodge a protest, but he gave her a half smile and waved it away.

"No need to lie. Daniel has told me often enough lately. Every morning, in fact."

"I think he's just concerned," Harry said.

"Yes, he's a good boy," Mr. Castillo said, and sighed. "A very good boy."

Harry didn't think a man in his mid-thirties ought to be referred to as a "boy," but she let it pass. Mr. Castillo had given Daniel his first role when the actor was in his twenties, and she supposed that gave him license to call Daniel a "boy."

"He cares about you a lot," Harry said.

She wanted to leave, to get to work, to keep her head down and stay focused and not get emotionally involved, but Mr. Castillo just stood there like a broken robot waiting for a new program.

"Well, I should get to it," Harry said, gesturing toward the house.

"You also look terrible," Mr. Castillo said suddenly, his gaze sharpening. "Is your apartment hunt not going well?"

"I just haven't found the right place yet," Harry said. She completely, one hundred percent did not want to have this discussion. There was something else she had to say, though, had to start laying the groundwork. She took a deep breath then, and took the plunge. "I'd like to talk to you about my position here."

"Yes?" he said, looking wary.

He had to be expecting Harry to leave, especially after Daniel had told him that it was unreasonable to expect her to put up with the constant questions. She decided to ease into it instead of saying flat out that she wanted to quit. *Coward.*

"It's been very stressful trying to get into and out of the house when I come for work. It's not just that there are reporters out in front of the house. One of them has been following me."

The wary look disappeared, followed by outrage. "That, my dear, is harassment. Who is this person?"

Harry shook her head. "I don't know his name or who he represents. He saw me coming through the back door the first day and then he tried to get me to talk to him the day you gave your statement."

"And did you?" Mr. Castillo asked.

"Did I what?" Harry had lost the thread.

"Talk to him. Give him any information that would intrigue him and make him interested in following you."

"No," Harry said, offended that he would even ask. It seemed an awful lot like victim-blaming, like she'd done something to attract this reporter to her. She quickly decided to turn the tables, though, and keep laying that foundation to leave this job without guilt on her part or surprise on his. "Of course not. I don't have anything to tell, anyway. I just work here."

She saw the pain in Mr. Castillo's eyes, an instant bloom that he immediately suppressed. She was sorry to hurt him. It wasn't in her nature to hurt someone for no reason. But this was a branch that needed to be pruned. It wasn't good for her or Gabe.

"Of course," he said, a hint of his old brisk nature returning. "We must identify this person and report him to the proper authorities. It's unacceptable for you to be followed home."

"I don't want Gabe getting involved," Harry said.

"I understand completely. You are a good mother, to try to

protect your son." His eyes went faraway again, and his lower lip quivered.

Danger, danger, she thought. They were on the verge of a talk about Michael and Lena.

"So what should I do?" Harry asked, trying to move away from that potential subject. "The next time he follows me? Should I confront him? Or call the police or what?"

Mr. Castillo looked contemplative. "I shall call the police now, myself, and ask their opinion. I have the number of the detective who came to investigate . . ."

He trailed off, gesturing vaguely toward the top of the house.

"Okay," Harry said, not wanting to get into Amina's death, either. "I'll start cleaning the top floor then, is that all right?"

She inched toward the door that led into the rest of the house, trying to silently encourage him to do the same, to move on with the day. He nodded and led the way, and Harry breathed an inward sigh of relief.

Going to work shouldn't be so emotionally exhausting, she thought. This had started off as the easiest job in the world—clean stuff for an employer who barely ever spoke to her. Now she was mired in the swamp of this man's past and present, desperately trying to reach shore, to escape him forever.

It's not unlike one of his horror movies. I'm the desperate heroine trying to leave the cabin in the woods or the nest of the vampires, Harry thought with a little smile as she climbed the stairs to the second floor and passed through the blue room. She heard Mr. Castillo's office door close down below. She gave the Sten costume a good hard stare as she passed through the room, but there was no response, and Harry was glad. Maybe she could finish off her time at Bright Horses with no more hauntings.

Harry was just finishing up with the third floor when Mr.

Castillo appeared in the doorway at the end of the hall. She paused in the act of wrapping the cord around the vacuum cleaner.

"Detective Hojknowski gave some extremely unsatisfactory information," Mr. Castillo announced. "He claimed that they could only act in the moment, so if this man continues to harass you then you need to call them when the action is actively occurring. At that time, if the police feel you are in danger, they could come to your aid and you could make a report with them. But otherwise—"

He shrugged his shoulders and raised his hands in the air, the universal gesture for *there's nothing that can be done about it.*

"Sure," Harry said.

It was more or less what she had expected. If it came down to it, the man could probably argue that he was simply doing his job and that the police shouldn't impede the press. Or just say that it was a coincidence that he took the same route as Harry. If he didn't actually approach her then he could make out that Harry was paranoid or making something out of nothing. And Harry knew that men tended to get their way in these scenarios, that women were passed off as crazy.

"I'm not prepared to accept that this is the extent of the matter, however," Mr. Castillo said. "I'd like you to see if you can identify this man from my security footage."

Of course Harry knew there were cameras all around the house, but reviewing the footage hadn't occurred to her. "It should be easy enough if you go back to the first day I came after—"

She stopped, because saying Amina's name appeared to be verboten, based on Mr. Castillo's own behavior that morning.

"Anyway," she said hastily, "he actually approached me the first day I had to go in through the garage. He's always wearing a trench coat."

"Does he think he's Columbo?" Mr. Castillo said, with a hint of a smile. It was the first time Harry had seen an emotion besides grief or guilt cross his face for days.

"I thought the same thing," Harry said.

"Great minds," Mr. Castillo said. "I'll find the correct day and time while you continue on to the blue room. After you review the footage, I'll assist you with the dusting. I've been leaving too much in your hands these last two weeks. It's not really a job for one person."

"It's okay," Harry said, though she was secretly relieved. The house really *wasn't* a job for one person. And besides, the haunt seemed to keep to itself whenever Mr. Castillo was around.

I wonder why that is? Harry thought as she followed her employer down the stairs to the blue room. Mr. Castillo appeared to be completely unaware that his house was haunted. The entity had appeared not only to Harry, who was there frequently, but also before Gabe, Daniel and Amina, even if Daniel and Amina hadn't actually seen it. Mr. Castillo had never indicated that he had noticed supernatural occurrences. Was it only that the haunt didn't want outsiders in the house?

Harry gave the Sten costume a speculative look as she started work in the opposite corner of the room. When Mr. Castillo joined her he could dust the damned costume.

As Harry cleaned, her mind drifted to Gabe. She wished she knew how to bridge the gap between them, how to get back the son she'd had before their argument. He'd never held on to a grudge against her for so long.

She was thinking so hard about Gabe that she didn't look around, didn't pay attention to her surroundings. She should have known better.

Harry turned to pick up the bucket with her cleaning supplies to move to another part of the room and the Sten costume was *there*, right behind her. It suddenly didn't look like a costume any-more, not a latex mask with curving plastic horns but something real, something terrifying, maybe an actual messenger from hell.

It smiled and reached out its long, long fingers toward her and Harry backed away, an act that she realized was a mistake as soon as she did it because the creature inched closer and Harry didn't know how, didn't understand why it moved so smoothly and flu-idly now when before it had struggled just to turn its head to look at her.

The fingers stroked over her cheek and Harry heard herself whimper, felt the cold sweat running down her back. Her only hope might be to stay still and small, to prevent its anger. Harry had Gabe. She couldn't leave Gabe all alone.

The distended face with its long chin and spiked teeth leaned closer to her, and Harry was sure she could feel its hot breath, see the life in the previously dead glass eyes. It seemed to pulse all over, warm and real and not in any sense a prop. She felt paralyzed by her fear, a terror she had never known before. The fingers, with their sharp-tipped claws, brushed down the side of her neck and Harry felt blood there, not enough to kill, not yet, but enough to scare, enough to make her feel that if it wanted to it could slash her throat open without a second thought.

The stairs creaked, followed by the sound of Mr. Castillo puff-ing as he came slowly along. The glass eyes slanted toward the stairs, back to Harry. The mask smiled wider, impossibly wide.

And then in a blink it was back on its stand, not a whisper of silk out of place, its joints stiff and assembled in the set pose that Mr. Castillo had designed. The eyes were dead glass again, no hint of malice.

For a moment Harry stood there, staring at the costume. Then she slapped her hand to her face, expecting to feel wet warmth there, the rise of blood from her scratched face. But there was nothing.

Am I really imagining all this? Was that all in my head, like the vision I had upstairs?

She stared at the costume, wondering. Maybe it didn't actually move at all, but only created the illusion of movement. Maybe she and Gabe had seen the same parlor trick.

When Mr. Castillo reached the top of the stairs he found her staring at her hand.

"Harry, did something happen?" he asked.

Harry's eyes flicked toward the costume, and she wondered what Mr. Castillo would say if she told the truth. But she couldn't tell the truth. There was too much of a chance that he'd think she was crazy. And while she didn't want this job forever, she wanted to leave it on her own terms.

She could edge close to the truth, though. "I must have come a little too close to the Sten costume. I thought his claws got me."

She gave a shaky little laugh at this, and Mr. Castillo stopped at the top of the stairs, frowning at her.

"But you haven't even cleaned that part of the room yet," he said.

Harry inwardly cursed. She should have realized that Mr. Castillo would notice. Mr. Castillo noticed everything to do with his precious collection.

"I thought it had gotten pushed out of place," Harry said, thinking fast. "So I walked over there real quick to check on it and I dropped my duster. When I bent down to pick it up I was closer to the costume than I thought."

Mr. Castillo stared at her for a little longer, his eyes searching—though for what, Harry didn't know. Finally he said, sounding much more like his old and grumpy self, "You should be more careful. Not just for your own safety, either. Many of these objects are irreplaceable relics."

It did not escape Harry's notice that Mr. Castillo included a prop from his own movie in the category of "irreplaceable relics."

Harry heard footsteps coming down from the third floor, and Daniel appeared, looking rumpled.

"What's going on?" he asked, looking from Mr. Castillo to Harry.

"Harry nearly knocked over the Sten costume," Mr. Castillo said.

She almost protested, but then decided not to get into it. If Mr. Castillo wanted to be upset about his costume, even if she didn't actually go near it, then fine. As long as she didn't have to explain that she was having delusions.

"Javier," Daniel said in a tired voice. "It's only a costume. Not the Rosetta stone. I've seen the care Harry takes in this house. Whatever happened, and it appears nothing bad *actually* happened, I'm sure it was nothing but an accident."

Harry threw Daniel a grateful look.

Mr. Castillo frowned. "Of course Harry takes care. She's a cinephile. She understands the value of the objects in this house."

There were a lot of things to remark upon here, but she held her tongue. Daniel had as much as told Mr. Castillo that he took his things too seriously and the director had responded by taking the objects even more seriously. She didn't consider herself a cinephile, but she let that, too, pass. All she wanted now was for them both to go away, or in lieu of that, for Mr. Castillo to clean silently while she also cleaned silently.

"I'm sure she does," Daniel said, also appearing to realize that arguing with Mr. Castillo about the importance of his stuff was a losing proposition. "Are you going upstairs to nap?"

"No," said Mr. Castillo. "I normally assist Harry in this room, though we have another task first."

"Why don't I do that?" Daniel suggested.

A brief spasm of horror crossed Mr. Castillo's face. "These items must be cleaned a very particular way. I couldn't possibly allow it."

"Harry can't teach me?" Daniel asked.

"It's best if teaching is done from the source," Mr. Castillo said, again behaving as if Harry wasn't just dusting some movie props.

"So show me," Daniel said. "I'm staying here. I can help."

Harry thought that Daniel wanted less to learn how to clean than to divert Mr. Castillo's attention away from her supposed infraction. No matter what the reason, Harry was grateful. Her blood felt like it was rushing through her body at eight zillion miles an hour. Whether or not the costume had *actually* moved, she certainly felt as if it had. The touch of its claws on her cheek seemed to echo there, a phantom memory.

Mr. Castillo had led Daniel toward the cleaning supplies. Daniel threw Harry a wry *help* glance over his shoulder. She smiled, though it was a little forced. It was so hard to act *normal* sometimes, so hard to pretend nothing was happening.

And maybe, she thought as she touched her own face, still expecting the hot welling of blood that never came, *nothing is. Maybe it's all an illusion.*

Harry spent a lot of the day alone. The only factor that seemed to give the ghost any pause was the presence of Mr. Castillo. Besides Gabe, no one else had seen the costume do anything.

Daniel was set to work at the opposite corner from Harry, and Mr. Castillo went over to the Sten costume. He didn't have a duster, though. He was studying the costume from every angle, and Harry realized what he was up to. He was making sure his precious collectible hadn't been damaged. He bent over, his glasses very close to the clawed hands.

While he did this Harry stared into the mask's eyes. But the eyes remained fixed and glassy. The mouth did not move. There was none of the usual threat and menace that Harry felt.

Why doesn't it show itself to Mr. Castillo?

"Well, the costume doesn't seem to be damaged," Mr. Castillo said, straightening. "Try to be more careful in the future."

Harry didn't say anything, only nodded.

"Daniel, can you continue here for a few moments while Harry looks at some security footage?"

"Sure," Daniel said, though he gave Harry a quizzical look.

She followed Mr. Castillo down to his office, where he quickly called up the video footage from the day the reporter had first shouted at Harry. She confirmed that was the correct man and then they both looked at the current video feed, which showed he was still outside with the rest of the crowd.

"It can't be a good use of their time to keep standing outside your house," Harry said.

"It is if they think I might make another statement," Mr. Castillo said, sounding grimmer than usual. "I thought that if I was firm and clear they would go away. Daniel told me they wouldn't, that I had given them just enough information to keep their attention. I think, deep down, I knew this. I wasn't thinking clearly at the time. I was only thinking of Amina, and that we had argued before she died."

Harry was standing beside Mr. Castillo, who sat in his desk chair with the laptop before him. She gave his shoulder an awkward pat.

"You shouldn't feel responsible for what happened to Amina," Harry said. She hoped the conversation would end there.

"But I do," he said. "I should have noticed how much wine she had, how emotional she was getting. She was in my home and she was my responsibility."

Harry felt her insides squirm. The longer she stayed here, the more Mr. Castillo would want to talk about Amina. Harry didn't want to talk about any of it. She wanted to get back to work and try not to think about the ghost. She let the silence stretch, hoping Mr. Castillo would take the hint. When he didn't say anything else, she edged around the desk and gestured vaguely toward the rest of the house.

"I should get back to—" she said, but Mr. Castillo cut her off.

"I have been thinking, Harry. Perhaps you and Gabriel should come and live here temporarily."

Harry's eyes widened. *Me and Gabe, in this house, with a ghost and an emotional sinkhole of an owner? No way.* She wasn't fast enough to hide the look of horror she felt at the suggestion, because Mr. Castillo's eyes darkened in response.

"It would save you some degree of worry at this time," he said, his voice cold and imperious—his default setting. "You would have a place to stay while finding an appropriate home for Gabriel. And you wouldn't have to worry about that reporter following you home every day."

"But how would Gabe get to school? Those people would follow him instead."

Mr. Castillo's eyebrows knit together, as if he hadn't considered this part of the question. Then he said, "I will hire a driver to take him to school every day."

Harry held up her hands. "Oh, no. Mr. Castillo, I appreciate the offer. I really do. But I don't think it's appropriate for us to live in your house. And Gabe doesn't need to get used to being chauffeured to school every day. He'd never want to take the city bus again."

"Is that so terrible? The bus is hardly an appropriate form of transportation," he said.

"What do you mean?" Harry asked, her temper rising.

"The kinds of people who take the bus," he said, his hand waving in airy gesture that seemed to say it all.

"I'm one of those people who take the bus," Harry said. All her half-buried resentment of rich people rose up. What did Mr. Castillo know? He was so wealthy he could hide away in this haunted house, keep himself insulated from the struggles of real people.

"Well, of course there's nothing wrong with *you*," he said, apparently unaware that he wasn't helping his cause.

"There's nothing wrong with anyone who takes the bus," Harry said. "Unless you think it's a sin to be poor."

He looked startled. "No, I don't think that—"

"And some people take public transportation because it's impractical to have a car in the city, or because they don't want to contribute to pollution by driving everywhere. I don't want my son to think he's above everyone else, that he's somehow better than taking the bus."

"Of course," Mr. Castillo said. His expression was frozen now. Harry couldn't read the emotion behind it. Was he angry? Annoyed with himself for sounding like a snob? Secure in his convictions that he was right?

"I'm going to finish in the blue room," Harry said stiffly.

Mr. Castillo nodded, and she went upstairs. She was slightly out of breath because her heart was racing—from anger, for a change, instead of fear.

He's just like that reporter, Harry thought, resisting the urge to stomp on each step. *He wants his own way and doesn't understand why I won't just let him have it.*

The idea of her and Gabe living at Bright Horses—it was too awful to contemplate. The only thing saving her sanity now was that she got to return home to her own space at the end of the day, away from the ghost and the miasma around Mr. Castillo.

She rounded the corner and saw the Sten costume in its place, just a prop again.

Don't even try to fuck with me, she thought, wagging her finger at it and breaking her own rule about swearing. *I am not in the mood.*

Harry thought that she saw the mask's eyes widen, as if it could read her thoughts, but then the impression went away and it was inanimate again.

Maybe it wore itself out with the performance earlier. She uncoiled the cord from the vacuum cleaner and slammed the cleaner down with an unnecessary amount of force.

Daniel, who'd been carefully brushing the duster, looked at her askance. "Javier?"

"Yes," Harry said, though she did not elaborate. She'd had enough. She'd absolutely had enough of everyone today, even Daniel, who didn't do anything wrong.

Mr. Castillo did not return to assist with the cleaning as he normally did, and when she left for the day he led her through the garage and let her out the back door without a word. That was fine with Harry. She didn't have to indulge his sulky mood. She just had to do her job and collect her paycheck.

She was in such a towering temper that she didn't bother with the usual machinations on the way home. When she stomped into the apartment Gabe looked up from his homework in surprise.

"You're home early," he said.

It was the first thing he'd voluntarily spoken to her in days, and she was too angry to respond like a human being.

"This is when I'm supposed to be home. Sorry if it cramps your style," she said, throwing her sneakers onto the mat.

"I just thought—" he began, then stopped and looked down at his work.

"Thought what?" Harry snapped.

"You know, that guy," Gabe said. "The one who was following you."

She was in the act of hanging up her jacket and she paused. Had she been stupid? Had that reporter managed to track her because she was too angry to shake him off her tail?

No, she thought. *I didn't see him at all, and I'm sure I would have noticed him.*

"It's fine," she said to Gabe.

"If you say so," he said, and returned to his work and his customary silent treatment for the rest of the night.

FOURTEEN

THE NEXT DAY HARRY and Gabe were both at home. It was her day off and one of his remote school days. Harry used her phone for a job and apartment search, since Gabe needed their only laptop for school. She marked down several possibilities in a notebook and began the laborious process of calling contacts to see when she could view apartments.

She'd only managed to complete three calls—one message left, two bored voices saying the apartments had already been taken—when someone knocked at the door. Harry checked through the spyglass and saw the distorted image of one of her upstairs neighbors. The woman was wrapped in a puffy coat and her face was distressed. She held a plastic Jewel bag with bananas and bread sticking out of it.

"Tiffany? What's up?" Harry said as she opened the door. Harry and her neighbors weren't unfriendly, but they didn't volunteer communication very often. Generally Harry only saw them if she needed the washing machine in the basement and one of them had left their laundry behind, which would necessitate a trip upstairs to remind them to move it to the dryer.

"Harry? There's all these people outside in the front." Tiffany's eyes were wide. "Like, people with cameras and reporters and stuff. They tried to stop me when I came back from the store. They were asking for you."

"What?" Harry's heart sank. She'd screwed up. She'd been so angry at Mr. Castillo the day before that she hadn't watched out the way she should have and now that frigging reporter had found her.

Harry's apartment faced the back of the building. The apartment door opened onto a stairwell with a window at each landing. Tiffany gestured and Harry followed her into the hall, both of them peering out toward the front lawn.

There were maybe ten people outside, including the curly-haired, trench-coated jackass. They stood in groups of twos and threes. Harry thought she recognized some of them from the crowd that had been camped outside of Bright Horses for the last few weeks.

"What did you do, murder somebody?" Tiffany asked with an awkward little laugh.

"No," Harry said, moving away from the window before anyone looked up and noticed her. "The guy I work for is kind of famous."

"Ooh, who do you work for? Tom Skilling?" Tiffany asked, naming the very beloved local Chicago weatherman with an intense fan club.

Now it was Harry's turn to laugh. "No, though I'd love to work for Skilling."

"He's the best," Tiffany said, nodding. "So who is it then?"

Harry hesitated for a minute, then said, "Javier Castillo."

For a second Tiffany looked blank, then she said, "Oh my god! That movie director? The one whose son is a murderer and who went on the run? You work for *him*?"

Harry rubbed her forehead with the back of her hand, feeling the blood rising in her face. "Uh, yeah. I mean, Mr. Castillo didn't murder anyone."

"I didn't even know he was living in Chicago until a couple of weeks ago when that girl from his movie fell out of the window of his mansion. Holy shit! Were you *there* when that happened?"

Harry was regretting mentioning Mr. Castillo's name. Tiffany had an avid look that Harry didn't like. She needed to extricate herself from this conversation. Tiffany might just decide to repeat things Harry didn't want repeated to some of the lurking journalists.

"No," Harry said shortly. "Listen, Tiffany, I was just in the middle of something."

"Okay," Tiffany said, looking disappointed. Then she pointed toward the window. "But what are we supposed to do about them?"

"I don't know," Harry said. "Ignoring them is probably best. It's not like you know Mr. Castillo. They want information on him."

"I guess it's good we're moving out this weekend," Tiffany said. "It would be really annoying to deal with this every time I go out to the gym or whatever."

"Oh, you already found a place?" Harry asked, her heart sinking. It would be just her and Gabe in the building and a pack of wolves outside. *But surely they can't stay out there forever. There's just no justification for it, like there is at Mr. Castillo's house. They'll give up soon enough.*

"Yeah," Tiffany said. "The rent is higher, but it's a three-bedroom and we got another friend to come in so the increase isn't too bad."

"Oh, that's good," Harry said. "Staying around here?"

"Nah, closer to Lincoln Square. I love all the little shops down there."

Harry tried not to feel the burn of jealousy. Tiffany had somewhere to go, a nice neighborhood where she wouldn't be harassed every time she stepped outside.

"That's great," Harry said.

"Did you find anything yet?" Tiffany asked.

"Still looking. That's what I was doing when you knocked, actually."

"Okay, well, I'll leave you to it. Good luck with the search." Tiffany peeked out the window again, her nose wrinkling. "I'm going to call Mr. Howell about this. Maybe he can get rid of them. It's his building."

Harry didn't think Mr. Howell had any power to move the reporters off the sidewalk if Mr. Castillo didn't, but she didn't say anything. Let Tiffany call if she wanted.

"See you later," Harry said, ducking back inside the apartment.

She shut the door a little harder than normal and leaned against it, trying to slow her racing heart. She felt like a mouse in a maze, trapped on all sides, scurrying for safety. The looming threat of homelessness, the unbearable weight of her job, Gabe's teenage sulk, reporters everywhere she turned.

And at the center of that maze was the blue room. Everything in her life seemed to revolve around Bright Horses and the one place inside the house that had consistently been a threat to her safety.

Gabe had gotten up from the kitchen table and come to stand in the archway to the living room. He looked half-worried, half-triumphant.

"That guy followed you home last night, huh?" he said.

Harry closed her eyes, drawing up all of her willpower so she wouldn't snap at Gabe. She was in no particular mood to deal with a smug teenager.

"It appears so," she said, and was impressed with how measured her voice sounded. Everything inside her seemed to be rioting. She felt she could barely breathe, barely stand.

"How am I supposed to get to school and stuff?" he asked.

"The same way you always do," Harry said, a little bite in her tone now because the question forcibly reminded her of her riding-the-bus argument with Mr. Castillo.

"But what about all the people?" Gabe said, gesturing toward the door that Harry leaned against for dear life.

"Just ignore them. Don't answer any of their questions. Don't respond to anything in any way." Then, for good measure, she added, "Mr. Castillo would never speak to you or me again if we talked to the press."

It was a little cruel to drag Mr. Castillo's potential disapproval into the conversation. But Harry knew that Gabe was more likely to listen if he thought his chances of returning to Bright Horses were on the line.

God knows he wouldn't do it for me, she thought bitterly.

"Yeah," Gabe said. "Okay. I hope we don't have to deal with it for long, though."

Harry thought of the determined crowd outside Bright Horses, lurking for days that had become weeks, and said nothing.

HARRY DIDN'T BOTHER MENTIONING the crowd outside her apartment to Mr. Castillo the next day when she went in to work. He was still cold to her when he let her in the back door. This honestly suited Harry fine. If he wanted to have a temper tantrum and ignore her, let him. It would just make things easier when she finally found a new job.

She'd had a couple of promising leads, even managing to obtain an interview at a restaurant not too far from their current apartment. It was a position that required helping with packing take-out orders and also acting as a part-time hostess. The hostessing part couldn't be too onerous, Harry thought, since restaurants were really only allowed capacity on outdoor patios. Many of them had built temporary shelters with portable warmers to protect against the bitter Chicago winters. Harry didn't know why anyone would want to sit on a sidewalk in a tent when it was twenty-five degrees outside but if people were that desperate to eat at a restaurant she'd take the job. Anything to get away from Bright Horses.

The morning went about as it normally did at Bright Horses— or at least, the way it normally had before the haunting began. She and Mr. Castillo went around the house cleaning the prop rooms together, not speaking to one another. Daniel was conspicuously absent, though she heard his voice coming from the guest bedroom. The door was closed and Harry assumed he was on business phone calls. Some film productions, temporarily shuttered by the pandemic, were probably starting up again. Harry wondered how long Daniel would be able to hang around and act as Javier Castillo's personal valet. Surely he would want to go back to work if it was offered to him.

Harry cleaned the upstairs rooms by herself, and at lunchtime she went into the kitchen to eat her bagged lunch at the kitchen table and check her phone.

There was a notification showing that she had three voicemails. She tapped over to her voicemail box, terrified that something had happened to Gabe, and saw that the calls were from Howell Jr. Her terror didn't leave, merely switched direction. She tapped on the button to play the message and put the phone up to her ear.

"I've had a call from Tiffany regarding some reporters that appear to be outside the building because of you," he began without preamble. "The new owners don't want any kind of bad press associated with the location."

Bad press associated with the location? Harry thought. It wasn't as though a body had been found in the basement or anything. She forced herself to pay attention and listen, though, because Howell was still talking.

"Tiffany and Jennifer are moving out this weekend and I want you out, as well. You've had more than enough time to find a new apartment and the builders are ready to come in and start the conversion."

He hung up, and Harry stared at the phone in shock. He couldn't force her to leave, could he? He'd given her two months' notice and she still had time. She had rights as a tenant, rights that were protected by the city.

She listened to the next message in a state of numb shock.

"Don't think about trying to sue to stay in longer. You have no money for a lawyer and by the time you got a hearing with the City of Chicago you'd have to be out of the apartment anyway. I don't have time to deal with a court case so don't even try unless you want me to leave a terrible reference with the next landlord who calls to check on you."

Harry felt her face flush in anger. She'd been a very good tenant to Howell Jr.'s father. She'd always paid her rent on time even when she'd had to dodge phone calls about the gas and electricity bills. She'd taken scrupulous care of the apartment so there wouldn't be any damages to pay. Now Howell Jr. was threatening to make her sound like an undesirable tenant and torpedo her chances of getting a halfway decent apartment.

That goddamned snake, she thought, her hands shaking now. She pressed the button for the last message. It was one sentence long.

"I expect you to be moved out of the apartment by Sunday at five p.m."

The dam broke. Harry burst into tears and put her head on her arms on the table. What was she supposed to do? Just what was she supposed to do? She'd been looking for a new home and hadn't found anything else she could afford, never mind paying for the cost of the move and the security deposit.

It was illegal for Howell to do what he was doing, but he was right. Harry was poor. She didn't have the money or the resources to fight him, and so he would just get his way. Harry and Gabe would be out on the street.

On the street, again. It was one thing to live in squats and sleep on the lakefront when you were a teenager on your own. At that time Harry had thought she could endure any hardship so long as she was free of her parents and their stifling beliefs. It was quite another to consider the same possibility when she was a mother herself, when her son had just started high school. How was he supposed to study if they had no home? How was he supposed to do his remote learning if they had no electricity? They might be able to stay in shelters, but Gabe would be mortified to have other students see that the background of his Zoom window was a homeless shelter instead of his own kitchen.

I've failed, she thought. No matter how much she'd struggled, no matter how hard she worked, no matter how many sacrifices she made—she was a failure. Harry thought of the day she'd seen Pete going into Northwestern, all those years ago. She thought of his shiny shoes, the clean, well-fed sense of prosperity around him. She wondered if she could find him, if he could be persuaded to take in Gabe.

It stuck in her craw, the possibility that she would have to beg for help from somebody who'd walked out on her and their child without a backward glance. She'd beg if she had to, though, for Gabe. She'd do almost anything for Gabe.

But even if Harry were able to find Pete, and even if she was somehow able to convince him to take a nominal interest in his own flesh and blood—how long would it take to convince him to help out? Too long to prevent Gabe from ending up in a sleeping bag under a Lake Shore Drive overpass, that was for sure. She only had five days to sort out something before Howell Jr. had them bodily removed from the building. She wouldn't put it past him to have scheduled demolition of their apartment for 5:01 p.m on Sunday afternoon.

"Harry? What's wrong?"

Harry's head flew up, and she swiped at her face with her sleeve. Mr. Castillo stood in the kitchen doorway, his previous frostiness gone. It had been replaced by an expression Harry couldn't quite read.

"Nothing," Harry said, hastily bundling her lunch back into the paper sack. She had no desire to eat.

"Is it Gabriel?" he asked, moving toward her, his eyes concerned.

"No, no, it's not Gabe," Harry said, standing up from the table and indicating that she was going to put her lunch and phone back in her bag in her hallway cubby. "Don't worry about that."

"Then what is it?" Mr. Castillo blocked the door, his eyes boring into her like he was trying to read her mind.

He wasn't going to let her pass, Harry realized, until she gave up her secrets. And she was tired, so tired of trying to shoulder everything on her own, tired of pretending everything was fine when it wasn't.

And this is his fault anyway, Harry thought fiercely. *His fault that reporters are hanging around outside my building, following me on buses, making my life miserable.*

"Remember that reporter that was following me?" Harry asked. "The one that I showed you on the security feed?"

A kind of wariness tightened around Mr. Castillo's eyes. "Yes?"

"Well, he managed to follow me home a couple of nights ago. I didn't realize until yesterday when my upstairs neighbor told me that a crowd of reporters had stopped her on the way back from the grocery store. There's a bunch of people out there now, outside my building, and my l-landlord . . ."

To her horror she started blubbering again, unable to speak. She put her hand over her mouth, appalled at herself. She never lost control like this. Never. Now that she'd started crying, though, she couldn't seem to make herself stop.

Harry hunched over, one arm around her middle, the other hand clamped over her mouth like she was trying to keep the sound of her grief stuffed inside her throat. She hated that she couldn't stop crying, hated that Mr. Castillo was standing there watching her break down like she was an exotic animal at Lincoln Park Zoo.

He patted her shoulder, awkwardly. She felt his hand going *pat, pat, pat* the way a very small child pets a dog—tentatively, checking to make sure they were doing it right. Mr. Castillo wasn't a toucher, wasn't one of these people that were always hugging and putting their hands on other people's arms in concern. He was always careful not to accidentally brush up against Harry when they worked in the same room. She realized that it took him a monumental effort just to offer this much comfort, and some-where, deep down beneath her fright and her grief and her failure, she appreciated that.

"It's all right," he said, putting his hand under her elbow and leading her back to the table so she would sit down. "Please, calm yourself."

She was making a fool of herself in front of her boss. Harry drew in a breath, ragged and shuddering, and tried to speak clearly, though her tears wouldn't stop flowing no matter how hard she tried.

"My landlord gave us two months to move out of the building—initially, anyway. Now that there are reporters hanging around he's decided it's my fault and says he wants me and Gabe out of the building by Sunday."

"That's illegal," Mr. Castillo said. "He can't do that."

"He can't, but he is," Harry said. "He knows I'm not in a posi-tion to challenge him, to force him to let us stay out the remainder of the time he originally promised. I can't afford a lawyer. I can't even afford a security deposit for a new place, if I'm honest."

A silence followed this, and Harry wondered if Mr. Castillo felt it was some kind of rebuke, her bringing up her lack of savings. He paid her a very fair wage—more than fair, really, considering she only came in three days a week. She swallowed, trying to think of a way to smooth over the moment, but Mr. Castillo spoke before she could.

"So what will you do now, Harry?"

"I'll, well, I'll . . ." She trailed off, put her hand over her stomach where the few bites of lunch she'd managed to get down were riot-ing. "I'll get a storage place for our stuff, I guess. And Gabe and me will go to a shelter for a few days."

Emotion flared in Mr. Castillo's eyes. "Is that what you want for Gabriel? To have him live in a homeless shelter?"

"Of course not," Harry snapped, feeling defensive. "But there's no shame in a roof over your head, however you get it."

"Exactly," Mr. Castillo said, and this time Harry saw triumph all over his face. "So there's absolutely no reason for you and Gabriel to stay in a shelter when I have perfectly good guest rooms here. Granted, Daniel is in one of them right now, but I imagine Gabriel wouldn't mind sleeping somewhere else in the house. Perhaps a cot in the upstairs library."

The feeling of being a mouse in a maze returned, scurrying frantically but encountering obstacles in every direction. What could she say? *I'm sorry, I don't want to live in your haunted house and I'd rather risk not having a bed to sleep in?* How could she possibly explain that?

"I realize that it is, in some way, a violation of your privacy and independence," Mr. Castillo said, his manner stiff and formal. "I gathered that when I first made the suggestion. But the fact remains that you are in an untenable situation and I am in a position to assist. You would lose much privacy and independence were you to enter a homeless shelter—assuming, of course, that there is available space for you. There are many people with no homes at this time. You are, of course, free to continue to look for your own living space in the meantime."

Daniel entered the kitchen at that moment, obviously looking for a snack. He looked from Harry to Mr. Castillo, taking in Harry's tear-streaked face.

"What's going on?" he asked.

Harry didn't want to explain it to another person. She felt if she said the words aloud that she'd start weeping uncontrollably.

Luckily, Mr. Castillo's natural instinct to dominate every situation took over. He quickly explained Harry's predicament to Daniel, who sat down at the kitchen table with them.

"I've offered Harry and Gabriel a place here until their situation is resolved," Mr. Castillo said.

Daniel watched Harry carefully throughout this explanation. He seemed to sense that Harry wasn't too sure that this was a good idea.

"That's very generous of you, Javier," Daniel said.

"Yes," Mr. Castillo said, and looked at Harry expectantly.

"Didn't you have a video conference to attend shortly?" Daniel asked Mr. Castillo.

Mr. Castillo glanced at his watch—analog, with a leather wristband, no vulgar digital smartwatches for him—and started. "Yes, I do. Harry, I'll speak to you later."

He rushed out of the kitchen, leaving Harry with Daniel.

"You don't look thrilled," he said.

"I'm not," she admitted.

"Because you want there to be a line between your work and your personal life, and this might cross it."

"Yes," she said, and thought, *That, and there's something at work in this house that wants my help and I don't want to give it.*

"But it sounds like you're caught in a bad situation."

"That's the understatement of the century," Harry said.

"Surely it would be better to stay here temporarily than to try to find a homeless shelter?"

"Of course," Harry said, but she felt like she was being backed into this decision, both Daniel and Mr. Castillo arguing that it only made sense for her to stay there.

"Look, it won't be so bad," Daniel said. "At least you won't have to run past the reporters every day. And you and Gabe would be safe here."

Safe, but haunted, Harry thought.

Harry realized she didn't truly have a choice. She wanted the best for Gabe, and the best for Gabe was the most permanent situation she could find right now. The only option was to take up Mr. Castillo's offer.

And Gabe knows there's something weird going on in the house. He'll know to watch out for signs.

She felt more than a little sick now, not sure if she was making the right decision but also unsure what other decision was even possible.

"All right," Harry said. "I'll tell Mr. Castillo later."

"And I'll make sure he understands it's only temporary," Daniel said. "He can get attached to his ideas of how things should be."

"Thanks," Harry said, relieved that Daniel had offered. She already knew how imperious Mr. Castillo could be when he didn't get his way.

It's only temporary, Harry repeated to herself later, when she told Mr. Castillo that she and Gabe would take him up on his offer.

"I can pay you rent," Harry began, wanting to establish some kind of professional boundary, but Mr. Castillo waved her away.

"I don't need your money," he said. "And besides, it doesn't make sense for you to pay me when I pay your salary. Why send the money on a carousel?"

"Sure," Harry said with a weak smile. "Of course."

"Well, that's settled," Mr. Castillo said. "I will arrange for you to have your personal items put into a storage space. Tell me where I should send the movers."

"Oh, no, I don't need movers, and I'll call a storage place and all that," Harry said, foreseeing that Mr. Castillo would completely take over the proceedings if she allowed him to do so. He was a director in search of a project, and she had no intention of becoming a cog in his machine. Besides, she didn't want to be any more indebted to him than she was about to be.

"If you insist," he said, looking disappointed. "You can move in anytime."

"It'll have to be in the middle of the night, when all the reporters are gone," Harry said, only half joking.

"I hope you will allow me to hire a driver for Gabriel to take him to school," Mr. Castillo said. "I understand that you would prefer him to take the bus, but under the circumstances—well, it would hardly be comfortable for him to have questions pelted at him every time he left and returned."

"Sure," Harry said. All the objections she'd had to Mr. Castillo's offer rose up inside her again, but the looming threat of their forced move counterbalanced everything.

And he'll be thrilled to move in here, Harry thought, with a bitter taste in her mouth. *Maybe even thrilled enough to start talking to me again.*

Sure enough, when Harry told Gabe about Mr. Howell's insistence that they move by Sunday and Mr. Castillo's repeated offer to let them stay, he whooped in delight.

"It's going to be so cool to live in that house," he said, his eyes shining. "With a ghost and everything. Maybe I'll even be able to solve the mystery of where it came from. I might be able to *talk* to it."

All of this sounded terrible to Harry, and her misgivings threatened to swamp her. *Just think of Gabe. Let him have this for a couple of weeks while you find a better place for him to live.*

"I hope all those books you've been reading tell you how to protect yourself from ghosts," Harry said lightly.

"Oh yeah," Gabe said, with more enthusiasm than she'd seen in him for a long while. "I can, you know, do some things to make sure they don't cross the threshold of our rooms, stuff like that. I don't want anything to wake me up in the middle of the night."

She saw a little bit of his fear then, the fear he'd been hiding so well under a teenage sulk. She grabbed him and pulled him close and gave him such a tight hug that he grumbled, "Mom, come on. I'm not five." But he let her hold tight anyway, just for a little while.

FIFTEEN

THE DAY HARRY AND Gabe came to stay at Bright Horses should have been momentous, Harry thought later. She was Jane Eyre looking up at Thornfield, or the second Mrs. de Winter outside Manderley. She was Eleanor Vance entering Hill House for the first time. There should have been dramatic music, and ominous clouds. There should have been a pause on the threshold, a sense that her life was to change irrevocably.

There was none of that.

Harry and Gabe had spent three days frantically packing up all their things and then Harry rented a U-Haul to take all their furniture and most of their personal belongings to a Public Storage facility on Western Avenue. The one upside was that the storage space was significantly cheaper than her rent, and the savings would help her with a security deposit on a new place.

Then, almost before she knew it, they were washing the floors and windows, doing a last walk-through with a completely indifferent Howell (who promised to mail her security deposit to Mr. Castillo's address), and climbing into a taxi to take them to the alley behind Mr. Castillo's house. As Harry suspected, 90 percent of the reporters had given up on her building as a bad job early on. The only one who stuck around was the Trench Coat Jerk, and that was only because it was obviously personal for him.

She never said a word to him, no matter how persistently he dogged her every time she left the building. She pretended he wasn't there all through the slow loading of their U-Haul truck, even as Gabe opened his mouth to tell the guy to take a hike. Harry had shaken her head and Gabe's mouth had snapped shut like a cartoon character.

"I'll get a quote from you yet, Miss Adams," Trench Coat Jerk had said, looking from Gabe to her as Gabe had climbed into the back of the U-Haul with a box full of old horror film videotapes.

Could you sound more like an antagonist from a bad movie? She'd have loved to say that, but it went against her principle of pretending that he wasn't there. She'd walked past him with dead eyes.

When they'd returned to the apartment to collect more stuff Gabe had chortled.

"What?" Harry said, grabbing another box.

"You've heard of resting bitch face?" Gabe said.

"Are you trying to say your mom has resting bitch face?"

"No," Gabe said, shaking his head. "You don't. You have Active Murder Face."

Harry smiled a little as she and Gabe rode from their old apartment to Bright Horses. The sun set so early that it was well dark when they each carried out a suitcase and a backpack to the cab. Harry had insisted that they each bring the bare minimum of items to Mr. Castillo's house. She didn't want Gabe, in particular, getting comfortable and thinking the situation was permanent. She wanted him to think of Bright Horses as a way station, not a home.

Trench Coat Jerk was nowhere to be seen. Harry assumed that he had tripped off for dinner, or perhaps he'd finally surrendered to the notion that she was never going to speak to him. When they arrived Mr. Castillo hurried out of the back door to pay the taxi driver before Harry could take the money from her purse.

"Uh, thanks," she said as they climbed out. This wasn't a good start. She didn't want to be even more indebted to Mr. Castillo, not when he was providing them with rooms and meals for free.

He waved away her thanks and beamed at Gabe as Gabe and the cabdriver unloaded their suitcases from the trunk.

"Is this all your things?" Mr. Castillo said, frowning as he picked up Harry's suitcase and carried it inside while she slung her backpack around her shoulders. He put the suitcase down once they were in the garage and looked at them expectantly.

"Thanks for letting us stay here, Mr. Castillo," Gabe said.

Mr. Castillo beamed, a beneficent lord receiving his due. "Of course, Gabriel. I am so pleased that your mother agreed. You know the way, Harry."

He indicated that they should precede him into the main part of the house. Harry picked up her suitcase, swallowed her pride and the nausea that seemed to accompany her everywhere these days, and led the way through the hall that passed by the kitchen. The scent of tomato sauce and cheese wafted from under the door.

"Something smells good, Mr. Castillo," Gabe said as he and Harry removed their shoes.

"Lasagna and fresh sourdough bread for dinner," Mr. Castillo said, pausing by the door. "I'll finish getting it all ready while you put your things upstairs. I decided that the best situation for now was to put a twin bed in the small library. I hope that's all right for you, Gabriel."

He disappeared into the kitchen while Harry and Gabe continued on to the main stairs. Harry did not look at the Sten costume as she passed through the blue room, giving it the same treatment that she gave Trench Coat Jerk. She heard Gabe's footsteps pause behind her, though, and she said, "Don't give it any of your attention."

A second later she heard his socks sliding across the carpet again, the jingle of the many charms that hung from his backpack zipper. She breathed out in a rush, not realizing until she did that she'd been holding on to all the air in her lungs.

If I'm like this now, how will I be after I spend a few days here? A week? Her shoulders had climbed practically to her earlobes, a sure sign that she was retaining stress. Harry thought longingly of the days when Bright Horses had just been a place she came to work.

I wonder if Mr. Castillo will want me to work every day now that we live here. Harry realized she might have put herself in a very bad position. She hadn't talked to Mr. Castillo about his expectations, and if he wanted her to help with the housework even on her normal days off, she didn't see how she could possibly refuse. He was letting Harry and Gabe stay in his house rent-free.

But how am I supposed to leave to look at other apartments if I have to work all the time? Then she firmly told herself to stop borrowing trouble. Mr. Castillo might not expect her to act like a live-in maid.

The guest room was, of course, spotlessly clean since Harry had prepared it herself. She indicated that Gabe should go into the little library. She peeked into the room before moving on to her own. Mr. Castillo—and presumably Daniel—had moved the armchairs out of the room and replaced them with a twin bed and a small side table that held a clock and a lamp.

"Okay?" Harry asked.

Gabe nodded. "It's better than the alternative."

Harry put her suitcase in the room where she'd often heard banging on the wall, though she hadn't heard a thing since the day she'd had the vision of a man strangling a woman. That day seemed so long ago, almost another lifetime.

The haunt seemed to have decided that banging and visions weren't the best way to get her attention. But it was hard to reconcile the voice that had whispered *Help me* with the malicious look that the Sten mask had given her when it scraped its claws over her (*or not really, because it didn't actually touch you*). Was the ghost angry at Harry now because she hadn't provided the help it required? Why hadn't she thought about this before?

Oh, maybe because you were being hounded by reporters and forced out of your home and your son wasn't speaking to you and everything else.

She sat on the edge of the bed and rubbed her temples. She was so exhausted, beyond exhausted. Her whole body felt wrung dry by crisis after crisis, and even now she couldn't relax. She couldn't relax when she knew that there was some other presence in this house trying to get her attention.

Gabe came to the door and hovered there, not saying anything.

"What's up?" she asked.

"I know you didn't want to come here, and I know you did because of me," he said in a rush, like he'd been holding the words inside for a while. "And I just want to say thanks, and I'm sorry I was such a little shit."

"Oh, Gabe," she said, her eyes welling. She felt some of the knot in her chest loosen, even if it didn't completely unravel.

"Don't cry," he said, looking alarmed. "I didn't apologize so that you would cry. I was hoping it would make you feel better. You looked really upset."

Harry wiped her eyes with the back of her wrist. "It does make me feel better. And don't swear in front of Daniel and Mr. Castillo."

He grinned at her. "See you downstairs."

He disappeared, and Harry almost called him back, told him to wait for her so that he wouldn't have to pass through the blue room on his own.

Am I going to hold Gabe's hand every time he walks through that space? Would he even let me? And really, who would I be doing it for—me or him?

Harry went into the bathroom, splashed cold water on her face, and marched downstairs. She paused in the doorway and gave the Sten costume a stern look, then lifted her chin and didn't glance at it again. Best to begin as she meant to go on, and not let it think it had any power over her. As she rounded to the steps leading to the first floor, though, she stopped.

Stopped, and gasped for breath.

The costume had not moved. The eyes did not glitter with malice. But Harry felt a wave of malevolence coming from that part of the room, and she was sure, just for a moment, that hands had closed around her throat, that those hands were squeezing tight, squeezing until she couldn't breathe and her hands were pulling frantically at her neck, looking for wrists to pull away so she could breathe again, but there was nothing, there was only the feeling of her air disappearing into the ether, into the malignant cloud emanating throughout the room.

"Hey, Mom, hurry up," Gabe called. "Mr. Castillo just put the lasagna on the table."

It was as if Gabe's voice was a talisman. The hold broke immediately, and Harry stood there, gasping, rubbing her neck, sure she could feel bruises forming. But then again, she'd thought the costume had scraped her cheek and it hadn't. And this time it hadn't even moved.

Maybe I should finally tell Mr. Castillo that his house is haunted and that we need to leave.

Then she thought of Gabe's grin, of his obvious pleasure at staying in the house of his hero. She thought of Gabe huddling in the cold instead of warm and fed inside a shelter. That was the reason why she'd come here in the first place, why she'd put herself at risk. She needed to protect her child from the world.

I'm sure there's some information online about dealing with ghosts. You can Google anything. And Gabe said he knew some protective things from his research.

Then she did the thing that she always did, ever since the moment when she realized she was about to have a baby and that her child would come first. She pretended she wasn't scared. As she left the blue room there were no emanations of hatred, no physical threats. But Harry resolved to look up ways to protect herself from the ghost before going to sleep that night. It might not actually be able to hurt her, but it seemed like it wanted to give things a try.

Mr. Castillo was their hearty host again, all traces of the grief and guilt that had hung over him since Amina's death gone. The change wrought in him was almost miraculous, but Harry wasn't foolish enough to attribute it to herself. It was Gabe who brightened him up, Gabe who hung on his every word as he told stories about the various scripts he'd written and the films he'd made and the challenges he'd faced.

This is what he had before, Harry thought. *He had people hanging around him, telling him he was wonderful all day long, an artist, a genius. This is what he's missed the most.*

Harry wondered if Mr. Castillo's wife had adored him in the same way, if she'd looked up to him and thought all his notions perfectly delightful, or if she'd been an equal partner in their relationship.

She felt, in some way, that she hadn't given enough consideration to Lena Castillo and her part in the tragedy that surrounded Javier Castillo. This was a woman who had, apparently, chosen to take their son and run from his potential indictment. And Lena had hidden herself so thoroughly that no one seemed to be able to find her and Michael.

Harry gave Mr. Castillo a speculative look. From all accounts, Lena had not been employed for several years. Which meant that any income had come from Javier Castillo's work. That also meant—probably, unless Lena was an heiress—that the couple had joint checking and savings accounts. Lena would need money—lots and lots of money, and in untraceable form—to accomplish what she had done. How could she withdraw that money without Mr. Castillo's knowledge? Had Javier Castillo played a part in their disappearance?

Why hadn't Harry thought of this before—or really, why hadn't anybody? The police might have looked into it, but there didn't seem to be any public comment on the subject. In all of the speculation surrounding Michael and Adelaide Walker, no one ever seemed to imply that Mr. Castillo had been involved with Michael's disappearance. Perhaps it was because he was so obviously hurt by being left behind.

Maybe he's just a really good actor, Harry thought.

Mr. Castillo seemed to notice her attention, and he gave her an inquiring look.

"Is something wrong, Harry?" he asked.

Daniel, who'd been silent for most of the meal to let Mr. Castillo take center stage, looked curious. She wondered if he suspected some of what she thought. He was a pretty perceptive guy.

"No, just spacing out," she said, hurriedly taking a bite of bread.

"She does that," Gabe said. "This is perfectly normal behavior."

Mr. Castillo and Gabe shared a conspiratorial glance that Harry did not care for at all. She didn't want her son to team up with Mr. Castillo against her. It would make it harder for them to ever leave Bright Horses, and they *were* going to leave Bright Horses. Eventually.

HARRY HOPED THE HAUNT had somehow exhausted itself trying scare her before dinner. It definitely had the power to exert itself on its surroundings in some way, but that power wasn't constant. Before bed Gabe did some kind of speech that sounded like a lot of nonsense to Harry over the threshold of each of their rooms. He was careful to do this when both Daniel and Mr. Castillo were downstairs. Harry had a feeling he wasn't entirely certain it wasn't nonsense himself.

He assured her it was a charm to keep away malevolent spirits, and he also gave her a handful of crystals to keep by her bedside table.

"Where did you get these?" she asked. What she was really asking was *Where did you get the money for these?* and Gabe knew it.

"I saved up my allowance," he said. "They weren't super-expensive, don't worry. Anyway, the black tourmaline shields you from negative energy and the smoky quartz protects you from outside chaos and disturbances."

Harry looked at the objects in her hand. They just looked like cheap rocks to her, but Gabe was in earnest and she knew he was trying to keep her feeling comfortable in this house. It was hard not to shy away from the symbolism, though. Her parents had put their faith in crosses and Bibles and prayers, and Harry had run from that belief, literally run into the night, and had never put her faith in anything again. The idea of unbending enough to believe in the power of these small things to keep her safe . . .

There's a ghost in this house. You'd better start believing before it's too late.

"Thanks, bud," she said, and kissed his cheek. "I'll pay you back for these, okay? You should use your money for something fun."

"It really wasn't a big deal," Gabe said, ducking his head the way he always did when he was embarrassed. "I've been wanting to give them to you for a while but I didn't think you'd, like, carry them in your pocket or whatever. I thought you wouldn't believe enough to use them."

He knows me, that's for sure, Harry thought ruefully, and privately vowed to put all the belief she had into the crystals.

Gabe turned to go back to his room, but before he did, he leaned close to her and whispered, "Hey, what's up with that room at the end of the hall?"

Mr. Castillo had disappeared into his office with Daniel after dinner, and Harry didn't know if they were trying to establish a boundary or if they were just giving Harry and Gabe some privacy while they accustomed themselves to staying in the house.

"That's the room that I told you about," Harry said. "The one where the noises come from."

Gabe appeared more interested. "Have you ever tried to get in there?"

"No," Harry said. "And you shouldn't even think about that room. Mr. Castillo has it locked for reasons of his own, and if you want to stay in this house you should respect that."

"But what if the reason why all the weird stuff is happening is because of something in that room?" Gabe asked. "What if a murder happened in there, or there's some object in the walls? What if it's like 'The Tell-Tale Heart'?"

"If that's the case I'm not sure how we would find out about it," Harry said. "Are you really going to take a sledgehammer to the drywall in somebody else's house?"

Although, Harry thought later, after Gabe had returned to his own room and she stood in front of the mirror brushing her teeth, *it's not a bad theory. In ghost stories there's always something left behind that keeps the ghost hanging around—the body under the floorboards, or a wedding ring, or whatever. But I still don't see how the fact of such a thing could help us, unless Mr. Castillo knew about the ghost and chose to open up that room.*

But Mr. Castillo didn't know about the ghost, and the door was always locked.

He's probably got his most valuable film props in there, things he would never want to risk damage by other people.

Or maybe it's the room where he keeps Michael and Lena's things, hoping against hope that one day they will come back to him.

Harry slid underneath the duvet, trying not to remember that Amina had slept in this room. She turned out the light and stared at the crystals she'd placed on the bedside table, their edges gleaming slightly in the light that filtered through the blinds from the streetlamps. The sheets were crisp and smelled like the Spring Fresh fabric softener that Mr. Castillo liked Harry to use when she did the laundry. The mattress was just the right balance between firm and soft, but the pillow felt too squishy to Harry. It was down and she'd never had the money to afford a down pillow, only the ten-dollar synthetic ones from Target.

Everything felt wrong, including the profound silence that settled over the house. Harry's old apartment building had always made noise—the sound of the steam in the heaters, the padding of footsteps from the neighbors above. She'd been able to hear music playing from the building next door or people shouting in the street outside, but that wasn't the case at Bright Horses. The lot was so large and the house so set back from the street that it was somewhat insulated from the ambient city noise around it.

Close your eyes, she told herself. *Go to sleep.*

She obediently followed her own instructions, closing her eyes, but she couldn't get comfortable. They didn't belong in Bright Horses, she and Gabe. This vast house and all the resources that went into it weren't for people like her, and she didn't want them. She felt like a piece of grit in clean gears. And as soon as her brain started to relax she remembered the feeling of hands on her throat, of dark anger pulsing all around her, and her eyes flew open and she stared at the ceiling.

It wanted to harm me, she thought, her hands rubbing the place where it had touched. There had been no marks on her neck when she looked in the mirror, though she'd been sure there would be.

Does that mean the ghost can't hurt me, only make me think it can hurt me? And if I believe it then will that make it true?

These were the kinds of questions that made Harry want to run in circles, screaming and holding her head with both hands. How the hell was she supposed to know how ghosts worked? No amount of horror film knowledge could help her here, except that the ghosts always lost power when they received some kind of personal resolution. Personal resolution couldn't arrive unless she knew the identity of the ghost and its unresolved life issues.

In the movies the heroes were always helped along with a deus ex machina—a conveniently discovered diary, or a local legend that told the tragic story of the houses' former occupants. There was none of that with Bright Horses. Gabe had exhausted all the avenues available to him, trying to find out if anything terrible had ever happened in the house. If it had, the house was keeping its secrets.

Harry rolled onto her right side, but this meant she was staring at the window. The window made her think of Amina falling, Amina screaming, so she turned to her left side, looking at the door instead. Her eyes had adjusted to the dark, so she could see the outline of the doorframe and the silver knob clearly.

The doorknob rolled slowly to the left.

Harry sat bolt upright in bed, staring into the dark, her heart hammering.

The knob wasn't moving. It was just her imagination, just the twitchy feeling that she'd had ever since their arrival giving her brain worms.

She stared at the door for a moment longer, then slowly lay back again, trying to calm her racing heart. Her fingers reached out for the crystals that Gabe had given her and she clutched them in her fist. She couldn't bring herself to believe that they had any intrinsic power, that these particular objects were inherently protective. But her son had cared enough to buy them, to give them to her to keep her safe, and that meant something.

Gabe gave these to me. He gave them to me with love and that love will protect me.

This time she heard the knob turning, heard the faint squeak of the bolt sliding through the connector in the frame. Harry held the crystals tight and thought about her child, about all the love and happiness that had ever flowed between them.

The door rattled in its frame, like something was on the other side trying to push it open, but it did not crack an inch.

Harry threw the covers off and went toward the door. She wasn't stupid enough to open it, wasn't stupid enough to invite the thing outside in. She knew better. She clutched the crystals in her hand even tighter, felt the sharp edges digging into her skin.

"Go away," she said, in a voice that was firm and clear and didn't reveal any of the terror she felt crawling under her skin because she knew it was out there and that it wanted her, that it wanted to hurt her, that it had come up the stairs hoping to push her through the window and hear her fall, screaming and screaming and screaming.

The door rattled again, the knob turning back and forth faster and faster.

"Go away," Harry said again. "You don't belong here. You can't hurt me."

There was a bang on the other side of the door, like someone had slammed a hand in frustration against it.

"Go away," Harry said for a third time, and the rattling abruptly ceased.

Harry stood there for a moment, a little dazed. *Threes*, she thought vaguely. *Things come in threes in stories, three bears and three wishes and three days to break a curse. I told it to go away three times, and it did.*

But she stood at the door for a long while anyway, waiting to see if anything else would happen, if the ghost would try again.

After a time she unclenched her fist and transferred the crystals back to her bedside table. The rocks had left an impression of their shape in her palm and she touched it with her other hand, tracing the marks.

She started to believe.

SIXTEEN

LIVING AT BRIGHT HORSES answered many questions that Harry had about Mr. Castillo's life. He never went out—never, for any reason whatsoever. He never took a walk, never seemed to want to. He spent many hours holed up in his office, ostensibly working. Harry assumed he was working on a new screenplay. Sometimes she heard him on the phone when she passed by the office. Often he seemed to be in conference with Daniel about various things. Somehow the two of them never ran out of subjects to discuss.

She was always careful not to try to listen, but occasionally words would seep out that made her think Mr. Castillo was trying to finance a new project. She wondered if he'd thought that all the way through. If he got backing for a film then he would have to leave the house, fly to places for meetings and to scout locations. He would be exposed to the world again in a way that he wasn't now.

If he thinks it's annoying to have reporters outside the house, how will he feel if they're dogging him when he's trying to shoot? But that wasn't Harry's problem, and she wasn't about to take it on. Hopefully she and Gabe would be out of Bright Horses by then.

Everything was delivered to Mr. Castillo, clothes and groceries and new books, and Harry reflected that the pandemic delivery boom certainly benefited people like him. A landscaping crew came once a week to rake the leaves.

And a doctor visited once a week on Thursday to give Mr. Castillo a checkup.

The first time this happened Harry had been in the upstairs library reading Mr. Castillo's copy of *Imajica* with her back against the wall and her feet hanging off Gabe's twin bed. It was her day off, and she'd discovered soon after she and Gabe moved in that Mr. Castillo definitely did *not* want Harry to work on any days except those she already had scheduled.

"I do not wish to impose on you," he'd said.

Harry had felt a little guilty then about all the suspicious thoughts she'd had about moving into Bright Horses. Her first instinct was always to suspect the worst of people, even when they'd demonstrated otherwise. Mr. Castillo could be imperious, yes, and often demanding, but he'd never been unfair to her.

On the day the doctor came to visit, Gabe was in Harry's room doing his remote schoolwork with Harry's laptop. Though his door was closed and she was across the hall she could still hear the murmur of his voice or the slightly staticky sound of his teachers coming through the tinny laptop speakers.

She'd spent a couple of hours that morning doing a search for a new apartment on her phone, but hadn't had any more luck than she'd had before they moved into Bright Horses. Since the initial terrorizing on the night they'd arrived, the ghost had kept to itself, though Harry wasn't foolish enough to think that meant it was gone. It was only in a kind of lull period, either too weak to exert its will on outside objects or plotting its next move.

Harry still wasn't sleeping well, despite the lack of haunted interference. She couldn't settle down at night, no matter how physically exhausted. As soon as she lay down all of her worries and fears would crowd in, and somehow the ghost was the least of them.

Mr. Castillo grew more animated by the day, seemingly rejuvenated by Gabe's presence. He took a deep and abiding interest in Gabe's schoolwork, his cross-country race times, the stupid videos that Gabe watched on TikTok. There was no aspect of Gabe's life that was too minor for Mr. Castillo, and even though they'd only been at Bright Horses for a few days Harry could feel jealousy burning in every pore of her body. Gabe was so much more open with Mr. Castillo, telling him things that he never told Harry.

She tried to convince herself that this was because Mr. Castillo was a father figure, that Gabe had never had anyone like that in his life. But it was extremely hard not to feel that she was losing her son to this man they barely knew, and who, she was increasingly convinced, had played a larger role in his wife and son's disappearance than originally suspected. Harry knew that Lena couldn't have succeeded without money, and Mr. Castillo had to have provided the funds.

These and other thoughts crowded into her head at night, keeping her from sleeping restfully, so she was half drowsing and half reading when she heard voices on the stairs. She sat up a little straighter, then saw a man she did not know pass in front of the doorway. She only had a fleeting sense of him—tall, dark-haired, slender—before he continued on. He was followed by Mr. Castillo, who seemed to sense her presence in the library and paused in the doorway.

"I have a weekly checkup with my doctor," he said. "Please do not disturb us at this time."

Harry nodded. She wondered if Mr. Castillo had a heart condition or something, something that would require constant monitoring. She expected to hear them enter the master bedroom next door, but the footsteps continued down the hallway. There was the unmistakable sound of a key in a lock, a door opening and then closing, then the sound of the lock being shot home again.

Harry's book dropped into her lap, completely forgotten. They hadn't gone into the master bedroom. They'd gone into the locked room at the end of the hall. Was Mr. Castillo hiding medical equipment in there? Was he ashamed of his condition, whatever it was?

It's not your business, she told herself, picking up the book again. She glanced at her watch. It was just after eleven a.m., and Gabe ate his lunch around eleven thirty during his break. Sometimes Daniel joined them, which Gabe also enjoyed. Daniel had adopted a bit of a fun-older-brother role with Gabe. Harry was the only one who hadn't slid neatly into a role in the house, who still tried to hold herself apart from the others. Daniel noticed, but he didn't say anything. If Mr. Castillo noticed then he didn't care. As long as Gabe watched him with shining eyes, Harry could disintegrate for all he cared, probably.

Harry wondered what Gabe would say if he saw Mr. Castillo coming out of the locked room. She wished she could warn him to keep whatever thoughts he had to himself, but she couldn't interrupt his class. If she sent him a text it might make him curious.

Harry decided it was best not to say anything at all and hope that the doctor left when Gabe was otherwise occupied.

The bedroom door popped open at eleven thirty, right on schedule.

"Going to make a sandwich, okay?" he said, sticking his head inside the door. "You want one?"

Harry would normally jump at the chance to sit with Gabe, even if it was only to get one-word answers from him. But she wondered how long the doctor was going to be with Mr. Castillo, and she was curious enough to want to stay and find out.

"I'm okay right now," she said. "I'm sure you'd rather look at your phone or hang with Daniel than talk to your mother, anyway."

"Love you, Mom," he sang out as he hurried down the stairs. She could hear the pounding of his feet all the way to the bottom floor. Gabe did not know how to move quietly.

A few moments later the locked door at the end of the hallway clicked open again. Harry had a strong desire to get up and run to the end of the hall so she could peek inside the room, but she suppressed it. It was a childish impulse and one that couldn't be fulfilled, in any case. The door was locked again before she could even stand up. She pretended to be absorbed in Clive Barker as the doctor and Mr. Castillo passed by again. She thought she felt Mr. Castillo's eyes on her as they went by, but she didn't look up.

About a week after Harry and Gabe moved into Bright Horses the media interest seemed to abruptly dry up. Harry didn't know if the companies had suddenly decided there wasn't a story to be found hanging out on the sidewalk in front of a recluse's house, or if the change in weather had prompted the move. It snowed in Chicago on Halloween and then the temperatures plummeted. Harry didn't mind the lack of nosy crowds—it meant that she'd be able to go outside and take a walk, at least—but she did mourn missing the trick-or-treaters. Mr. Castillo, naturally, did not give away candy at the door during the holiday. That would mean exposing himself in a way that he clearly did not want to do.

Harry couldn't blame him. It was a certainty that some journalist—maybe Trench Coat Jerk—would show up at the door with a prop kid in a costume in order to try to corner Mr. Castillo into giving a quote. So no trick-or-treating at the biggest, gothiest, most naturally Halloween-y house on the block. It made Harry sad, because she really liked seeing all the kids in their costumes. She'd missed her favorite holiday completely, having never put up the decorations in their old apartment.

Mr. Castillo had, as promised, hired a driver to take Gabe to school every day. Harry thought that once the reporters were gone there would be no need for this, but when she'd tentatively broached the subject with Mr. Castillo he'd frowned at her.

"It's very cold out," he said. "I don't think Gabriel should be standing at a cold bus stop if I can prevent it."

Harry felt that her authority over her own child was being undermined, but again felt powerless to do anything about it. They were in Mr. Castillo's house. He was giving them room and board for free, and paying for her son to have a comfortable ride to school. To say "other kids stand at the bus stop in the winter" would make her sound churlish and ungrateful, and Gabe loved getting picked up. It meant he could sleep a little later in the morning, especially on practice days.

"And no exposure to weird germs, Mom," Gabe said when she pointed out that he could tell Mr. Castillo he didn't need the car. She'd thought that would solve the problem, if the impetus came from Gabe, but he didn't want to give up his comfy ride. "Less possible COVID and all that. Mr. Castillo is a super-germaphobe, right? He probably doesn't want me bringing anything home."

Harry had reluctantly conceded, but she hated it. She didn't want Gabe resenting her when they left Bright Horses and he didn't have these little luxuries anymore.

Two weeks passed, three weeks, then all of a sudden it was Thanksgiving and Mr. Castillo ordered a turkey that probably weighed more than Harry and spent the whole day in the kitchen, humming the musical themes from *Close Encounters of the Third Kind* and *Halloween* and preparing enough food to feed an army. Every time Harry tried to enter the kitchen to help he waved her out, clearly enjoying himself, but the extravagance of the meal made her feel guilty. They didn't need all of that food for four people. Harry had thought Daniel would go elsewhere to see his own family for the holiday, but when Harry broached the subject Daniel had said that he had always spent Thanksgiving with Mr. Castillo before the pandemic.

Before Michael did what he did, Harry thought, and did not pursue the subject any more.

She and Gabe usually volunteered at a food bank on Thanksgiving and then had a small dinner with the other volunteers. She'd never even had a chance to bring this up with Mr. Castillo, who had just assumed that they would want a massive feast.

We've got to get out of here, Harry thought desperately as she climbed the stairs to the third floor, the smell of cooking turkey wafting through the house. The ghost had been very quiet and Harry didn't trust the quiet. She was sure it meant some terrible thing was in the offing, and waiting for it was far worse than the actual thing happening. She still wasn't sleeping through the night and she felt wiped out all the time. It was hard to think when she was this tired.

Gabe was lying on his bed on his stomach as she passed by. He was tapping away at his phone.

"Playing a game?" she asked, and he nodded without looking up. "Mr. Castillo said everything should be ready in about an hour and a half so I'm going to try to take a nap."

He waved his hand at her to indicate that he understood and Harry frowned at him. Gabe usually at least responded with a "yes" or "no," no matter how absorbed he was in his task.

"Something wrong?" she asked.

"No," he said, his voice sharp and short. "I'm in the middle of something, okay?"

Harry thought about letting it pass. She was tired and it didn't always feel worth it to argue about little things. But Gabe was being rude and if she let it go once it would be harder to get back her authority later. She already felt like she'd given away a lot of status to Mr. Castillo that she might never get back.

"Hey," she said. "There's no need to talk to me that way. Your phone is a privilege, not a right."

She expected Gabe to apologize. He was a good kid and she thought this must be a hormone flare-up or something. Instead he turned such an ugly look on her that she stepped back involuntarily.

"'Your phone is a privilege, not a right,'" he repeated, in a high-pitched, mocking voice. "Why can't you just leave me alone? You're always nagging me about everything. It's like you can't stand to see me happy."

These accusations were not only shocking to hear, they were completely unfair. Harry didn't nag him constantly. She tried, always, to talk to him instead of lecture. She couldn't, however, let him get away with this kind of behavior.

"All right, mister," she said, marching over to the bed and taking the phone out of his hands. "I guess you'll have to live without this until you learn how to behave like a decent human being."

"Hey!" he shouted. "That's mine."

"No, it isn't," Harry said. "It's mine. I bought it. I pay for the wireless service. And if you want it back you'll think about what you've done and whether or not an extra second's attention on your game was worth talking to your mother that way."

"'Meh meh meh meh meh meh meh,'" Gabe said, again in that high-pitched tone, like he was mocking what she said as meaningless babble, an adult speaking on a *Peanuts* cartoon.

Harry felt herself getting really angry then. Was Gabe becoming a spoiled little monster? He didn't have to do any chores in Mr. Castillo's house, because Mr. Castillo wouldn't let him. He had much less responsibility and a lot more leisure. She deliberately slid the phone in her pocket and Gabe gave her a mocking look.

"I don't know what good you think that will do," he said. "Javier will buy me a new phone if I ask for it. A new one, too, not some crummy refurbished thing that's four models old."

Harry's face flushed, both because of the implication that Mr. Castillo would give him what he wanted and also because she couldn't afford any better. "No, he will not. I won't allow it."

Gabe smirked at her. "You think it matters at all what you want? He *loves* me."

Harry stared at her son, at this stranger openly mocking her, seemingly completely unconcerned by her anger or her attempts at discipline. There was a dark gleam of malice in his eyes that reminded her of something.

"No," Harry said, a chill washing over her as she realized what she was looking at. "No."

"Yeah, he does," Gabe said, clearly thinking she was responding to his statement about Mr. Castillo. "He thinks I deserve so much more than I've got."

Harry felt herself backing away, knew she was ceding ground, but it was too horrible to think of, too horrible to contemplate as Gabe smiled a wide, complacent Joker smile.

She turned and fled to the second guest room—she could never think of it as her own room, no matter how many nights she spent in it—and shut the door, leaning back against it and breathing hard.

The ghost is inside Gabe, she thought, and closed her eyes tight, trying to wash away the image of Gabe smiling with the same smile that the Sten mask had done.

What was she supposed to do now? It was one thing to deal with a disembodied haunt, even one that was able to occupy inanimate objects. But sneaking into her son? How had it even managed to do that?

When had it happened? Soon after they came into the house, or was it more recent? And how was she supposed to get rid of it now?

Where's Father Karras when I need him? She gave a shaky little laugh. *The Exorcist* was supposed to be fiction, not a life blueprint.

"Calm down," she told herself, but her body ignored her and started pacing back and forth across the room anyway. "Think, think."

She pulled out her phone and typed "spirit possession" in the search bar. The first article to pop up was from Wikipedia, and Harry eagerly scanned it. But all it did was list off a bunch of cultures and religions that believed in spirit possession and the forms that possession took in those religions. It didn't have any suggestions for dealing with possession.

Were you expecting a how-to? She found a link to a medical abstract from 1994 in which the author claimed "exorcism-resistant ghost treated with clopenthixol." Harry didn't know what clopenthixol was or even how to get hold of it. It sounded like a treatment for a psychiatric disorder. There was no time to try to get Gabe diagnosed with a psychiatric disorder, and no guarantee of the desired result in any case. A therapist might just say that Gabe was acting out because he was a teenager, and that it was developmentally normal and healthy. Harry was the one who would sound crazy if she tried to tell a doctor that her son was possessed by a ghost.

She kept scrolling. There was a YouTube video that claimed to demonstrate the "16 signs of a REAL demonic possession." She skipped this, as it appeared to be a performance by a religious person using the Bible to prove his own particular beliefs. That was the kind of thing her parents might have done. Harry realized, without any enjoyment in the irony, that her family had been convinced that she'd been controlled by Satan when she bought *Fangoria* magazines and Stephen King books. Now her own child was *actually* possessed by something malevolent and she had no tools whatsoever to deal with it. She didn't even have any faith to fall back on, because she'd deliberately given that up years before.

A surprising number of results were just academic papers studying the phenomena of spirit possession or the belief thereof. At the bottom of the second page she found an ad for a "Sorcerer for Hire—Protect Yourself Against Spirits & *Ghosts*. Learn More Now! Curse Removal. House Clearing. Services: Clearing Haunted Houses, Curse Removal, *Demon* Removal, Energy Healings."

Useless, Harry thought. It was probably a scam, and on the off chance that it wasn't a scam, she didn't have the money for it anyway.

She sank onto the bed, tossed the phone aside and let her head fall into her hands. The situation was ridiculous, absurd, beyond belief. Her child, her beautiful boy, the love of her life was possessed by a murdering ghost.

There was a tentative knock at her door. "Mom? Can I talk to you?"

Harry stared at the door, wishing she could see through to the other side. It sounded like Gabe, like the old Gabe, but maybe it was a trick.

What are you going to do, avoid him? She stood up and went to the door. Before she opened it she steeled her face so it wouldn't show her fear or her grief.

Harry pulled the door open. Gabe stood on the other side of the threshold, his head down.

"I'm sorry," he mumbled to the floor.

"What?" Harry asked, putting her hand to her ear like she hadn't heard.

He picked up his head. He looked miserable. "I'm sorry. I . . . I don't know what came over me. Truly. It was like I was outside of myself, watching me say all these horrible things to you. I didn't mean it."

His eyes welled up, and Harry stared at him in suspicion. Was this a ploy of the ghost to get her to trust Gabe again? Or had its power been limited? Harry put her hands on both sides of Gabe's face and peered deep into his eyes, searching for that spark of malice.

"I mean it," he said, and a tear slipped out of his right eye and rolled over his cheek. "I'm really sorry."

Harry looked and looked, and found only Gabe.

"Okay," she said, and put her arms around him. He crumpled into her, the way he had when he was very little and had done something wrong. "It's okay."

After a few minutes he pulled away and wiped his face with his sleeve. She held out his phone to him and he put his hands up, backing away.

"No, you hold on to it for the rest of the day," he said. "At least the rest of the day. I deserve that."

She nodded and put the phone inside her room on the bedside table. "Let's try to brighten up for Daniel and for Mr. Castillo. He's really putting a lot into this meal and he won't want to see our long faces."

"Yeah. Yeah. He's really excited about today. I'm going to eat *so much*," Gabe said, and his stomach rumbled as if in response to this wish.

They both laughed, but the terror that had clutched Harry when she'd seen the malice inside Gabe hadn't dissipated. The ghost had gone (she hoped), but it could return. It could do much more damage from inside a human body than it could from inside a horror movie costume. And once it had hitched a ride, it could hitch right on out the door with her child, which meant that leaving Bright Horses wouldn't solve the problem.

Harry put on her best perky waitress smile and went downstairs with Gabe. The costume in the blue room didn't matter anymore and she passed by it without a second thought.

She had heard the phrase "the table was groaning" before but had never seen an actual example of the phenomenon. Mr. Castillo had truly cooked for about fifteen people rather than four. There was a twenty-pound turkey, an enormous casserole dish overloaded with cornbread stuffing, a two-quart bowl filled with cranberry sauce, another casserole with macaroni and cheese and a third with roasted brussels sprouts. He'd made dinner rolls from scratch and baked three pies—an apple, a pumpkin and a French silk. Daniel had clearly been drafted as sous-chef, because he sat down at the table still wearing an apron and he appeared slightly frazzled.

"We'll be eating Thanksgiving leftovers until Christmas," Harry said, but she tempered it with a smile so Mr. Castillo wouldn't take offense. She felt he had gone way too far but kept that to herself.

"This looks amazing," Gabe said.

"Eat, eat," Mr. Castillo said, waving them to the table.

They sat down and Mr. Castillo dished out generous helpings to everyone, including himself. Then he poured out some wine for himself and Daniel and Harry, and even, over Harry's objections, for Gabe.

"Just a little bit," he said soothingly, as he put about three tablespoons of wine in Gabe's glass. "When I was his age my parents would give me a little taste at the dinner table. It makes alcohol less of a temptation when you're older then, when it's not treated like forbidden fruit."

Again, Harry wanted to say Gabe was a little young for that, though she believed in Mr. Castillo's point in principle. She would have waited until he was sixteen, at least. But it was a holiday and she didn't want to spoil it with an argument.

A second argument, she thought as she remembered the scene with Gabe upstairs.

Mr. Castillo sat down and raised his glass, and everyone did likewise. "Happy Thanksgiving. And may I say, on this day that we give thanks, how grateful I am for the three of you. My life has been made better by your presence in this house."

Harry knew her cue, and she took it. "And thank you for letting us stay here. I don't know what we would have done without your generosity."

Mr. Castillo smiled widely, basking in his due praise. "It is nothing. I had the means and the ability. Now, let us feast."

They dug in to their meal. Harry could appreciate, in a distant sort of way, that all the food had been expertly prepared. She wished she could taste it, though. Her mouth was filled with sour bile, and she could barely swallow, even after chewing until her food was mashed enough for a nine-month-old.

She couldn't help watching Gabe (in what she hoped was a surreptitious way) for signs of behavior that did not belong to him. It was easy to do this since Mr. Castillo usually saw every meal as an opportunity to Hold Forth on the greatness that was Javier Castillo, and he didn't really expect her participation other than affirmative nods. Daniel was able to chime in for many of the stories since he'd worked so much with Mr. Castillo, and Gabe had many of his normal excited questions. But for the duration of the meal there was nothing that made her antennae stand up. He was just her usual smart, funny, eating-fifteen-helpings Gabe, his eyes glowing as he listened.

Mr. Castillo regaled them with stories from the famously difficult set of *The Devil Knows,* and made it all sound like an adventure in the jungle rather than an overtime and over-budget nightmare, which it actually was. Harry remembered reading stories at the time that made it sound like the filming of *Apocalypse Now.*

After dinner Gabe convinced Mr. Castillo to play Clue, which meant Harry and Daniel got dragged in as well. Gabe loved to play board and card games but most of his games had been put away in their storage unit. He'd brought only Clue and Uno to Bright Horses, reasoning that they were both easy to play and that Mr. Castillo might join in.

Harry put her brain into the game for a while, but it soon became clear that she and Daniel were superfluous to requirements. Gabe and Mr. Castillo were getting really competitive and it couldn't be clearer that they both really wanted to win.

Which is weird, Harry thought as she watched Gabe move his piece around the board. *Gabe likes a friendly competition, but he doesn't usually care this much.*

"All right, I *accuse* Professor Plum of committing the crime in the conservatory with the rope," Gabe said.

"Are you sure you wish to accuse, Gabriel?" said Mr. Castillo, smiling slightly. "If you make an accusation and you're wrong, you're out of the game. You could always make a suggestion instead."

"Don't try to bluff me, old man," Gabe said as he picked up the envelope to check the cards inside.

Harry looked up from her own cards as she heard the tone in his voice. *Not Gabe,* she thought. *The ghost. It's been inside him all day, just waiting.*

Her heart fell, but that was nothing compared to Mr. Castillo's reaction. All the blood had drained from his face, and no wonder. Gabe had been incredibly rude, and Mr. Castillo was accustomed to nothing but adulation from Harry's son. Daniel appeared shocked, his eyes wide as they went from Gabe to Mr. Castillo.

Gabe pulled the three cards from the envelope and threw them on the table. "Ha! Read 'em and weep."

Mr. Castillo looked from the cards to Gabe, then silently dropped his hand of cards, stood up and walked out of the room.

The flush of triumph in Gabe's face faded, leaving the same bewildered and sorry look that he'd had upstairs when he'd apologized to Harry. The ghost had returned just long enough to cause trouble, and then disappeared again. He looked at his mother.

"I didn't mean—I didn't mean to get so caught up," he said. "I hurt his feelings."

Gabe stood up and ran after Mr. Castillo, who must have retreated into his office as he so often did. Harry heard the sound of knocking on the office door, and Gabe calling, "Mr. Castillo? I'm really sorry."

"That was so strange," Daniel said. "It's not like Gabe to behave that way."

"No, it isn't," Harry said. She wondered if she dared to take Daniel into her confidence, to tell him that she thought Gabe was possessed by something supernatural that lived in the house.

How would I explain such a thing? Where would I even begin?

Daniel looked toward the doorway that led into the hall, where Gabe continued entreating Mr. Castillo.

But Javier Castillo did not answer. Harry cleaned up the board game, listening to the sound of Gabe knocking on the door in vain.

SEVENTEEN

HARRY HAD EXPECTED MR. Castillo to say something to her about Gabe's behavior, but the next day he stayed holed up in his office. The following day Gabe had a cross-country meet, and Harry and Daniel went to watch. Outdoor sports were still on at a lot of schools, at least as much as they could do.

Daniel and Harry watched Gabe line up at the start and shoot out when the gun went off. Harry saw her son pull into a front pack of eight or nine runners, their legs churning at a pace she couldn't imagine. Harry was not much for recreational exercise. She felt like she got more than enough movement during the day, carrying buckets and vacuum cleaners up and down stairs.

The start and finish line were in the same place, but the runners quickly disappeared onto the course, and Harry and Daniel, along with the other spectators, were left to linger until they returned.

Harry sighed, watching the space where her son had disappeared into the crowd. He'd been himself today, for which she was grateful. She hoped it stayed that way.

"Harry?" Daniel asked.

"Mm-hmm?" she said, thinking about Gabe and the ghost (*or whatever,* she couldn't stop herself from mentally adding).

She hadn't seen any sign of the haunt since Thanksgiving night, and she was spending all of her free time trying to research spirit possession. This meant that she encountered a lot of questionable information. There were lots of websites advertising mediums who promised to speak to the dead or professional exorcists who promised to scrub your house and being of the presence that haunted you. There were also a lot of people just holding forth about their beliefs and the supposed evidence for them. It was incredibly time-consuming trying to sort through the nonsense and find credible accounts.

And who knows what's credible, really? There was no verified evidence, just anecdotes everywhere.

Daniel took a deep breath, which made Harry look up at him. Long inhales were usually a sign of uncomfortable conversation to come.

"What is it?" she asked, giving him her full attention.

"The other night, Thanksgiving night." He stopped, seeming unsure how to go on.

"You want to know why Gabe acted so out of character," Harry said.

"I was wondering if he'd had something personal happen—a person he likes not liking him back, something of that kind? Or maybe that Javier had done something to anger Gabe? I know he can come on strong sometimes."

"He can come on strong oftentimes," Harry said.

"Yeah," Daniel said, with a little smile. "But Gabe doesn't seem to mind, usually. If anyone minds—"

"It's me," Harry finished.

Daniel appeared stricken. "I didn't mean to imply—"

"It's okay," Harry said, waving him away. He really was a nice man, and he seemed to care so much about Mr. Castillo. "I do mind, sometimes. Oftentimes. I feel like Mr. Castillo is trying to take over, to become Gabe's parent when he's not. And before you say anything—I know. I know he lost his son and it devastated him. But Gabe isn't his, and all he's doing by pretending is setting himself up for more heartache."

"The thing is," Daniel said slowly, like he was picking his words with care, "I'm not so sure Javier *was* devastated by the loss of Michael. Lena, yes. Michael . . . let's just say the two of them hadn't gotten along for a long time. In fact, I don't think they'd gotten along since the boy hit puberty."

This startled Harry. She knew that Michael had been a Problem Child—all of the news articles had made that extremely clear—but something about the way Mr. Castillo behaved had made her think he missed Michael desperately. Whenever the disappearance came up, even obliquely, it was always Michael that was mentioned.

Or at least, Harry conceded to herself, *if he wasn't actually named then his name was implied. The only time Lena ever came up was the first time Gabe asked Mr. Castillo if he missed them, and Mr. Castillo said "yes."*

"And the thing is, the other night, when Gabe was acting so strange," Daniel continued, "he was acting a lot like the way Michael did, when he and Javier weren't getting along."

Harry frowned. "That would explain why Mr. Castillo hasn't spoken to Gabe since Thanksgiving."

"It was the 'old man' that did it," Daniel said. "Michael always used to say that to Javier. He stopped calling him 'Dad' years ago."

A cheer went up from the crowd, and Harry saw that the first runner had reappeared. She glanced at her watch.

"Jeez, they've only been gone about fifteen minutes."

"Hey, there's Gabe!" Daniel said.

Gabe and another runner were very close to each other, about thirty seconds or so behind the leader.

Harry and Daniel called Gabe's name and cheered loudly as he placed third, and for a little while Harry forgot about what Daniel had said, about Gabe acting like Michael. But she found herself brooding on it as Daniel drove them back to Bright Horses in Mr. Castillo's car.

When they got home, Mr. Castillo was reading in the downstairs library. He called to them when they came through the front door and they all crowded in the doorway.

"How was the meet, Gabriel?" he asked, as if nothing had happened between them at all.

Gabe gave Harry a *Should I say something?* look and Harry gave him a little head shake *no*. If Mr. Castillo wanted to pretend nothing had happened then Harry was fine with that.

"It was pretty good. I came in third overall," Gabe said.

"That is excellent!" Mr. Castillo said, putting his book aside and clapping his hands. "I think this calls for pizza."

"Wow, thanks!" Gabe said. "That's really nice of you."

"Go take a shower," Harry said. "No one wants to eat pizza while sitting next to your stinky sweaty butt."

Gabe rubbed his cheek against hers and Harry pretended to shriek in disgust.

"No, you're gross! Go! Go!" she said, though it really wasn't that bad.

Mr. Castillo smiled at them indulgently and Gabe ran upstairs to shower and change. Daniel followed him upstairs, carrying his sneakers in one hand. Harry waited for the sound of water running in the pipes before speaking.

"Mr. Castillo?"

"I've told you many times, Harry, to call me Javier," he said, frowning at his phone. He had a food delivery app open and was clicking around on it. "Does Gabriel like mozzarella sticks? Chicken wings?"

"Gabe likes anything," Harry said, then corrected herself. "Except calamari."

"He just hasn't had it prepared properly," Mr. Castillo said absently. "I don't think it's at its best when it's fried. Two pizzas, one pepperoni, one mushroom, an order of mozzarella sticks, an order of loaded potato skins . . . what else?"

"That's plenty," Harry said. "Mr. Castillo, I just want you to know that Gabe is really sorry about what he said the other night. He just got caught up in the game and it got a little out of hand. He didn't mean to hurt your feelings."

Mr. Castillo's expression darkened as he listened, but he didn't look up or respond while he finished placing the order. Harry hovered in the doorway, wondering if she should have brought it up at all. It just went against the grain for her to pretend there hadn't been an argument. Mr. Castillo obviously liked to be an ostrich, but Harry couldn't live that way.

Finally, Mr. Castillo said, "You're right. He wasn't himself. Perhaps I should have listened to you and not given him the wine."

Harry doubted that a mouthful of wine taken at the beginning of the meal could be credited as the culprit, but if that was what

Mr. Castillo wanted to believe, then fine. Better than Harry trying to explain that the ghost that haunted his house was occasionally speaking through her son.

"Okay," Harry said. "Thanks for being so understanding."

Mr. Castillo looked like he wanted to say something else on the subject, but thought better of it. "Gabriel is a good boy. You've raised him well. Everybody makes mistakes from time to time."

"Yeah," Harry said, then thought she'd better make space for any potential future troubles. Until she figured out how to get the ghost away from Gabe there was more than a good chance that this could happen again. "And he's fourteen. His brain is being bathed in chemicals. It can make boys impulsive."

"Yes," Mr. Castillo said, appearing broody again. "It certainly can."

Just like that, the specter of Michael Castillo hung over the proceedings, and Harry regretted bringing up the subject at all.

"Let's watch a film while we eat," Mr. Castillo said. "What is Gabriel's favorite?"

"Oh, I don't know. He could go for anything," Harry demurred, even though she knew his favorite movie was John Carpenter's *The Thing*. She didn't want to say it wasn't a Castillo film.

Gabe must have wanted to make up for his behavior during the board game, because when he came downstairs, freshly showered, he said he wanted to watch *A Messenger from Hell*.

"Oh, unless you don't want to," Gabe said, suddenly realizing he might have stepped in it again. "Because of Amina."

Mr. Castillo's eyes brightened. "No, you're right. We should watch it. As a tribute to that young lady and her powerful performance."

"I notice you don't mention my powerful performance," Daniel said, trying to lighten the mood.

Harry went to the gate to fetch the pizza when the delivery driver rang the buzzer. It was astonishingly cold and she shivered inside her coat as she took the food and thanked the driver. She was hurrying back up the walk when a movement on the upper floor caught her eye. She glanced up and then stopped dead in the middle of the walk, steam rising from the pizza boxes in the chilly air.

There was someone upstairs, someone looking down from the locked room at the end of the hallway. Harry couldn't make out any features, or even whether it was a man or a woman. But there was definitely someone standing in the window.

Harry blinked, and the person was gone.

You've got to be kidding me, she thought. *Another hallucination? Or the ghost? Or has there really been someone in that room all this time, the way I thought there was months ago?*

"Mom? What are you doing? The pizza's gonna get cold!" Gabe stood in the doorway, his arms wrapped around himself in an attempt to protect against the cold night air.

"Yeah," she said, and forced herself to move.

She handed the pizza boxes to Gabe, and then placed the plastic bag with the other items on top.

I've got to get inside that room.

The thought shot across her brain like an arrow, and there was a conviction in it that she'd never had before. That room was the key to everything. The haunt had first manifested from there. She'd allowed herself to be distracted by the spectacle, by the costume, by the possession of her son and the death of Amina. But those were symptoms, not the disease itself. The locked room was the source, and no matter how badly it violated Mr. Castillo's privacy, she had to get in there.

But how? She didn't know a thing about lock picking, and Mr.

Castillo never left the house. When would she even have the opportunity?

"Come on, come on," Gabe said as she slowly took off her coat and shut the front door.

"Go ahead," Harry said. "I just want to get something from my room. Another layer. You guys can start the movie and I'll be down in a second."

"Okay," Gabe said. "I'm so hungry."

"Such a surprise," Harry said.

She went to the bottom of the stairs that led up to the second floor, and stood there for a moment, listening to the distant sounds of men murmuring in the screening room as they opened the pizza boxes.

Then she ran up the stairs, dashed through the blue room and up the second flight to the third floor. She went to her room, took out a flannel shirt as cover for her story, then went out into the hall.

She walked slowly toward the room at the end, trying not to step on any squeaky part of the floor. The door seemed to grow bigger as she approached it, like something was pushing at it from the inside.

Don't let your imagination run wild, she told herself. Reality was quite enough. The door wasn't changing size. It was all in her head.

She stopped in front of the door. It was just like the other doors on the floor, white and heavy with a silver knob. The only difference was that this one had a keyhole inside it.

Harry touched the knob and tried to spin it, but of course it didn't move. It was too much to hope that Mr. Castillo would have forgotten to lock it the last time he was in the room.

She got down on the floor and tried to peer under the crack, but couldn't see anything except more floor. She stood again and leaned her head against the door, trying to hear any sounds of movement inside. There was nothing—no rustle of clothing, no creak of furniture.

I imagined it, she thought. There was no one in the room. It was probably just another space full of Mr. Castillo's private stuff, and he brought the doctor in there every week because—

"Help me help me HELP ME HELP ME"

The words seemed to explode out of the room, roaring in Harry's ears. They were followed by a giant push of air pressure that exploded from under the door. It lifted Harry off her feet and threw her against the wall opposite. She crumpled to the ground, all the breath stolen from her lungs.

She tried to stand up but her ears were ringing and she fell again.

"Mom? Are you okay?" Gabe. Calling from downstairs.

She couldn't answer, couldn't speak. Harry pulled herself across the floor, boneless, barely able to move. She felt nauseous and no matter how hard she tried the sound of that voice screaming *"HELP ME"* seemed to fill up the empty space inside her ears.

Got to get away from this door, though, she thought. She couldn't get caught. There was no reason for her to be at this end of the hallway. She had to at least pull herself to the doorway of her own bedroom before Gabe and Daniel and Mr. Castillo made it upstairs. The sound of their feet on the stairs carried to her as she dragged herself, sweating and sick, to the proper doorway. Then she closed her eyes, and everything went away for a while.

SOMEBODY WAS ARGUING. TWO male voices, one younger, one older. No, they weren't arguing. They were screaming at each other.

Gabe and Mr. Castillo, Harry thought. *But Gabe wouldn't talk like that to Mr. Castillo. He wouldn't speak like that to anyone.*

Harry opened her eyes. They were a few feet away from her, practically nose to nose, snarling at one another. She blinked, and realized it wasn't Gabe at all.

It was Michael.

"Stop this," she heard herself say, but it wasn't her voice. She looked down at her hands, at the heavy, old-fashioned diamond engagement ring over the gold wedding band, at the neat and tasteful French manicure. She wore dress pants and a cashmere sweater. Harry didn't even own dress pants and a cashmere sweater.

"You're finally going to face consequences for your behavior," Javier Castillo said. "You wanted to be wild and you never would listen to me or your mother, and now your rope has run out. They're going to indict you for the murder of that girl and, god help me, I hope that the jury convicts you and the judge throws the book at you. Twenty years to life should be long enough for you to think about what you've done."

"No, Michael," Harry said, but she knew it wasn't her, it was Lena, Lena's voice filled with unshed tears. "Of course we don't want that for you. We love you."

"*He* doesn't love me," Michael said, sneering. "He never has. Don't even pretend."

"That's not true," Lena said, even though in her heart she knew it was true, that Javier had never wanted Michael, that he'd said so from the first.

"Why would he have hit me in front of his entire crew if he loved me?" Michael said.

Javier's face contorted. "How many times are you going to throw that in my face? Besides, a slap was the least of what you deserved. You behaved like a brat and you ruined the shooting schedule."

"See?" Michael said. "All he cares about are his movies. He doesn't love you or me as much as his work."

"I love your mother very much," Javier said.

Lena knew that Javier thought he did, but he'd never love her as much as he loved his movies. Moreover, it hurt her that he didn't love Michael at all and he'd as much as said it.

"Besides," Javier continued. "My behavior hardly matters now. It's your behavior that does. There are witnesses that heard you arguing with that girl, heard her screaming, saw you leaving the house. You will be arrested and I will not be bailing you out of jail. You can stay there."

"Juvenile detention. Big deal," Michael said.

"Not if they decide to try you as an adult," Javier said, and there was a grim complacency in his gaze. "And given the brutality of her death and the fact that you are nearly eighteen, they just might."

Lena felt terror grip her heart. Her boy, her darling boy. She couldn't believe he'd done this terrible thing he was accused of, couldn't believe that Javier thought Michael had done it, too.

"Javier," she said, the tears falling thick on her cheeks, "how can you say such a thing? How can you believe that Michael would do this, would commit a m-murder?"

Her mouth stuttered on the last word. Her son was not a murderer. He was not.

"He did it," Javier said. "And he should be punished for it."

"I'm not going to be punished for anything," Michael said. "Your fancy lawyer is going to get me off, and when he does I'm going to court and I'm going to have myself legally emancipated."

"Good luck with that," Javier said. "You wouldn't know the first thing about living without a silver spoon in your mouth. And as for that fancy lawyer—once you're charged you can have a public defender."

Lena saw fear leap into Michael's eyes, the same fear that she felt herself. "No, Javier, you wouldn't. He's your son. What would people think if you couldn't be bothered to pay for a lawyer when you live in this enormous house surrounded by all these things?"

"I don't care what they think!" Javier roared, turning his ire on her. She shrank back. "You always take his side. Always. You never stop to consider how I might feel. It's always about Michael."

"He's my child," she said, staring at him in shock, and she realized something she should have realized long before. Javier was jealous. He was jealous of his own son.

"Yes, and your child is going to jail," Javier said. "I'm going to call the detective now and tell them to come and pick you up."

"Like they'll listen to you, old man," Michael said.

"They'll listen to me when I tell them I found the murder weapon in your bedroom," Javier said, his face triumphant.

"The murder weapon? In Michael's bedroom?"

Lena looked from Javier to Michael. Michael's face was frozen, all his sneering arrogance gone. And she knew then, knew that it was true, knew her son had killed Adelaide Walker and there was no justification for it in the world. Her son was a murderer, and her husband couldn't wait to send him to jail. Her heart felt like it was falling, falling into a deep well that had no end.

"Nothing to say?" Javier said, his face flushed. "I thought not."

He turned away from Michael. Michael's face twisted, turned his handsome features into an ugly, distorted mask. He reached behind him, and Lena saw he had the fireplace poker in his hand.

"No!" she shouted, and her warning gave Javier enough time

to turn so that the blow glanced off his shoulder instead of his head. Michael lifted the poker again. "Stop! Michael, stop!"

Javier grabbed a heavy statue from an end table and swung it at Michael before Michael could slam the poker down. The thick base of the statue struck the side of Michael's head. There was a terrible *crack*. The poker fell from Michael's hand. His eyes rolled up white, and he fell to the ground.

"Michael!" Lena cried, and ran to him. Blood poured from the side of his head. She put her hands over it, trying to staunch the flow. Michael's face was very pale. His eyes were closed. "Javier, call 911!"

Javier did not move. Lena bent over Michael, calling his name.

A few moments later, he stopped breathing.

"Michael!" she screamed. "Michael!"

Still Javier did not move. When she looked up from the still body of her son, her beautiful boy, she saw a strange and terrible expression on Javier's face.

"You killed him," she said. "You killed your own son."

Javier shook his head slowly. "No. I was defending myself. You saw that."

Lena hunched over Michael then, crying, because she'd seen the look on Michael's face. Michael would have killed Javier. He'd wanted to. But Javier had wanted to kill Michael, too.

After a while she heard Javier speak again.

"We'll have to hide the body," he said.

"Wh-what?" she said. "What are you talking about? We have to call the police."

"We can't call the police," he said. "They'll think I'm a murderer."

"But you were defending yourself, like you said," Lena said. "I'll tell them."

Javier shook his head, and she recognized the stubborn intransigence in his eyes. "I'll never work in this town again. It was bad enough when my son was accused, but if it gets out that I killed my own child . . . well, no one will want to fund any of my scripts in the future. It won't matter that it was an accident. We'll have to hide the body. We'll say that Michael ran away. People will believe that. He was a rebellious little brat and he wouldn't want to go to jail. He'll just disappear and we'll pretend we know nothing about it."

Lena felt her anger growing and growing as Javier spoke. She couldn't believe what she was hearing. It wasn't possible. He wanted to pretend that he hadn't just murdered his son, wanted to keep it quiet because nothing was more important than the brilliant Javier Castillo continuing to make movies.

"We might not even have to go so far as to hide him," Javier said. "I have some preservation materials for taxidermy in the attic. Remember when I thought I might like to do a film about a taxidermist? We could preserve him and hide him away in the basement among the props. Even if the police searched we could lock him in a prop coffin or something like that. There's no reason for anyone to suspect."

Lena stood up slowly, feeling in some way like she was seeing her husband for the first time in their marriage. She'd always explained away his faults, always pretended she didn't see them because she loved him. And she knew that he did love her. He really did.

He just didn't love her more than his movies. Michael had been right about that.

"But they will suspect," Lena said. "They'll suspect because I'll tell them what happened. I won't do this, Javier. I won't cover up the death of our child just because you want to make sure you get funding for your next project."

Javier's mouth pressed into a thin line, and when he spoke it was through gritted teeth. "Lena, be reasonable."

"I am being reasonable," she said, taking her cell phone from her pocket. "I'm calling the authorities. That's what normal people do when something like this happens."

Javier snatched the phone out of Lena's hand and threw it into the fireplace. She heard the sound of glass shattering.

"You can't stop me," she said, turning toward the front of the house. "I'll just drive down to the station."

"No, you won't," he said, grabbing her arm and yanking her back. "You're still doing it. He's dead and you're still taking his side."

"You *killed your own son*, Javier," Lena said. "I'm not taking his side. You told Michael he had to face the consequences of his actions. So do you."

"No," Javier said. His eyes were wild, unfocused. "No. I won't let you do this. I won't let you ruin me. I won't let *Michael* ruin me."

And then his hands were at her throat, squeezing, squeezing.

He's killing me.

She gasped for air, tried to pry his hands off her. He didn't even appear to see her anymore. His eyes were like the monsters in his movies, inhuman, faraway.

He's killing me.

Michael, she thought. *Help me. He's killing me.*

EIGHTEEN

HARRY OPENED HER EYES. She lay on her side in the bed in the second guest bedroom. The first thing she saw were the silly crystals that Gabe had given her on the bedside table, the ones that had protected her the first night. She reached out for them, and Mr. Castillo spoke.

"How are you feeling?"

Harry sat bolt upright. It was a shock to hear his voice, so calm and measured and unlike the monstrous snarl that still echoed in her head.

Mr. Castillo had brought a folding chair from somewhere else in the house and placed it at the foot of her bed. Gabe dozed in the armchair in the corner. Daniel paced back and forth at the foot of the bed. At the sound of Harry's voice Gabe sat up, rubbing his eyes.

"Mom? What happened? You were passed out cold in the hallway."

Harry looked at Daniel, then at Mr. Castillo. There could be no more pretending now.

"Gabe, I want you to go and pack your things. We're leaving."

Mr. Castillo's gaze sharpened. "What are you talking about? It's the middle of the night and you have nowhere to go."

"Mom, we can't leave," Gabe said. "Did you hit your head or something?"

"Yes," she said, watching Mr. Castillo carefully the whole time. "I did hit my head. Lena threw me against the wall. She's been trying to get my attention for a while now, and I've finally gotten the message. It's not safe for us here. We're leaving."

"Lena?" Gabe said, looking from Mr. Castillo to his mother. "Who's Lena?"

"Harry, what are you talking about?" Daniel asked, looking from Harry to Mr. Castillo and back again. "Lena's gone, and nobody knows where she is."

"He does. He knows where Michael is, too." Harry realized then that what Daniel had told her earlier had stuck in her brain, though she couldn't figure out why at the time.

Old man, Harry thought. Daniel said that Michael always called Javier Castillo that instead of *Dad*.

"Michael's been trying to get my attention, too," Harry added. "Trying so hard that he used my own son when I pretended not to notice."

Mr. Castillo's face had whitened at the mention of Lena, but he still tried to brazen it out. "Harry, you're confused. I wonder if you have a concussion."

"You're not going to gaslight me," she said. "I've done enough of that to myself. You killed them. You killed them both."

"Harry, stop this," Daniel said. "I don't know what happened while we were downstairs, but you must have had a strange dream. Javier would never hurt his family that way."

Gabe looked frightened now, and terribly young. "Mom, what are you saying? Mr. Castillo didn't kill anyone."

"Yes, he did," Harry said. "He hit Michael over the head with a statue and the boy died almost instantly."

"H-how . . . ?" Mr. Castillo said, and swallowed reflexively, unable to finish the sentence.

That one word was enough to have Daniel turning toward Mr. Castillo in dawning awareness. "Javier? This can't be true."

"How did I know that?" Harry said. "Lena told me. No, that's not right. She *showed* me. And the last thing she ever saw on this earth was your face as you choked her to death."

Gabe gave Mr. Castillo a horrified look. "The ghost? The ghost has been your wife all along? You *killed* her?"

"What ghost?" Daniel said. His face was a mixture of horror and disgust. "Are you telling me that the ghost of Lena is in this house? And that Javier killed her? Killed her and Michael?"

Harry felt so sorry for Daniel, sorry that she had to be the one to reveal Mr. Castillo's true character to him. She thought of all the time Daniel had spent in the house, tending to Mr. Castillo, making sure he was okay. All that time he'd been looking after a murderer.

"No," Mr. Castillo said. "No, I didn't kill her."

"Don't lie," Harry said. "I saw it. She showed me everything."

"Not everything," he said. "Lena is still alive."

"How can that be?" Harry said. Then she thought about the doctor that arrived once a week for Mr. Castillo's "checkup." Could Lena really have been in this house the whole time?

"Where is she?" Daniel asked.

"Is this real?" Gabe said, his voice barely above a whisper. His look plainly said that he couldn't believe it of his hero, Javier Castillo.

"Gabe, I want you to go to your room and pack your things. Right now," she said in a voice that brooked no argument. "As soon as you're finished I want you to go downstairs and wait for me in the foyer."

Gabe stood up slowly, moving like a sleepwalker.

"No," Javier Castillo said, grabbing Gabe's wrist.

Harry was off the bed in a second, prying his fingers from Gabe. "Don't touch my son."

"No," Mr. Castillo said again, his face desperate. "No, I don't want you to go. Don't leave."

"He's my child, and I'm going to do what's best for him," Harry said.

"I thought," Mr. Castillo said, half to himself and half to Harry. "I thought we could share him. He could be like the son I never had. He's such a good boy. A really good boy. Not like Michael."

Harry stared at Mr. Castillo in disgust. "He's not a toy that can be passed between people. He's a person, and he doesn't belong to you. Go, Gabe."

Gabe was staring at his wrist, at the place where Mr. Castillo had grabbed him. Then he ran from the room, a little choked sob emitting from his throat.

"Don't take him from me," Mr. Castillo said. "I was so alone before he came."

"You mean before *I* came, and brought him with me," Harry said. Then she took a deep breath. "Show me what's in the room at the end of the hall."

Daniel looked at Harry and then at Mr. Castillo. He seemed completely unmoored, a lost child.

She heard the sounds of drawers opening and closing in the

next room. *Good,* she thought. *Gabe's packing up. As soon as I have proof of what happened in this house we're leaving and I'm calling the police. Daniel will back me up.*

Mr. Castillo gave her a shattered look.

"Show me," she repeated.

"I can't," he said, in a pleading tone. "I can't."

"What's in the room at the end of the hall?" Daniel said.

"Amina went in there, and I had to—I can't," Javier Castillo said.

Harry felt bile roiling in her empty stomach. "Amina went in there? When? The night you argued with her?"

Daniel stared at Mr. Castillo, recognition in his eyes. "You killed her."

"I had to," Mr. Castillo said. "She went in the room. She was going to tell."

"You *pushed* Amina out a window because she went into a locked room?" Any trace of disbelief, any remnant of affection in Daniel had disappeared. "You killed her. It was your footsteps I heard that night. You pushed a young woman, a young woman who worshiped you, out the window because you thought she might *tell?* What was she going to tell, Javier?"

"Show us what's in the room, Mr. Castillo," Harry said. She was glad that Gabe wouldn't see this, but relieved that Daniel was there. She didn't want to be alone with Mr. Castillo.

He closed his eyes, and shuddered. Then he nodded and stood. "Yes. Yes. If you see, you will understand. If you understand then you couldn't possibly leave."

Harry and Daniel followed Mr. Castillo down the hall, watched as he pulled the key from his pocket, saw him turn it in the keyhole. He tried to indicate that they should go before him, but Harry shook her head.

"You first," she said, and held her hand out for the key. "You're not locking us in here."

Mr. Castillo gave her a long and measured look, then dropped the key in her hand. He was obviously still thinking there might be a chance that Harry and Gabe would stay, that he might bring her around if he cooperated. She didn't know what he was thinking about Daniel. Daniel didn't seem to figure in Mr. Castillo's plans at the moment.

Harry's hand closed on the key and she dropped it into her own pocket. Then she followed Mr. Castillo into the room, giving him a wide berth. She knew what he was capable of, and she wasn't going to give him a chance to knock her on the head and pretend it was an accident.

There was a twin bed in the middle of the room, slender, childish, though it dwarfed the woman who lay in the middle of it. She was very, very thin. The skin of her face pulled tight around her cheekbones. There was an IV drip attached to one arm and a series of sensors on the other. These sensors attached to a monitor that showed Lena Castillo's heartbeat and oxygen levels. Next to the bed was a small refrigerator, which Harry presumed held IV packs, and a stiff-looking hardbacked wooden chair.

On the other side of the bed, tucked in the far corner, was a collection of crates. These crates had various labels for props on them, but Harry was sure that at least one of them contained the taxidermied body of one Michael Castillo, the boy who seemed to have disappeared into the ether. Javier Castillo had disguised his son's remains as a horror movie prop, and who would question him?

"How did you get away with this?" Harry whispered, looking at Lena Castillo's shrunken form. "How did you move her without anyone knowing?"

"Carefully," he said. "I enlisted the help of a doctor friend of mine who helped me have her admitted under a different name in a hospital here in Chicago. We transported her here and she had round-the-clock care while I packed up the house in California."

"And just what did you tell your doctor friend had happened to your wife?" Harry said, unable to keep the anger out of her voice. "Did you explain that you'd strangled her in a fit of rage because you were jealous of your own son?"

"Of course not," he said, his nostrils flaring. "I said that Michael had attacked her while I was not at home, that Michael had fled, and that I didn't want any more negative press while my wife was gravely ill. He sympathized, and agreed."

"So you lied," Harry said. "All for the sake of your stupid career."

His eyes widened at that, and she saw a flash of the temper that he usually kept hidden.

"Stupid career? Is that what you think it is? I'm an artist. I make films that change people's lives."

"It doesn't matter what you make if you run over the people around you," Harry said. "And Lena doesn't want to be trapped inside this body anymore. She's in a coma. She's clearly not going to wake up. She's been calling to me, banging on the walls, sending me visions, asking me to help. I didn't understand for a long time, but I do now. You have to disconnect her from the machines. You have to let her go."

"No," Daniel said. He was staring at Lena in horror. "It's worse than that. It's so much worse."

"What?" Harry said.

"Look at her," Daniel said, backing away. "Really look at her."

Harry walked a little closer to the bed, and she realized what Daniel meant. The machine beeped, but the graphics never changed. The needle for the IV drip was taped to her arm. Lena Castillo's chest did not rise and fall. Lena Castillo's skin was stretched over her bones because she was dead, but Mr. Castillo had preserved her, was pretending she was still alive.

"What the *actual fuck*?" Harry said. "You're pretending she's still alive? You killed her. You killed your wife and your son and even your foolish colleague."

"Javier, how could you?" Daniel said. He sounded weak, dazed. "Who the hell has been coming in this room with you every week?"

"My doctor friend. He checks up on Lena," Javier Castillo said.

Harry understood then. Whoever it was that came in this room every week was, for some reason of their own—compassion? Money?—letting Mr. Castillo get away with his illusion that his wife was still alive.

Money really can buy anything in this country, Harry thought. *It can buy any damned delusion you want.*

"Lena is *dead*, Javier. Look at her!" Daniel shouted.

"No," Mr. Castillo said. "That's a lie. Lena would never do that."

"Let's get out of here, Daniel," Harry said. "We can call the police from a taxi."

The real terror in Bright Horses wasn't a ghost, or even two ghosts. It was the live madman who'd killed at least three people, who refused to believe his wife was dead, who wanted to take and keep her son forever.

She was worried about Gabe now, worried that he would get curious and try to come back inside the house. She didn't know what kind of desperate ploy Javier Castillo might try to keep her son, and she didn't want to find out. It probably involved pushing her and Daniel down the stairs.

"Where is Gabriel?" Javier Castillo said.

"He's gone," Harry said.

"No, he can't leave. He can't leave, because Michael is inside him."

Harry stared. She had no idea that Mr. Castillo realized a ghost had occupied Gabe's body. She felt a momentary worry that Michael might continue to cling to Gabe, even after they left.

I'll deal with that if it comes, she thought. *A ghost is easier to deal with than a murderer.*

"I knew it as soon as I heard Gabriel say 'old man,' knew by the look on his face. Michael always clung to his mother's skirts, tried to use her to protect him. He wormed his way inside Gabriel. He's been trying to hurt you so that I'll be blamed. He was the one who wanted me to push Amina from the window, so that the scandal would destroy me."

Harry didn't know what to do in the face of such mad conviction. There was no reason to stay here for even a moment longer.

"Come on, Daniel," Harry said, preceding him out of the room.

"You're going to jail, Javier," Daniel said. "I'm going to make sure of it."

She walked out of the room and toward the bedroom. She'd just throw everything in her suitcase and go, never mind organizing it. All she really had were clothes, in any case. All her personal items were in the storage center.

Her phone buzzed in her pocket, and she saw it was a text from Gabe.

I'm packed up and outside. I don't want to stay in the house anymore.

Be right there. Just need a few minutes to grab my stuff. Put on a hat, Harry typed, because she was sure he was standing out in the cold weather without one.

On second thought, she didn't need those clothes, really. It was all cheap stuff acquired from Target or H&M, nothing for which she had an emotional attachment. Her purse and coat and shoes were downstairs in the cubby by the front door. All she needed to do was walk out, get away from the murder house.

She kept going down the hall. She reached the top of the stairs that led down to the blue room and realized Daniel wasn't behind her as she'd expected. Then she felt a hand in the middle of her back shove *hard*.

Mr. Castillo can walk so silently when he wants, Harry thought as she tumbled down the full flight of stairs, her arms and limbs flailing out of control. Her ankle bent underneath her and she heard a cracking sound. The sound connected to her brain and she screamed in pain but she kept falling until she finished in a heap on the carpet of the blue room. Mr. Castillo followed, his steps slow and measured.

"You know I can't let you leave, Harry. Not when I did so much to get you and Gabriel here in the first place," he said.

Harry felt herself trapped in a nightmare loop, trying to pull herself across the floor as she had done a couple of hours earlier. There was no way she could put any weight on her ankle. Just the friction of the floor rubbing against it made her whimper in pain. Where was Daniel? Had Mr. Castillo quietly killed him while Harry was walking down the hall?

"I tried to get you here nicely, but you wouldn't cooperate. You'd rather have taken that wonderful, sensitive boy of yours to a homeless shelter than live in this beautiful house with me. I knew if you felt trapped you'd have nowhere to run but here. And once you were here I could work on Gabriel. I knew if he was happy and content here you wouldn't want to take him from me."

"We're . . . not . . . staying," Harry said, pulling herself away from him. She didn't want to be near him. She could hear the madness in his voice. "No . . . matter . . . what."

"Oh, Harry," Mr. Castillo said. "You'll stay. I'll make sure of it."

Sure, she thought. *In the third bedroom with Lena and Michael, preserved forever.*

She sensed rather than saw the movement behind her, and managed to roll out of the way just in time as Mr. Castillo swung down with a baseball bat. A surge of adrenaline rushed through her and it powered her to her feet, though her ankle wanted to buckle underneath her. She held out her hands in front of her.

"He's not yours," she said for the second time that night. "He doesn't exist to provide you personal adoration."

"But he will," Javier Castillo said. "I haven't been able to make a movie since Lena became ill. I need Gabriel. He thinks I'm wonderful."

"She didn't 'become ill,'" Harry said, backing away from him and clinging to the banister that ran along the edge of the room. "You killed her and turned her into a doll. And Gabe doesn't think you're so wonderful now. He's standing outside in the freezing cold because he's afraid to stay here a second longer."

"No," Javier Castillo said. "He will return. He'll return to me and he will be my son. He will help me become a great filmmaker again. I'll be able to trust him to stay here and look after Lena while I begin anew. And he will want to help me do this, because Gabriel believes in me. He believes in my films, in my genius."

Harry inched along the banister as he spoke. If she had to fall down the stairs a second time, so be it. She wasn't staying here a moment longer. Just then there was a creak on the stairs, and

Daniel Jensen staggered down them, holding the back of his head. Mr. Castillo had obviously tried to knock him out with the bat.

"Daniel!" Harry said. She wanted to rush toward him, to help him, but she was barely keeping herself upright.

Javier Castillo turned toward Daniel, the baseball bat raised.

Then she smelled it, and her need to get out of the house immediately took on even greater urgency.

"Is something burning?" she said.

"What?" Javier Castillo said, his arms relaxing, the bat falling to his side. He turned his head toward the third-floor stairs and sniffed. "Michael? Michael, no!"

Javier Castillo made for the steps, to knock Daniel out of the way, this time so he could run up to put the fire out.

The Sten costume came to life once more. Michael Castillo gave Harry his Joker grin, wide and malicious, and then he ran for his father. Harry saw the stunned look on Daniel Jensen's face.

The clawed hands came around Javier Castillo's arms and chest, holding him in place. Daniel hurried past them, his walk listing. Harry worried that he had a concussion. She could barely stand upright from the pain in her ankle.

"No, Michael, no! Your mother! Your mother will burn!"

There was so much anguish in Mr. Castillo's voice that Harry almost, *almost*, felt sorry for him. Black smoke was rolling down the stairs now, and Harry realized the whole third floor must be aflame. Michael Castillo had finally decided that he was never going to be able to destroy his father by any other means.

"Lena!" Javier Castillo shouted. "Lena!"

He tried to wrench away from the costume, but it held him tight, and Michael Castillo had one more surprise on offer.

As Harry watched, the Sten costume lit up like a bonfire, and Javier Castillo lit up, too.

Time to leave.

It wasn't Harry's thought, though, but Lena's voice. Harry felt a little push on her shoulder, gentle this time, apologetic.

Harry put her arm around Daniel and they stumbled down the stairs, coughing as smoke filled the air, past all the movie posters that she'd admired so much on that long-ago day when she'd first come to Bright Horses.

She threw open the front door and paused only to grab her coat, purse and shoes from the cubby in the hall, though she didn't take the time to put them on. She staggered out into the cold, still wearing her slippers.

Daniel clung to her like a drunk, his words slurring as he spoke. "He's a murderer. A murderer. I treated him like my family, and he's a murderer."

Gabe stood by the front gate, his suitcase and backpack beside him. He turned when he heard the door open and ran toward Harry as she lost her grip on Daniel and fell forward onto the sidewalk. Daniel stood beside her, swaying.

"Mom! Daniel! What happened?" he shouted, helping her up. Then he saw the smoke billowing down the hall and through the open door. "Oh my god."

"Yeah," Harry said. "Let's get away. To the sidewalk, anyway."

Gabe put one arm around her and one around Daniel. They limped down to the gate. She heard the sound of sirens, distant but coming closer. One of the neighbors must have called the fire department. Harry was vaguely aware of people coming out on their own front porches and walks to stare.

Once they were off Mr. Castillo's property Harry sat down on the sidewalk and turned around. Daniel collapsed beside her. The whole third floor was aflame now, Bright Horses burning like Manderley.

"You know," Gabe said, and he sounded sadder than Harry had ever heard him, "Mr. Castillo moved here because he was afraid of his stuff, all his props and things, burning in a California wildfire. He told me that once."

"Yeah," Harry said. "Mr. Castillo said a lot of things."

The rearing, snarling horse on the corner of the house was surrounded by fire. Harry hoped it burned clean and bright, and that all the bad things inside turned to ash and blew away.

Photo by Kathryn McCallum Osgood

Christina Henry is a horror and dark fantasy author whose works include *Good Girls Don't Die*, *Horseman*, *Near the Bone*, *The Ghost Tree*, *Looking Glass*, *The Girl in Red*, *The Mermaid*, *Lost Boy*, *Red Queen*, *Alice* and the seven-book urban fantasy Black Wings series. She enjoys running long distances, reading anything she can get her hands on and watching movies with samurai, zombies and/or subtitles in her spare time. She lives in Chicago with her husband and son.

Ready to find
your next great read?

Let us help.

Visit prh.com/nextread